Also by J. A. Henrikus

The Clock Shop Mystery Series
(by Julianne Holmes for Berkley Prime Crime)

Chime and Punishment (2017)
Clock and Dagger (2016)
Just Killing Time (2015)

a CHRISTMAS *Peril*

a CHRISTMAS *Peril*

a **THEATER COP**
— *Mystery* —

J. A. HENNRIKUS

MIDNIGHT INK
WOODBURY, MINNESOTA

FIRST EDITION
First Printing, 2017

Book format by Bob Gaul
Cover design by Kevin R. Brown
Cover illustration by Bill Bruning/Deborah Wolfe Ltd.

Midnight Ink, an imprint of Llewellyn Worldwide Ltd.

Library of Congress Cataloging-in-Publication Data
Names: Hennrikus, J. A., author.
Title: A Christmas peril / J. A. Hennrikus.
Description: Woodbury, Minnesota: Midnight Ink, [2017] | Series: A theater
  cop mystery; 1
Identifiers: LCCN 2017017353 (print) | LCCN 2017029576 (ebook) | ISBN
  9780738754789 | ISBN 9780738754154 (softcover: acid-free paper)
Subjects: LCSH: Women detectives—Fiction. | Murder—Investigation—Fiction.
  | GSAFD: Mystery fiction.
Classification: LCC PS3608.E56454 (ebook) | LCC PS3608.E56454 C48 2017
  (print) | DDC 813/.6—dc23
LC record available at https://lccn.loc.gov/2017017353

Midnight Ink
Llewellyn Worldwide Ltd.
2143 Wooddale Drive
Woodbury, MN 55125-2989
www.midnightinkbooks.com

Printed in the United States of America

To Jason Allen-Forrest, my first reader, fellow theater lover, prime cheerleader, and dear friend.

· One ·

*Y*ou could kill him without getting caught, couldn't you, Sully?"

I assumed Dimitri was referring to Patrick King, Scrooge in our production of *A Christmas Carol*. I'd considered killing Patrick myself, but purely for stress relief. The considering part, that is. Some people do yoga. I try to plan the perfect crime, and then I figure out what would trip me up. A cop may retire, but she never really leaves the job.

I'd stopped listening to Dimitri ten minutes earlier, so his question caught me off guard. How did we go from production problems to murder? When I realized I'd forgotten my dry cleaning in the office, I'd thought, foolishly, that I could get a head start on my to-do list before the Whitehall funeral. Forgetting what was in which office was commonplace these days, since I was working out of three offices at the moment—a temporary one at the high school, where the Cliffside Theater Company was performing *A Christmas Carol*; one at my house; and one here in the basement space that our company rented from the town for our costume shop, prop storage, and administrative center. I'd been hoping to find my dry-cleaned suit, and expecting to find a pile of paperwork. What I hadn't counted on was the artistic director being here. Listening to his dramatic rendition of our production woes as he paced in our cramped space was too much this early in the morning. I chose to nod appropriately and tsk in sympathy, assuming that the diatribe was directed at our star. I hoped for a break from another long story about why our Scrooge deserved a dire end. Or why he deserved said dire end so early in the day. Now Dimitri was questioning my murder competence.

"I might get caught," I said, choosing to take his question seriously. I stood and removed my skirt from the dry-cleaning hanger, slipping it on over my workout pants. "I doubt I'd get convicted though. I'd leave too many holes for reasonable doubt."

Dimitri stopped pacing and turned toward me. "So you've thought about killing him?"

"Dimitri, how could anyone work with you for three years and not think of murder?" I asked with the most serious look I could muster. I reached under my skirt and removed the workout pants. The skirt fell very low on my hips, exposing the top of my underwear.

"You had me going for a minute, you really did," he said. His ego normally never would have let him believe I'd want to kill him. But these days he was off his game. I felt guilty when I looked at the dark purple smudges under his eyes from the stress of the past few weeks of rehearsal.

"We can't kill Patrick, Dimitri," I said. "His name is over the title. We would have to refund the tickets."

Dimitri sighed and flung himself across the too-short loveseat I'd impounded from prop storage. His knees hung over one arm while his head rested on the other. I'd selected a loveseat rather than a couch so Dimitri wouldn't be tempted to nap in our office. It hadn't worked. But at least he could only sleep solo. Dimitri might be getting older—with his hairline beginning to recede, a little more flesh around his jowls, and a slight roll over his belt—but the animal magnetism that made him a brilliant director and catnip to investors was only growing stronger. I'd inoculated myself against the Dimitri charisma—years of dealing with crooks and liars will do that to you—but I still appreciated it.

When I was sure his eyes were closed I pulled my fleece off and replaced it with the silk T-shirt that went with the suit. It was too short to meet the top of the skirt. Damn. I had to leave in ten minutes if I wanted to get to the funeral on time. Going home for another outfit wasn't an option. Besides, this was "the suit" I always wore to funerals and court appearances. Though I still topped off at almost six feet and was far from model thin, I was in better shape than I'd been in years. On one hand, I was absurdly pleased the skirt was too large for me. On the other, I didn't want to invest in a new funeral suit, and I didn't want to taint anything else.

Calling a funeral a social event might seem crude, but it was appropriate with this one. Peter Whitehall was a very rich, very important citizen of Trevorton, Massachusetts. Hell, he ranked up there in all of New England, and that was saying something. Peter's financial generosity would be missed by many, including our theater, but the man himself? Not so sure about that. I'd seen him many times since I'd moved back to Trevorton, and found him charming, but it was the same type of charm I'd found in the con artists and sociopaths I arrested in my previous career.

Of course, I was prejudiced. Most of what I truly knew about Peter Whitehall came from his son, Eric. And it was for Eric that I had wrestled my funeral suit from the back of my closet after five years. Because even if your father is a son of a bitch, his death is a blow. And murder makes it worse.

"Sully, what are you doing?" Dimitri asked as I searched my desk for a stapler or a binder clip.

"I'm trying to fix my skirt."

"Is that what that is? Good God woman, it looks like a sack. You can't go out in that."

"Thanks. You know how to charm a girl." I tried to create a fold of material and maneuver the stapler toward it. "This is my funeral suit. I need to fix it, and if I go into the costume shop to borrow one they'll make me take it off so they can press it. I'm already running late."

"Whoa, whoa. If you insist, let's use this." Dimitri lifted a roll of gaff tape. Gaff tape is like duct tape without the sticky residue. Theater techs use it to tape down cables. But like duct tape, it has a million other uses. Dimitri surveyed my waist and ripped a piece off. While I gathered the fullness as artistically as I could, he wrapped the tape around the skirt, creating a new waistband. He held my waist for a minute to secure it, and then stepped back to survey his handiwork. He nodded appreciatively.

"I thought the funeral was Saturday," he said.

"Today is Saturday."

"Damn. I'm going to hell, joking about killing Patrick today of all days. I'm such a ... listen, should I go with you? Eric's a good guy. I didn't know his father well, but still. Give me a minute to pull it together."

Dimitri attempted to smooth his hopelessly cowlicked hair. We both looked down at his beyond-wrinkled shirt and jeans that were a couple of days late for the washer. He looked up at me, and I shook my head.

"You're busy. Eric will understand if you don't come. It's fine." I took a sip of my now-cold coffee and winced. It was bad enough hot, but cold it was bile. I took a deep breath and gulped down the rest of the cup, knowing the caffeine would still work its magic. There was no time to brew a fresh pot, though it didn't really matter. I hadn't had a decent homemade cup since my divorce. I should've leveraged Gus for his coffee formula before signing the papers.

Dimitri flopped back on the couch, his foray with the gaff tape having used up his energy reserves. He sighed loudly and threw his left forearm over his eyes.

"Things with Patrick aren't getting better, are they?" I asked. It was as if Patrick King had a finite amount of charm coursing through his veins. He'd used it all up the first week of rehearsal. Since then, he'd become more and more like the character of Ebenezer Scrooge. Normally I'd think it was method acting, but I didn't give Patrick that much credit. He'd only showed his true colors once it was too late to fire him.

"Worse."

"Is he at least off-book yet?"

"No. I think his memory has been pickled. He can't remember more than a scene at a time. Thanks for suggesting Connie loop Frank into the situation. He has an idea that may help Patrick with his lines … although I still think it would be easier to kill him." Dimitri winced. "Sorry. Though the publicity wouldn't be a bad thing for the show. Sully, what in hell are you doing now?"

Dimitri watched as I pulled my pantyhose up, trying not to flash him in the process. With my inordinately long legs and too-short hose, it was probably an exercise in folly, but I persisted, trying to time tugging with small hops in my traditional pantyhose dance.

"Just finishing up getting dressed."

"Don't you have anything that fits?"

"I don't like to wear my regular clothes for funerals. I know it sounds weird …"

Dimitri shrugged. "I get it. It's your costume for mourning. A little big on you though."

"I haven't had to wear it for a long time, thankfully."

"Get it pressed, my friend. You'll need it opening night." Another sigh.

"If Frank can figure out a way to feed Patrick his lines, won't that help?" Frank was our tech director, the anchor backstage, with expertise ranging from electronics to fly systems to lighting. I was glad, and not surprised, that he'd come up with a solution to our problem.

"Would that it were only Patrick." Dimitri sighed as he plopped on the desk chair. "I'm afraid I'm going to need you to have another conversation with David. He's refusing to double as any other character in the show. Says he was only contracted for Marley."

"Oh, please. Everyone is contracted to double as necessary—"

"He's the worst Marley ever, by the way. The scenery has teeth marks he's chewing it so hard."

"I'll talk to him," I said.

"Connie thinks Lila is having an affair with him, by the way. Patrick, not David. Or at best, she's catching some of his bad habits. Scrooge and Mrs. Cratchit. It just feels so wrong somehow."

∞

My car was shuddering up the icy hill. Usually, bone-chilling cold didn't hit Trevorton until after the new year, but this year it had come early. We'd had a couple of storms already. The snow didn't last long, but the ice stayed. I saw Harry Frederick fighting the cold wind a block away as he biked up the hill. I caught up, tapped on my horn, and pulled over in front of him.

"Are you heading to the church?" I asked, knowing the answer. Harry was our Bob Cratchit. He was also Eric Whitehall's sometime boyfriend. Last I knew, the relationship was in an off phase, but I wasn't sure. "Want a ride?"

By taking the front wheel off the bike, we could fit it in the back seat of my car. We'd done this dance before, many times. I even had a special towel I laid out on the seat to protect it from grease.

"Thanks," Harry said, rubbing his hands in front of the heater to warm them up. He took his bike clip off and patted the crease out of his pants, and then pulled a tie from his knapsack and put it on.

"Not a problem," I said. "I should have asked last night if you wanted a ride, but ... "

"But you weren't sure if Eric and I were back together yet?"

"There's that, yes. Are you?"

"No," Harry said. "It may really be over this time. But I still think I should go to the funeral, show my support."

"My mother always said that you didn't go to funerals for the dead, you go for the living. She always went to funerals and dragged me along."

"Plus, I want to make sure the old man is really dead," Harry said.

Harry was one of my favorite people, due in no small part to his incessantly good humor. I paused to let him explain this harshness, but he watched the scenery going past the window.

"Now that sounds like my father," I said, trying to lighten the mood. "I can actually hear him now: 'Sully, my darlin', I heartily doubt that a thimbleful of sincere tears will be shed over a first-rate bastard like Peter Whitehall.'"

"So, your father knew him?"

I laughed. "He did indeed. My mother and Eric's mother were best friends. Also, first cousins. When I was little the families used to get together regularly, Sunday dinners, beach outings, Thanksgiving, Easter. The Whitehalls had a lot of money, even then, and I loved visiting the Anchorage. What a great name for their house. A sailor built it, did you know that? It was magical. But then one day my father came home and announced the visits were over. He wouldn't budge. So, they stopped. You couldn't even say the words 'Peter Whitehall' in my house after that."

"What happened?"

I looked over at Harry. "I really don't know. We never talked about it."

"And you never asked?"

"Nope. If you'd ever met my father, you'd understand. He was a truly lovely man ninety-nine percent of the time. The other one percent? Don't cross him. Peter Whitehall was in the one percent."

For the rest of the ride over to the church we were silent, and I thought about Peter's death. I admit I was surprised when I heard someone had shot him. Not necessarily that he'd been shot, but that the police claimed to have no suspects. I could immediately name at least three possible killers, and I didn't know the man that well. If ghosts could return, I would have added my own dear dad's name to the list. But ghosts were ghosts, and Dad was off the list.

∞

Five years ago, I'd moved back to the small town I had escaped years earlier. Ostensibly, it was to take care of my dying father. I'd already buried a career and a marriage that year, so I decided to stay in the safety of Trevorton and recreate my life, which I did. Now a murder had happened in my refuge, and I was as informed as anyone else who watched the news or read the paper, which is to say, not very. Even though the murder was in the news every day, there were few facts known beyond what was reported. One, Peter Whitehall had been shot and killed at home after midnight a week ago. He'd been on a conference call at midnight, which helped set the timetable. Two, his family and a few friends were the only people home at the time. I hadn't heard a lot of speculation that it was an intruder, and I didn't know why that wasn't being floated as the prime idea. Three, his youngest daughter, Amelia, had found the body. And four, she was hospitalized that night and sent home a few days later. Previous bouts with depression were alluded to circumspectly by cautious reporters, well aware of the deep Whitehall influence in the commonwealth. These were all facts.

But rumors were running rampant. Even if I hadn't wanted to hear about the murder, gossip would have seeped into my consciousness. It couldn't be helped. As a small coastal town, Trevorton swells at the height of the season when the summer folk descend. During winter, only the very hardy are in residence: the year-rounders. And by virtue of the fact that we've all decided to brave the New England winter together, we've formed a bond. This bond creates a link through which all gossip passes with such speed and accuracy that someone can get a tooth filled by the dentist and when they stop by the grocery store on the way home, the cashier will suggest a home remedy for the ache. Peter still had the canonized glow of the recently deceased, but I knew that would change soon after the funeral. Anyone's murder would take over the gossip mill, never mind the murder of the town's richest and most important citizen.

Gossip had it that Amelia was the prime suspect. Gossip had it that the family was using their clout to cover up the crime. Gossip had it that Emma Whitehall Holmes, Amelia's older sister and family matriarch since the death of their mother twenty years ago, had made a deal with the police to hospitalize Amelia rather than send her to jail.

The deal was doubtful, but not out of the realm of possibility. The Whitehall family was very, very rich. They had deep ties to the community. And the family might not put too much pressure on the police to solve the crime if it meant convicting one of their own.

I glanced over at Harry and wondered if he was as worried as I was that Eric might be involved somehow. If I were making a short list, Eric would be near the top. Question was, who should be at the top?

· Two ·

Though we got to the church in good time, finding parking wasn't easy. I finally found a space three blocks away on a side street, taking the time to write down its name on a deposit slip. Harry took his bike out of the back seat and reattached the wheel.

"I have rehearsal at noon," he said. "What are you writing?"

"In Boston, I could always remember exactly where I'd parked, but in Trevorton everything looks alike. I'm constantly forgetting where my car is." The quaint New England beauty of my hometown's clapboard houses, mostly painted white, blurred together. More than once I'd pretended to take a walk while desperately trying to remember where I'd left the car.

Harry and I walked together toward the Congregational Church. We slowed down as we turned the corner. The crowd was moving slowly into the building. The simplicity of the church, the oldest one in town and historically known as a Meetinghouse, was less familiar to me than the elaborate beauty of the Catholic Church in the next town over. I thought of my mother with a pang. She wouldn't be happy that I couldn't remember the last time I'd been in a church. But I was here today, in my funeral attire. The gaff tape was holding up so far, though I was hesitant to take a deep breath.

Harry went around to the back of the church to lock up his bike. I waited for him by the front door. Three limousines rolled up. I watched as the drivers opened the doors and Terry Holmes stepped out. He reached his hand inside, and I expected to see Emma appear. Instead, Terry helped Brooke Whitehall, Peter's young widow, out of the car. She snaked her arm through his and leaned heavily on him as they walked toward the church.

Even in grief, Brooke Whitehall was one of the most beautiful women I had ever seen: porcelain skin, curly hair with enough high-lights to give it a healthy, sun-kissed look, and a body that displayed both strength and sexiness, even through her funeral clothes. Her con-fidence made me hunch my shoulders forward, trying to minimize my six-foot height and not-inconsiderable frame. Looking down, I saw my size-eleven feet with my hose sagging at the ankles. Damn.

Harry came around the corner and stopped beside me. "Let's go sit," he said. Though the church was packed, Harry smiled and charmed someone into making room so we could sit together on the same pew. Other latecomers were reduced to standing in the back and in the aisles.

The tension was high. Peter's murder had changed the tenor of an event that is, by definition, difficult. Rather than having thoughtfully chosen readings or meaningful songs, the service felt rote. Even the eulogy, delivered by Terry, left little in its emotional wake. The only overt feeling came from the second pew, where Peter's children sat. Emma and Eric wiped tears, but Amelia sobbed. Her brother put his arm around her, pulling her toward his chest. The depth of her emo-tion moved me. Surely the gossip was wrong. Amelia was obviously distraught. How could she possibly have … or maybe that was why she was so distraught. Guilt.

I gave myself a mental shake and tried to concentrate on the service. No time to run through suspects. I'd been off the job for years, but at times like these I realized I'd never left. Not really. The police department had "retired" me, the word we'd settled on when we couldn't come to terms with "quit" or "fired," but a bad ending to my career did nothing to stop my curiosity, my suspicious mind, or my craving for justice. I needed to remember that I shouldn't get involved. No matter what. Or whom.

There would be no graveside ceremony for Peter Whitehall, either because of family wishes or, more likely, because his body hadn't been released by the coroner. The minister reminded the congregation that there would be a reception afterward at the Whitehall home, the Anchorage, to pay respects to the family. And before I knew it, the service was over and the family whisked out of the church to prepare to meet their public.

∞

"Why don't you come with me to the reception?" I said.

"Rehearsal," Harry said. He'd watched Eric get into the limo and drive off without looking around.

"I bet Dimitri would be all right if you missed a bit of rehearsal," I said. Especially since this was Harry's third year playing Bob Cratchit.

"I may need to cash in that favor another time. It's fine. I'll see you later," he said. He leaned over and kissed me on the cheek. Maybe he and Eric really were over? I hated the idea that I might have to choose sides between my two friends, but perhaps they'd be more mature than I'd been when Gus and I divorced.

Though work beckoned, I decided to go to the reception, partly to pay my respects, partly to see the Whitehall mansion again. The

Anchorage had been a major part of my childhood, a place of magic. I wondered if it would still feel that way.

For an unknown reason, the original builder, a sea captain of ill repute, had constructed the large mansion only a few yards from the high, rocky bluff. One hundred years later Peter Whitehall went further, building an addition that extended over the cliff, with huge windows on three sides. Window washers received monthly hazard pay to wash, sometimes scrape, the salt from the windows. This two-floor addition was Peter's domain: his study on the first floor and his bedroom and sitting room on the second. I knew Peter was murdered in the addition, but wasn't sure where. I'd heard rumors of sharp shooters on the beaches from Gene at the Beef and Ale, but this was dismissed by someone else at the bar as impractical because of the angles. Given that we live in a twenty-four-hour news world, there'd been remarkably little reported. The cops were doing a good job at keeping a lid on leaks.

Though it was visible from most of the Trevorton beaches, tall privet hedges hid the Anchorage from the road and camouflaged a large iron fence surrounding the property. Two large stone columns supported a huge gate. There were stories that a disgruntled business associate had tried to ram the gate with his big, heavy eight-cylinder SUV fifteen years ago, believing the loaded gun on the seat would help speed his entry into the house once he got past the gates. But he never made it, and his car was totaled in the effort.

The gate was open today but the circular driveway was filled with cars, so I drove past and parked on the side of the road. I considered leaving my coat in the car but didn't want to walk even the short distance to the house in the frigid wind. I waved to the guard on duty, a habit from my patrol days. As I made my way toward the house I kept mental notes of the cars parked in the circle, another habit from my early days issuing parking tickets. My fingers were nearly frozen, but I took out my cell and checked messages, emails, and texts. In a nod to funerary decorum I switched the phone to vibrate.

Two oversized, magnificently carved doors marked the entrance to the front of the house. I didn't think I'd ever used those doors before. We always went around back to the kitchen. The better you knew a family, the less likely you were to use the front door. At my parents' house, the front door had had a table in front of it where we'd put the mail.

One of the doors was open to the receiving line that was beginning to queue. The other remained closed, displaying a splendid wreath that probably cost as much as my entire holiday decoration budget for the theater. As I got closer, I noticed a black ribbon instead of a more holiday-appropriate red. The gesture made my throat tighten. Even if his *true* mourners were few, the Anchorage acknowledged Peter's passing.

Emma and Terry stood at the open door, seemingly oblivious to the cold, greeting their guests. Emma looked nervous as I approached, so I donned my most comforting smile and took her hand in both of mine. "I'm so sorry about your father."

"Thank you for coming, Sully. This is my husband, Terry Holmes, have you met? Terry, this is my second cousin … is that right? My mother's cousin's daughter … whatever. Sully Sullivan."

"Sully Sullivan?" Terry shook my hand as if we were long-lost friends. His reputation as a charmer seemed well founded.

"Born Edwina. My grandfather, Edwin Temple, died a month before I was born … "

"Sully's been Sully our whole life," Emma told him. "Only our mothers called her Edwina. God rest their souls."

"I wish I'd known them both. It's wonderful to meet you." His eyes seemed sincere, his voice wonderfully modulated. I wished I didn't know as much as I did about him.

"Nice to meet you, Terry." I said. "I'm surprised we haven't already met at the theater."

"Sully manages the Cliffside Theatre Company," Emma explained.

"Ah. No, you wouldn't see me there. I don't like theater. Happy to contribute to it, but thrilled Emma goes with Eric."

"Speaking of whom ... ?" I moved into the doorway, much to the relief of the frozen line of mourners behind me.

"Check the library. I'll see you later, Sully?" Emma said.

"Of course. Again, I'm so sorry. If there's anything I can do ... "

"Thanks, I'll be in touch." Something about her tone told me she meant it.

∞

I sidled through the crowd, looking for Amelia and Eric. The house was Federal style, with a center entrance and mirrored wings on either side. The entrance led to a grand hallway, a large, beautifully carved wooden staircase, and a glimpse of an upper hallway. Despite the grandeur of the home and the intricate period details, the rooms were not massive, particularly by current McMansion standards. There were a few grand spaces with high ceilings for entertaining. The less-formal rooms were smaller, with normal-height ceilings. Most rooms had fireplaces, all of which still worked despite the advent of central heat. The Anchorage had a simple elegance I preferred over the Newport cottages farther south. The spaces here were designed for use as well as for show. Today they would be well used, receiving Peter's mourners. And there were a lot of them.

For many people, this was more than an opportunity to show the family support; it was a chance to see the inside of the Anchorage, an opportunity few would pass up. Add a catered spread, and a turnout was guaranteed. I thought about my father's imagined remark about the thimbleful of tears and wondered how many of the people enjoying a repast in Peter Whitehall's home were genuinely sorry. I guessed very few.

I saw David Taylor the same moment he saw me. I might have let him off the hook with a wave, given where we were, but his pointed attempts to ignore my presence ticked me off. The conversation I'd planned for later got moved up. Until the Patrick King experiment, David had been our perennial Scrooge. Since he was a core member of the company who'd always been a joy to work with, we thought he would be okay with the role of Jacob Marley this year. Actually, Dimitri thought he'd be okay. But now, with fewer lines to deliver, he was playing the role of an actor wronged, and he was punishing us. Our production had a lot of actors doubling roles; it was part of Dimitri's conceit for the production. I needed David to double as one of the people in the Ghost of Christmas Future scene, either as one of the businessmen that Scrooge overhears talking or as Old Bob the pawnbroker. As I walked toward him, David looked around and realized that all escape routes were cut off. I smiled and slowed my pace.

"David, I'm so glad to see you. We keep missing each other at rehearsal," I said.

"Well, I'm not called for that many rehearsals this year."

"Connie has been trying to call you for a few more, from what I understand."

David shook his head. "I was only contracted for Marley."

"Come on, David. What are you doing? You're a member of the Cliffside—we need you to help get us through this, um, production, so we can start planning for next season."

"I'm sorry, but I can't. I was hoping to talk to you about this later, but I guess now is as good a time as any." He looked me square in the eyes and stood tall. "I'm leaving the production."

"You're what? You can't. You've got a contract."

"It's all in this letter. I got offered a role in a new movie filming in Boston. For more money."

Damn it. More remunerative employment. That was the clause in the contract that allowed an actor to break the agreement so he or she could take another gig. Because let's face it, almost anything would be more remunerative that working at the Cliffside. But most of the time we tried to work out schedules.

"I was going to leave this letter for you at the theater. Cowardly, I know. But I didn't want to risk you talking me out of my decision. You know how much the company means to me, but I can't do it, Sully. What was a joy has become a nightmare."

Normally I would chalk such a comment up to actor hyperbole, but he was telling the truth. Our production of *A Christmas Carol* had become a nightmare. I expected the ghost of Charles Dickens to haunt my dreams soon.

"Nothing I can say?" I asked. David shook his head. "All right, I'll tell Dimitri."

"You're not pissed?" he asked. He sounded disappointed.

I bit my tongue. David was one of my favorite actors. I wasn't going to burn a bridge for Patrick King, even though I was tempted. "Of course I'm pissed. But I'll get over it. Someday."

As David walked away, I pulled out my cell and checked for messages. Nothing. I sent a text to Stewart Tracy. It said *SOS. You have a gig for the next few weeks? We need you. Call me.* After a second I added a *XOXO, Sully* to the end of the text and hit send. I went to my email and found the draft I'd written to Stewart as a just-in-case measure; the email laid out the entire situation. I hit send and turned off my phone. Time to find the rest of the family, pay my respects, and then get back to work. I had a part to recast.

∞

I spotted Eric across the room and started toward him, then stopped. He was talking to my ex-husband. What was Gus doing here? I didn't walk over—as much for Gus's sake as for my own. Small talk was going to be a tricky business. Unlike some of my friends who'd become friends with their exes, I hadn't spoken to Gus since my father's funeral. Even the divorce was handled through our lawyers. I couldn't bear to try, and he'd given up. I would need more prep time, and a drink, before I attempted to talk to him today.

I found Amelia, looking tiny in a large wingback chair in the corner of the ballroom, oblivious to the humanity swirling around her. She stared at the untouched plate of food on her lap.

I walked over to her, wanting to get her attention without startling her. Amelia didn't register my presence until I crouched down and took both of her hands.

"Amelia, hi," I said in low tones. "My name is Sully ... you may not remember me. Our mothers were cousins, and I used to come over here to play a long time ago ..."

"Your mother was Sarah." Amelia's voice was loud, a little too loud given my proximity. Her eyes were dilated, and she seemed to be having trouble focusing. Most of the conversation around us stopped as people turned to listen.

"Yes ..."

"I remember her. She was very kind to Mother when she was sick…"

"She loved your mother very much," I agreed, hoping that she would lower her voice to my level.

"I loved my father like that." No such luck. Amelia stared at me as if daring me to challenge her. I had no response, at least not an adequate one. No matter. Amelia wasn't finished. "He wasn't an easy man to love, but I did. He loved me back. Called me his angel." With that she looked around defiantly.

Emma and Eric waded through the crowd toward Amelia. "Well, there you are, darling," Emma said. "You must be exhausted. I know I am. Why don't you come and lie down for a while? Sully won't mind, will you?"

"No, of course not." I lifted the untouched plate from Amelia's lap and held my other hand out to her. She took it, using it to lift herself from the chair. "Amelia, I truly am so sorry about your father."

"Thank you." Amelia squeezed my hand and then took Emma's, allowing herself to be guided toward the staircase. She'd only taken a few steps when she turned back toward me while addressing her sister. "Emma, didn't you tell me once that Sully used to be a policewoman? Maybe she can help us, Emma. Shall we ask?"

Emma hesitated and looked over her shoulder. She clearly wanted to say something, but not in a room full of people.

"Why don't you call me at the theater, Amelia? Anytime."

Eric stayed behind to talk with me. "Careful, Sully. We may take you up on that." He looked around, and then back at me. "Are you alone?"

"I am. Harry sends his best," I said.

"I'll bet," Eric said. "Frankly, I'm surprised either of you came to the funeral. My father wasn't one of your favorite people."

I got a whiff of Eric's whiskey-laden breath and took a long look at him. The bloodshot eyes and blotching skin were familiar signs that he'd been drinking. Hard. Aside from an occasional glass of wine, I hadn't seen Eric drink for months.

"Harry came to the funeral for you, dope. This isn't the best time to get into a pissing match."

"You're right. This isn't the time. Sorry. I don't know what's wrong with me … "

Deep breath. Months of anger management and meditation had to have done me some good, right? "Well, for starters, you just got back from your father's funeral. Grief, maybe some mixed emotions?"

"Yes, you're right, there's that. And Harry … do you think I should have had him come to the house?"

Eric, and most of Trevorton, had adopted a "don't ask, don't tell" policy about his love life. Harry hated the fact that he was never part of *all* of Eric's life. So I almost replied that having Harry at his side at the reception would have been a good way for Eric to tell the world that Harry was his partner. It also would have been a good way to win him back. But in a rare moment of diplomacy, I said, "That's not for me to say."

"Coward. I could use a chat, but now's not the time. Maybe later?"

"Of course. I need to go by the theater, but I'll be home tonight … "

"Oh, right. *Christmas Carol* rehearsals," Eric said. He was on the board of the Cliffside and usually stopped by our rehearsals, especially when Harry was in the cast. "Tell me, is it as bad as I've heard?"

"Shhh, not so loud. There's a lot of potential audience members here." Eric seemed appropriately chagrined. "Let's just say it isn't good, aside from our brilliant Bob Cratchit. But there's still hope. Not a lot of hope. But some."

Eric looked over my shoulder and pulled me toward him. "Whoa, evil stepmother approaching at six o'clock. Do you want to bolt?"

"Nah. Brooke's pretty harmless, at least to me. She never remembers me."

"Run now, Sully, or those days may be over. She's been on a tear today."

"I'll take my chances."

At that moment, Brooke Whitehall descended. There was no other word for it. One moment she was across the room, the next moment she stood beside Eric, her hand on his arm. The movement left a wake; everyone in the room was looking at her. She didn't seem to notice, but then again, given her looks, she was probably used to people staring at her.

As always, I was struck by her beauty. If I hadn't known as much about the woman behind the face, I probably would have been awed. But Eric had told me enough stories to tarnish the veneer. So rather than being vexed or awed by her, I chose to be amused.

"Eric, is this a *friend* of yours?" Emphasis on "friend." Brooke was either baiting Eric or she was clueless.

"Yes, Brooke. Also a relative. You've met Sully before, haven't you? She runs the Cliffside ... "

"I thought Dimitri ran the theater?"

Dimitri runs it into the ground, I thought. Aloud, I explained, "Dimitri is the artistic director. I'm the general manager. I run the business part. Dimitri does the creative work." A second diplomatic moment in as many minutes. And I hadn't had anything to drink. Yet.

"Oh, how interesting. I've always wanted to be more involved with the theater, but Peter didn't like it." She took a moment to dab her eyes. "Poor Peter," she said. She almost sounded sincere.

"Mrs. Whitehall, forgive me. I should have said straight off how sorry I am about your husband."

"Thank you, Sally. I appreciate it ... oh, Eric, the senator is leaving. Come with me and say goodbye. I don't know where Terry is ... "

With that, Brooke took her stepson by the arm and steered him out of the room. Again, all eyes watched their departure.

I had done my duty so I headed for the exit. I pulled my cell phone out, willing a message to have come in. Still nothing. I really wanted to make it out the door without seeing Gus, and I almost did. Almost. Just three more feet ...

"Sully?"

"Gus." I amazed myself with my ability to come up with scintillating conversation despite the circumstance.

"I didn't know you'd be here." That particular tone in his voice did what it had always done: got my back up.

"Are you surprised that I travel in these circles?" I asked.

"Yes. No. Sorry. I'm just surprised. I remember how your dad felt about Peter, and thought ... but of course you'd be here. Sorry. It's been a tough few days."

When Gus and I first got together, verbal jousting was foreplay. Later, it made me angry. Now, it made me sad. He'd been my husband, my lover, my best friend for so long. And now? He was nothing. No, not nothing. He'd always be something in my life. A regret. My biggest regret. Not for having married him, but rather for not fighting harder to keep him in my life. Of course, I'd be damned if I'd ever tell him that.

Another deep breath. If people kept pissing me off, I'd hyperventilate or pop my gaff-tape waistband. "Eric's a good friend and on the board of the theater." I tried my best to smile.

Gus's exhale seemed deep-rooted as well. "I'd heard you were running the Cliffside. How's that going?"

"Well, really well—"

"I was surprised when I heard. You never seemed that interested in theater while we were together. I mean, I had to force you into subscribing to the ART, and then you didn't go most of the time."

My therapist would have called this moment "an opportunity for choice." I could rise to the bait, pick a fight, and stomp out. Or I could ignore the bait, answer Gus, and keep the door open so that it might be less awkward the next time we met. The former, my normal modus operandi, hadn't worked well, so I decided to try the latter.

"My mother loved theater. She worked at the Cliffside for years—volunteering in the box office, acting in some of the shows. She used to bring me with her. I'd help her do whatever she was doing. She wrangled my father into helping out with sets, props… a few years after she passed, he joined the board. I think it helped him remember her. After he died I heard they were looking for a general manager, and I had the special requirements for the job."

"I didn't know you worked in theater before," Gus said.

"No, not experience. Requirements. First, with my pension from the force, I could live on what they could pay. Second, the artistic director couldn't scare me."

Gus laughed. "What do you do in the winter? Isn't the Cliffside a summer theater?"

"Technically, yes. But we do a production of *A Christmas Carol* every year at the high school. Dimitri ties the crew work into a class he teaches. It's a moneymaker, or it's supposed to be. The rest of the winter we plan the season and have board meetings, strategic planning sessions, fundraisers…"

"So it keeps you busy?"

"Busy enough. How about you? Are you ... were you working with Peter?"

"Yes. I've taken on some corporate clients."

"Given up on criminal law?" I asked. Gus was an amazing lawyer, with a passionate zeal for truth.

"I'd hate to say I've given it up. I'd rather say I've branched out," he said, studiously adjusting his cufflinks and avoiding looking at me.

"Still in Boston?"

"Yes, I bought a condo on Comm Ave." Obviously corporate law paid well.

"That's terrific, Gus. I'm glad things are going well."

"Sully ... " he said, taking a tentative step toward me.

Emma's appearance interrupted the moment. "Sully, I'm glad you're still here."

"Gus and I were catching up."

"Oh. I forgot you knew each other."

The smirk on Gus's face might have finally undone my therapy. "We don't know each other that well anymore," he said. "Good to see you, Sully. Em, call me if you need anything." He leaned over and gave her a quick kiss on the cheek.

"I'll be in touch. We need to move on the Century Project this week," Emma said.

"Emma, it can wait until —"

"No, it can't. Things are likely to get more complicated, and it may be harder to move forward."

"Fine, I'll call you tomorrow." Gus walked toward the front door, seemingly oblivious to Brooke, who was flapping both her wrists at him from across the foyer.

"Thank God for Gus," Emma said. "With him around I don't have to worry as much about the project, and I can focus on—"

"I can't imagine how difficult this has been, Emma." I touched her arm and a wave of grief flowed across her face. The wave was soon controlled, but she still looked drawn. I remembered that feeling too well.

I focused on the bright winter sun filtering through the windows around the front door, trying to get my emotions back in check. What was happening to me? Was the theater crowd finally wearing down my thick skin? If I didn't watch myself, I'd start hugging people instead of shaking hands. And from there, who knows? Perhaps an emotional attachment to another person? Doubtful. That would involve dating, and I wasn't ready. Besides, pickings were slim in Trevorton.

Suddenly I realized Emma was talking.

"So anyway, Sully, I know that you aren't a detective anymore … I don't know what you can do. I don't know what anyone can do, but I need help. I'd like to talk to you about—" Emma stopped.

"Don't let me interrupt, ladies." Terry appeared by Emma's side. "Did I see Gus leave?"

"Yes, he needed to get back," Emma said, putting her hand on her husband's arm. He shook it off."

"Damn, I wanted to talk to him. He told me he'd wait." Terry looked furious.

"Probably my fault, Terry," I said, trying to change the subject. "He wanted to escape." I was taken aback by the frustrated tone in Terry's voice. He was obviously a man accustomed to getting his way. "Gus and I haven't been in touch for a while. Seeing each other probably threw him off. I know it did me."

"You don't seem like a woman easily thrown anywhere." Terry gave me a brief up and down with his eyes and then turned toward his wife for a private conversation. Perhaps the up and down was supposed to intimidate me, or remind me that I wasn't a rail-thin supermodel.

26

Instead, it confirmed what I'd thought for a while. Emma had married a jackass.

I'd thought so the first time she'd told me about him, last spring. Eric had invited me out lunch with them. I'd thought the point of the lunch was to relive old times. And it was, until Emma poured herself another glass of wine and drank half of it in one gulp. Courage restored, she began, haltingly, to tell me the real reason for lunch. She didn't know where else to turn ... she knew that I used to be a detective, maybe I could help ... she worried that her husband was having an affair ...

I stopped her "Emma, I'm no longer a detective."

"But surely you could—"

"I don't know if this is going to make sense or not, but I'm going to ask you to hear me out. When I left the force, I made some hard decisions about my life. One of the first decisions was what to do next. I could easily have become a private investigator. A lot of people who take early retirement do. But I didn't want to go that route, so I chose a new path." I took a sip of water. "I hope you understand this, Emma, but I can't help you. It was hard enough while I was on the job, knowing more about people than I wanted to. Meeting an old high school friend at the mall and realizing that I'd busted her husband for drugs. Being part of an investigation where I knew some of the players. That blurring of the lines was hard, but it was my job. And it was worth it. But to be a PI means doing that part of the job without the reward of being on the job. It works for some people, but not me. I don't want to know if your husband is fooling around. You could never look at me the same way, never forgive me on some level, no matter what I found out. I can't deal with that flotsam in my life. I'm really sorry ... "

"Don't apologize," Emma said. "And don't blame Eric; this was my idea. I don't know what to do ... "

I pulled out my theater business card, wrote down a name and number on the back, and slid it toward her. "This is someone who was on the job and became a PI. His name's Jack Megan. He's a good man; you can trust him. I'm sure he'd be happy to help." Emma hesitated before taking the card. "He's discreet. I can call him and let him know you'll be in touch, if that helps."

I never knew whether Emma called Jack, but I was glad I hadn't gotten involved. Now I stopped daydreaming and half listened to Terry and Emma's conversation. They were engaged in a husband-and-wife exchange with the shorthand only couples knew.

"I told you I'd take care of it."

"That's what you said about the other thing, but you didn't."

"I didn't because of whatsit, you know that."

This part of marriage I didn't miss. "Emma, Terry, I've got to get back to the theater," I said, leaning in and giving her a kiss on the cheek. "We're having Jacob Marley issues I need to address. Again, I'm so sorry about your loss."

I turned to her husband and shook his hand. "Terry, it was nice to meet you."

"And you, Edwina."

"Sully, please. I hate that name." I gave Terry a look that I hoped would dissuade him from using my given name ever again. What had my mother been thinking?

"Happy to help," Emma said.

"Help?"

"I'm happy to help with that committee you talked to me about."

"Great news, thank you."

"Call me anytime, we can meet and talk about it." And with that, I finally made it the last three feet to the door.

· Three ·

Frigid air sliced through my coat as I left the house. I jammed my gloveless hands into my pockets and hunched my shoulders. I really needed to find my matching gloves and scarf for these public events. They didn't keep me very warm, but they sufficed for dashes from door to car. I was sure they'd resurface after the holidays when I didn't need them anymore. In the meantime, I should have worn my fleece mittens and ugly ribbed scarf. They weren't glamorous, but they were fabulously warm. I planned to put them on as soon as I could.

I walked to the right, to the horseshoe driveway, rather than down the more direct path to the front gate. It was a long driveway, and I felt the pull of a slight detour. I stepped onto the footpath that led toward the cliff, leaning into the wind. I considered turning back, but I wanted to see it again for myself.

And then, there it was. The glass addition of the Anchorage. Peter's pride and joy and final resting place. I'd seen it before, as a kid, and more recently from the town beach, but current events lent a different lens to my observations. Up close it was a monolith of rebar, cables, glass, and beams that flew over the large, rocky cliff. It looked like a giant erector set with tinted windows, a glass blight on an otherwise beautifully restored home. Other houses had walkways down to the beach below, but not the Anchorage. In order to get to the beach, the family had to leave the estate, go down the road, and use the public access. Not that they ever did—they used the pool on the other side of the house instead. With its beautiful water views and landscaping, it was like being in the ocean without the salt and sand.

I kept walking, careful to avoid any icy patches that might send me over the cliff. That would be a hell of a way to end the visit. I saw a piece of plywood affixed on the southern corner of the addition. Just one pane gone. I couldn't tell if the sparkling bits on the rocks below were ice or glass.

The finicky December sun peaked out from behind a cloud and I saw myself reflected in the short side of the addition, visible before it careened over the cliff. A perfect, mirrored reflection of my freezing, fashion-free form.

"Hello, Sully," a familiar dulcet tone shouted over the wind.

I walked toward the side of the house where Regina Roberts was hunkered down trying to get out of the wind. She was almost a foot shorter than I was, and almost that much wider. Regina was on the Trevorton police force. I'd heard she was first on the scene, but I was sure the case was out of her hands by now. Peter Whitehall was too important.

"Damn, Regina, you scared me."

"Couldn't stay away, huh?"

"I can't be the only person who's tried to sneak a peek of the room?"

"First one I've seen. Most people have better manners, I guess," she said, pushing her hands farther down into her pockets. Unlike me,

Regina was dressed for the weather. She was wearing a full-length navy blue down coat and an off-white fleece hat/scarf/mittens set. Still, her cheeks were purplish red and her eyes were watering.

"That must be it." I smiled. She'd caught me, but we both knew that if the shoe were on the other foot, she'd be doing the same thing. "I thought I saw you inside earlier," I said. "Are you on duty?"

"Yes. Most of Trevorton's finest are here, either officially or unofficially."

Regina and I had known each other a little in high school and had chosen similar career paths in life, though an early marriage had kept her in Trevorton. It wasn't until her son Gabe became an intern at the theater his freshman year that we reconnected. I'd wrangled her into a few nights behind the concession stand, but I suspected she'd be too busy with other things this holiday season.

"Must have been a hell of a shot," I said, looking out at the glass enclosure, trying to figure angles. I wasn't an expert, but it seemed to me that the possibility of the shot that killed Peter coming from outside the house was slim at best. To hit someone in the room through that corner pane, a shooter would have needed to be suspended in midair. Unless Peter was standing right in front of the window. But I thought I'd test the water, see if Regina responded.

She looked over her shoulder quickly, caught my eye, and shook her head slightly.

"He wasn't shot through the window, was he?"

"Did you notice how these windows look more like mirrors than glass?" she asked. "They're slightly smoked for privacy and sun filtration."

Information without giving me information. Regina was a good cop, and a good friend.

31

"Makes sense, I guess. It would be a fishbowl otherwise, out there over the cliff." I looked down toward the drop-off. "Well, I've got to go check in on rehearsal."

"From what Gabe tells me, I'm not sure who has the worse afternoon plans. Me doing driveway duty or you having to sit through rehearsal."

"You don't even know the half of it, Regina. David told me he quit the show."

"Really? That's a shame. I love his work," she said. "What are you going to do?"

"Plan G. At this point, no Jacob Marley is the least of my problems. I'll fill you in after the show opens. Maybe we can have a cup of coffee?"

"Screw the coffee, I could use a drink. But it may take a while." She tilted her head toward the house and rolled her eyes.

"Give me a call when you're free." I turned to walk back toward the driveway, looking at the fence that went partially down the cliff. A stunning, dramatic view. Did the cops suspect an intruder? I supposed it was possible that someone could have gotten up the cliff from the beach. I couldn't, but that was a low bar these days. I might have been able to five years ago. Maybe ten. Were they seriously considering the idea that it was someone outside the house? I wanted to ask, but I knew Regina wouldn't tell me anything more. I had no information to trade. Yet.

· Four ·

Although I'd planned to go to the high school, I decided to go back to our regular office instead. I had a mountain of mundane paperwork to wade through. Today's rehearsal promised to be a quiet one: the Fezziwig party scene. Patrick didn't need to be there, since Dimitri had reblocked the scene precisely so Scrooge merely observed rather than participated in the dancing.

I had to circle the block twice. Our theater company shared a building with several other nonprofits, including an after-school program. It made afternoon parking very difficult, navigating around well-heeled folks coming to pick up their offspring. Never mind the noise bleed we endured during the day. While we were grateful to have a place, I was starting to pin my hopes on the new production center we planned to build next spring, at the site of our outdoor performance space on the edge of the harbor.

The land for the new center was tucked away behind a large historic house, so the town had given us clearance to build without worrying about historical accuracy. Our current idea was that the center would look like a large barn and contain dressing rooms, shop spaces, and some administrative offices. Building it would be a game changer for the Cliffside. It would also be the first large-scale project the theater had taken on since it was founded.

Several years before my return to Trevorton, Dimitri Traietti—then a local personality of some note, one with more than a small amount of talent—was approached by the town council to reopen the outdoor amphitheater by the harbor, which had long ago lost its luster after its original purpose was eclipsed by band drills and troop meetings. Funds were raised to restore the theater and grounds. The council's hope was that a performance space of a particular caliber would attract tourists who would spend money in local restaurants and hotels. In this vision, the match between the Cliffside and Dimitri proved perfect, and their hopes were realized. Although the performance season was shortened by New England weather, the reopening of the amphitheater was a triumph.

Not surprisingly, the theater's success fed Dimitri's monster of an ego. He needed a general manager to keep him reined in, but he couldn't keep one on staff for more than a season. His tantrums, ego blasts, and crazed business practices wore them out.

When I heard about the job of general manager opening up once again, I felt a little tingle in my gut. It was a few weeks after my father had died, and I was lost, weighed down by grief and regret. Sometimes I wonder if my mother had orchestrated that moment. For the first time in months I saw a way to create a new life. Eric Whitehall, a Christmas-card-exchanging relative, had come to Dad's funeral and called me a few times to check in. Even though we didn't know each other well anymore, we fell into an easy friendship immediately, and his concern for me was sincere. So I decided to take him up on his "anything I can do?" offer and ask about the job.

"Sully, what makes you think you'd be … "

"Able to do the job?"

"No, of course you could do the job. Not that it's easy, mind you, but the board is strong and more than willing to help. It doesn't pay close to what it should. But that aside, it doesn't seem like your next step ..."

"Eric, that's the point. I don't have a next step. I have no idea what I want to do. I do know that some of my happiest memories were summers at the Cliffside while I was young. My mother loved Dimitri ..."

"Those were early days, Sully. Dimitri was still charming then. Now he's a nut. A talented nut, I'll grant you, but a nut. He gets a thrill out of making the general manager miserable. It's his summer sport."

"I'm pretty good at taking care of myself. I've dealt with some challenging characters in my life."

"Don't glamorize this, Sully. Dimitri may be a better class of character, but he's still tough. The last general manager implied he was a sociopath. I don't think he's that bad, but he does have his moments—"

"Eric, I need to get back into life. Before I forget how."

∞

Dimitri may have vaguely remembered me from some of my volunteer jobs when I was younger, but he misjudged the toll the years since had taken on me. He couldn't wear me down. He tried charm, tantrums, and threats, but none of them worked. I stayed focused on running the theater and learning my job. The board's help was invaluable, and eventually Dimitri and I established a good working relationship. I'd like to think it was because of my business acumen, but it probably had more to do with Eric's stories about me.

"What did you tell him?" I asked Eric one night over a shared plate of fries.

"I told him you have a hair-trigger temper, that you can kill a man with your bare hands, and that you pack a piece," Eric said, dipping a fry into Gene's homemade ketchup. He took a bite and closed his eyes in delight. The Beef and Ale's fries were nirvana.

"Eric, I don't carry a gun. Usually." I couldn't dispute the other two, though I was working on the temper. I had to smile. A little fear was probably healthy. Seemed to work for Dimitri and me.

I thought I'd only keep the Cliffside job until I got my life back together, but then the work became my life. I resisted this at first, but I was comfortable falling into my old patterns. Much as I liked to think otherwise, a nine-to-five job that stayed at the office didn't suit me. I needed immersion. So, despite the odds, I proved a good match with the Cliffside.

The biggest challenge was dealing with deficit funding for the theater. During the boom times of the '90s, a cocktail party, a couple of fundraisers, a few phone calls and these debts were easily resolved. Times had changed, and many of the private funding sources had slowed to a trickle or dried up entirely.

After my first summer as general manager, at the end of one of our more arduous budget meetings, Dimitri shared his vision for the next season: a post-apocalyptic *Romeo and Juliet*, with the entire theater and its grounds used as part of the set. We were sitting in our office, sharing a bottle of wine. He'd pulled a large portfolio out of his only locked drawer and was flipping through the pages of research and preliminary drawings he'd worked on. He stopped and ran his fingers over the drawings.

"Imagine it, Sully. Tanks parked outside the theater. Camouflage nets covering doorways. The staff in the same costumes as the actors. An immersive experience made all the more powerful because it supports the words of the greatest playwright..."

The budget kept climbing as he described his dream. I'd been hatching my own plan for a moneymaker in the off-season, and decided now was as good a time as any to run it by him.

"That would require a huge budget—"

"There you go, thinking like a businessperson again. I thought we had uncovered an artist's soul under all that—"

"Whoa! Hear me out. I have an idea I've been cooking. How about doing *A Christmas Carol* in December? We could use the high school—lots of seats and a state-of-the-art facility."

"I can't imagine what could possess you to even suggest complicity with that commercial dreck." Dimitri looked aghast.

"It isn't dreck. It may be overdone, but it's a wonderful story and open to interpretation." I let those last words hang in the air for a few seconds. Nothing tempted Dimitri like an opportunity to upstage his colleagues at other theaters. "You could do your own adaptation, hone it down to the core meaning of the book. It could be a cash cow for us. I've run some numbers ... "

"You've actually given this some thought?"

"I think we can make this a win-win. At least hear me out. I listened to your ideas for *Mad Max* meets *Romeo and Juliet*."

"You said you liked it." It was, and still is, difficult for me to reconcile the bravado of the difficult director Dimitri with the desperation of the vulnerable artist Dimitri.

"I do like it. Really. But you're talking about putting a tank in front of the theater. That takes money, Dimitri." I couldn't imagine the hoops we'd need to jump through to get a permit for a project like this, since tanks on the edge of the harbor wasn't the charm that Trevorton was going for with its occasional tourists. I'd deal with that later.

He sulked for another minute and then said, "Okay, I'll listen."

"We could have high school students to work on the production as part of your class. The gross potential is impressive, given the size of their theater."

Dimitri had been asked by the public school system to teach a theater arts class. Everyone was surprised when he'd agreed, and more surprised when he'd agreed to do it again. He referred to his students as future artists and patrons, and, in fact, the number of student interns at the Cliffside had increased dramatically since he began working in the schools. The stipend also helped him make ends meet. No one was getting rich working at the Cliffside.

"Think about how timely the story is, and what you could do with it," I continued. "What do you think the soul of the piece is? Maybe it's the Cratchits' story?" I thought I saw a light of inspiration spark in Dimitri's eyes.

"A modern version, in a city," he mused. "Scrooge could run one of those check cashing places … Bob Cratchit would be a woman, of course … "

Personally, I would have preferred a Victorian *Christmas Carol*, but if modernization got him to do it, then so be it. Nonetheless, I recognized the signs and realized that he needed to be reined in, and quickly, before our cash cow cost us more than its gross potential.

"Okay, Dimitri, here's the deal. This has got to be a thrifty production. The goal is to make money for the summer. You've got to keep that in mind. Think in metaphors." I spoke slowly, as if to a child, emphasizing each word so that I could be sure he understood. I wished I had turned on the recorder on my phone.

"But my audience expects a certain panache in my efforts."

"Panache, but on a budget. That's not something everyone can do. Remember your tanks. And the camouflage."

∞

It worked, for the first two years. Dimitri reworked the text, coming up with a version of *A Christmas Carol* that was both a critical and commercial success. He worked within a budget, used his pool of student talent well, and helped take some of the pressure off the summer fundraising efforts. Indeed, it worked as intended—until this year. He cast a star as Scrooge and all hell broke loose.

When Dimitri informed me he'd talked to Patrick about taking over the role of Scrooge, my gut told me to panic. I wasn't sure why.

"Dimitri, he's pretty well known. We can't afford him."

"He's willing to work for scale. And to come up early and work with my students." He sounded a little smug, which made my gut ache even more.

"Why?"

"Why what?"

"Why is he willing to do Scrooge in a shoestring production on a high school stage?" It was cold, I'll admit. Our production was more than fine, and I was proud to be associated with it. That said, I'd found over the years that if I pissed Dimitri off right away and he lost his temper, we cut through a lot of crap. This time, however, he didn't bite.

"He's interested in doing *Long Day's Journey Into Night*, possibly this summer. Don't look at me like that. You've got to admit he'd make a fabulous James Tyrone."

"Dimitri, we haven't finalized that yet." Getting the board to sign off on a four-hour drama at a summer theater was going to take some work. They'd "given" me a new play by a local playwright and a Gilbert and Sullivan in trade.

"Of course not."

Dimitri and I had agreed to wait until after *A Christmas Carol* to commit to *Long Day's Journey Into Night*, and thank heaven for that. I'd asked around about Patrick King before he arrived and gleaned that he had a difficult reputation. Difficult actors with talent were often worth the effort. But not always. Patrick King was decidedly not worth the trouble. He'd turned our simple fundraising production into a nightmare.

My gut had also told me to ask questions. Why was an actor like Patrick King available on such short notice? Why was he willing to work for so little? Why wasn't he doing a play in New York or London, or working on a television series, or making a movie? Why hadn't I seen him work recently? During the second week of rehearsal, the reasons for his availability came flying in at breakneck speed. They were, in no particular order: because he's a drunk, because he's a letch, because he can't remember his lines worth a damn, because he had an ego the size of Utah, and because he's lost the talent that made the ego palatable.

By the time we'd figured it out, it was too late. The run was sold out. His name was above the title. If we replaced him, we would have to offer refunds. The money already had been spent. I could have said "I told you so" to Dimitri, but it wouldn't have changed things. He'd been a Patrick King fan.

We cancelled the classes with the students, since putting him in the vicinity of females under the age of twenty-one was a liability. I kept him away from unchaperoned interns. I thought I had it covered, until he hit on Lila Allen, aka Mrs. Cratchit, a heretofore happily married woman. She was thrilled by the attention and had, of late, taken on some of his less admirable traits. Now, according to Dimitri, they were having an affair.

Add to that the continuing attrition of cast members like David and we had a full-scale disaster in the offing. The normally copious supporting cast, most of them volunteers, had dwindled to a spartan few. There weren't even enough Cratchit kids. Now I needed to convince Stewart Tracy to come to the rescue.

Stewart Tracy. Handsome, cocky, charming Stewart Tracy. Stewart Tracy was one of my favorite actors. He was a pleasure to work with, incredibly adaptable, and talented to boot. Stewart had been at the Cliffside for at least part of the past three seasons. The first season we became friends, with some harmless flirting that made life interesting. During the second season, the flirting started early and led to a full-scale affair. It didn't endure past Labor Day, but I hadn't expected it to, nor had he. Last season he'd only been in one show, and had come up with a girlfriend in tow. I was a little jealous, but mostly relieved. Our relationship had been cathartic, but it wasn't long-term material.

I considered Stewart a friend, a very good friend, and looked forward to seeing him again. He and his summer fling had broken up, and he'd called and emailed me a few times over the past few weeks for consolation. His career required, and received, most of his emotional focus, which was difficult for a lot of women to understand. Hell, if I'd been in it for the long haul, I wouldn't have been very happy about it either. But I'd been in the relationship for an emotional reboot, and I got a great friend in the process. I still got a stupid grin on my face every time I saw a Facebook post announcing his latest play, and I tried to travel and see it whenever possible.

Stewart's latest posts had chronicled a Broadway play that never got its legs and closed early. He was putting a good face on his forced vacation with a "the Universe will provide" Facebook post that got 426 likes and 123 comments assuring him he'd land on his feet. Stewart hated not working, which is why I'd taken the chance that he would join our merry troupe and texted and emailed him from the reception. He hated *A Christmas Carol*, and normally wouldn't have come near the piece, but my email told him how desperate the situation was. And I begged. I'd give him another half hour before the full email/phone call/text assault began.

I settled down at my desk and dove into the copious administrative work of a general manager. I'd barely finished sorting the mail when there was a knock on the door.

"What?!?" It wasn't the most pleasant greeting, but I was annoyed that my *Do Not Disturb* sign had gone unheeded.

It was Harry. "Just wanted to check in and see how the party went," he said.

I smiled despite myself. "It wasn't a party. And the reception was fine. You should have come with me."

"I should have been with Eric. If he had any backbone ... "

"Harry, don't. I'm not going to pick sides here." And if I were, I thought to myself, I'd choose yours. Even though Eric was a relative, and despite the genuine affection I felt for him, Harry and I had clicked as friends from the start. Though he made a good living doing film and industrial work and occasionally working at other theaters, Harry was a staple at the Cliffside. He spent hours volunteering in the office. He did help, but we also spent a lot of time talking, gossiping, and laughing. We shared the same sensibilities, used the same cultural references, and had similar backgrounds. We both tended to refer to the Brady Bunch as if it were Jane Austen, which in a way it was for our generation. Isn't that sad? And both of us were only children raised Catholic by happily married parents.

Harry and I had another thing in common: we were both orphaned. It doesn't matter how old you are when your second parent dies; becoming an orphan is a horrible rite of passage. Harry lost his father a few months after we met, and our shared grief provided a layer to our friendship that propelled it from friends to something akin to a soulmate.

Now Eric had joined the orphan club, but it was different. We both knew that his relationship with his father was troubled at best. I wondered if that made it more difficult for Eric to lose his father. When Peter was murdered, Eric lost his last chance to convince his father to accept him for who he was, rather than the son Peter made no bones about wanting him to be.

Harry picked up my pile of discarded mail and began to rip it into pieces, putting each of the fragments in a different pile to be discarded in different recycling bins. This was my doing, this paranoid mail discarding. I knew of far too many people who were undone by someone else pawing through their mail, stealing a credit card application or an insurance renewal, and wreaking havoc with their life. The Cliffside had enough troubles without getting its credit damaged by identity theft.

"Maybe I should buy a shredder." I'd always found a better use for the money, but this ripping ritual was ridiculous, though strangely therapeutic. And Harry was an amazing ripper, making sure to destroy addresses while somehow tearing things into fairly uniform squares.

"How was Eric holding up at the reception?" he asked after a moment. He said it a little too nonchalantly. I wondered when they'd last spoken.

"He wasn't his normal charming self," I said. "But he was wrestled away from me by Brooke. She's really something, isn't she? Is she always—"

"Had he been drinking?"

"Yeah, he had. But to be fair, there was an open bar. I was the only person not drinking." Eric and drinking had a rocky relationship. One might say that Eric didn't do it well, but that wasn't true. He did it very well. But he was a mean drunk. He'd quit drinking hard liquor last New Year's as a resolution and promise to Harry. He drank an occasional glass of wine with dinner, but he'd stuck to his resolution as far as I knew.

As if reading my mind, Harry offered me more information. "Something's been up at work. I don't know what—he wouldn't talk about it. He's been hitting the bourbon bottle a lot lately, falling into some bad habits. That's one reason we decided to take a break."

"I'm sorry. I didn't know."

"I thought it would blow over, but now … he's taking his father's death pretty hard. Harder than Peter deserved, you know?"

"You've been in contact?"

"Through texts. He won't talk to me."

"That's tough," I said. I hated texts. I texted, but I much preferred talking to people. "I'm not surprised he's taking Peter's death hard. He was a loyal son. And he's a very loyal brother."

"Yes, he's worried sick about Amelia."

"She seems a little, um, medicated."

"She's always on a different plain of existence. It's part of her charm. Her father used to call her his hippy. I'm not surprised she's a wreck. She loved the old bastard. And she's the one who found him. He was locked in his office, and no one else had been in there all night. Emma says—"

"Emma?"

"She and I have been talking every day. Talking, not texting."

"I didn't realize you were that close," I said.

The ripping was finally over. Harry took one of the piles and put it in his knapsack. He'd recycle it at home. Then he moved on to sorting the rest of the mail into piles.

"We're friendly, but we weren't that close until all this happened," he said. "I called to offer my condolences, and she opened up. She needed someone familiar with the players, but a little removed, you know? She's processing a lot right now. Especially if ... "

"If what?"

"If someone in the family killed Peter."

"Do they think it was the family?" I was getting hooked on the puzzle—it had started with my tour outside the Anchorage. My personality drove me to understand, and complete, puzzles. My strength lay in the fact that I never forced the pieces. Instead, I continued to look for new ones to complete the picture. "Maybe someone came in from outside."

Harry shook his head. "Impossible. Well, maybe not impossible, but unlikely. The fence around the property is secure, and there are security cameras inside and outside the house. Peter was a freak about security. Coming up from the cliff would be tough no matter what, but the Saturday he died was that storm, remember? The ice and sleet? No way someone could get up in that. Even if they could climb up the cliff to the windows of his study, what then? The windows don't open at the bottom. Only the transom windows open, on top."

"You've thought a lot about this," I said. I thought back to the windows, and my theory that the shot must have come from inside the house. If only family was there ...

"No one else went in or came out?" I asked.

"Not from what I've heard. Did you meet Terry?"

"Emma's husband, yes." Harry and I paused. I assumed that Harry probably knew about Emma meeting with me last spring, since Eric had set it up, but we'd never discussed it. I wanted to go there, to start dishing, but that would be betraying Emma. I let the moment pass.

"Anyway," he said, acknowledging the pause, "Terry is the son Peter always wanted, and got when Terry married Emma. Poor Em. She has the goods, you know. But Peter passed the reins to Terry when he decided Eric wasn't up to snuff. Emma could run the company, but he was a sexist old bastard. Anyway, Terry and Peter had a conference call around midnight the night Peter was killed. Amelia found her dad around seven the next morning. Coroner said he'd only been dead a couple of hours, but she couldn't be sure of an exact time of death."

"You said there were cameras?"

"The cops have the recordings. But from what Emma's heard, they aren't helpful. If someone was walking in the dark, it would be tough to identify them."

I took one pile of mail and put it in my bag, and threw away another in a recycling bin. I wanted to ask a million questions—how did they set the time of death? Were the recordings tampered with? Were they digital or on tape? Or both? Did they confirm the call? But I moved away from the murder details, tempting as they were. Harry's expertise was the family dynamic, not ballistics. "What did you mean by 'Eric wasn't up to snuff'?"

"You know ... a businessman like his old man."

"Eric has a great reputation."

"I'm not saying that Eric isn't good at business. I'm saying that he isn't his father's son. He's always fighting for the little guy, questioning the ethics of buying a small company as if you're going to fold it into your company and then squash it like a bug. He doesn't have the stomach for running the business like his father."

"Does Emma?" I realized that though I knew Eric as an adult, the Emma I knew, really knew, was about ten years old. I wondered how the Emma I'd met this spring fit into that picture. Was the wronged wife who wore her emotions on her sleeve part of the woman Emma had become, or an aberration? Was Emma a cold, heartless business-woman, a Peter protégé save the gender difference?

"Yes, she does, for the most part," Harry replied. "She listens to Eric, seeks his counsel, shields him from the really difficult decisions. And he lets her."

"She's the big sister." Sibling relationships intrigued me. I'd met siblings who'd die for one another, who'd kill for one another, and who'd gladly kill each other.

"To both Eric and Amelia. And Eric's the big brother to Amelia. There's no one in the world he would do more for than Amelia. No one."

"Does he think Amelia had anything to do with her father's death?"

"I have no idea. He's made it really clear that taking care of her is his priority right now."

"Which means?"

"Keeping her out of jail. Whatever it takes."

· Five ·

The phone call came Monday morning. I didn't recognize the number on my caller ID, which usually means I let it go to voicemail and deal with it later. But this time I picked up. Granted, since Massachusetts enacted the Do Not Call law, picking up isn't as hazardous to my mental equilibrium as it once was, but it was still a risk.

"Did I wake you?" Emma was on the line.

"No, I've been up for a while," I lied. I'd been up for the fifteen seconds since the phone rang.

"Thanks for coming to the funeral."

"Of course. Again, I'm so sorry—"

"So am I. My father was a pain in the ass and could be a world-class bastard." I smiled at that—the exact phrase my father used to describe Peter Whitehall. "But he was my father, and I loved him," Emma went on. "I hope he knew that. I've spent a lot of this past week, since it … happened, thinking about how he would have wanted things handled. I have a pretty good idea. He was always clear about prioritizing. Protect the business and the family at all costs."

"What happens if there's a conflict between the two?" I swung my legs over the side of the bed and stretched. Max took it as a signal to get up and get ready for his breakfast. He did his cat yoga on the bed, and then jumped down. We both left the bedroom together and walked into the kitchen.

"He didn't tell me how to handle that. Right now, the business is fine. It's Amelia."

"She seemed pretty wrecked."

"I believe my father loved all of his children, I do, but I *know* he loved Amelia. Which is why it's so ridiculous."

"What?"

"That she's under suspicion," Emma said. For the first time, I heard her voice break a little.

"You're sure?"

"I'm sure. I know you don't do this kind of work anymore, but I was hoping that you could help ... "

"Clear Amelia?"

"Yes," Emma said. "Listen, Sully, I don't know what to think. She doesn't remember anything from that night. She doesn't even remember finding him." Emma took a ragged breath and fought for control. She'd regained it when she spoke next. "I'm almost at the office, so here it is, all the cards on the table. I don't think Amelia did it, but someone in the house did."

"You know that for sure?"

"Yes, the police confirmed it. My father had an extensive security system. All the doors and windows were secured, and no one came in or left from nine until the police arrived the next morning. The list is short. And everyone on it is family, or close to. What I need you to do is to figure out what the police could use as evidence, so that we're ready."

"Ready for what?"

"To circle the wagons, if need be." Her sentence hung there for a while. I had no doubt the Whitehall family would, and could, "circle the wagons," whatever that meant. I questioned whether or not I wanted to be a part of it, but decided to cross that bridge when I got to it.

Who killed Peter Whitehall intrigued me. I wouldn't deny it.

"Emma, I can't promise anything. But I'll confess, the challenge of figuring this out is intriguing. Tell me about who was at the house."

"Terry. Eric. Mrs. Bridges. Clive Willis, a business associate. Hal Maxwell, I think you know him?"

"I've met him several times at the Cliffside. I know his wife, Babs Allyn."

"She wasn't there, but Jerry and Mimi Cunningham came. Hal and the Cunninghams left early because of the weather, but they were on the conference call later."

"Why was the call so late?"

"Foreign business."

"Anyone else in the house?"

"Brooke was there, of course. Mrs. Bridges sent the rest of the staff home while the roads were still passable."

"Emma, do you have an idea of who might have done it?" I asked gently.

Emma sighed. "Sully, this is between you and me, but I wouldn't be heartbroken to find out Brooke did it. I don't like her, never have, and I look forward to extricating her from our lives." The vehemence that dripped from her last statement was the strongest emotion I'd heard displayed so far in this conversation.

"Okay…"

"Sorry, sorry," Emma said. "She gets under my skin. When I left the house this morning, she was already half in the bag."

"She has a drinking problem?"

"She drinks, but it's never been a problem per se. The last couple of days, though, she's stayed pretty toasted. Listen, I've got to go into the office. I've told Mrs. Bridges I was going to try and talk you into looking around."

"No promises, but I'll go visit Mrs. Bridges, see what I come up with. I'm not an investigator anymore—"

"But you are family. Thank you, Sully. Oh, wait, before you go, one more thing."

"Yes?" I said.

"For the record, I didn't kill my father."

"I didn't think you did," I said. I may have been lying.

∞

I took a quick shower, fed Max, and headed into the theater as soon as the coffee was made and poured into my travel mug. During show weeks, Monday is usually dark, meaning there are no performances. Even during rehearsal weeks it's often the day off. But not this week. This Monday was the last Monday before we performed for a paying audience on Friday. We had five preview performances, then opened the next week. By this point the cast, crew, and designers were deep into technical rehearsals, focusing lights, practicing costume changes, setting the props, working on the set. Dimitri was at the helm, but now the pilot was Connie, our stage manager. All I could do was hold Dimitri's hand while refusing to throw any more money at this debacle.

So when I got to the high school, that is precisely what I did. I checked in with everyone and said no to a half-dozen requests coming from every department. I knew Dimitri had put the requestors up to it; their hearts weren't in it. Somewhere along the line, Dimitri had decided to up the ante with the production values like lights, costumes, sound, and set to help offset what some had nicknamed "A Christmas Dirge." He was trying to take our small show into the special effects world of Broadway, and I was running interference. I couldn't see how adding more lights and fog to the scenes would really help cover up the fact that Scrooge couldn't remember his lines or his blocking.

Trying to clear my schedule, Stewart texted as I made my way to the tech table in the middle of the theater. *Got a commercial. Be up tonight or early tomorrow a.m.*

Thank you! Keep me posted, I texted back.

I sat through as much of the rehearsal as I could stand, which wasn't much. Tech rehearsals are notoriously slow and exacting. I went out to the lobby and sipped my coffee while reading through emails on my phone. Who was I kidding? I couldn't concentrate. Finally I called Mrs. Bridges, the Whitehall family housekeeper.

When I heard her voice and the relief in it when she knew it was me, I knew I'd committed to looking into the murder. Mrs. Bridges invited me over for tea, and I accepted. For the second time in less than a week, I found myself at the Anchorage.

∞

I rang the buzzer at the gate and gave my name. Today mine was the only car in the large circular drive. The gray December sky added an ominous backdrop to the imposing house, but it suited the sepia palette of the place, with the landscape and the sky working together to enhance the house's majesty. Red ribbons had replaced the black ones on the wreaths. I would have spent a few more seconds looking around, but the door swung open and I found myself face to face with Mrs. Bridges.

I'd known her my entire life, and I was amazed at how little she'd changed over time. She was plumper now; not fat, just rounded out a little. Her hair was grayer, but her French braid was the same. Her wide-legged pants, unstructured jacket, and dark-colored shirt were simple but high quality. She remained neither fashionable nor unfashionable, but timeless instead.

"It's been a long time. Let me look at you." She held me out at arm's length and then folded me into her arms and gave me a hug. It caught me off balance. My initial instinct was to pull away, but I allowed myself to relax for a minute. It had been a long time since someone had held me that tight. I'd forgotten how safe it felt. She let go and took me by the elbow, guiding me toward the kitchen at the back of the house, her domain.

"It's good to see you, Mrs. B. It's been a while."

"Well, I saw you at the funeral, of course. And I've seen you at the theater a few times."

"You have? I didn't see you … "

"You're always so busy, I didn't want to interrupt."

"Please interrupt. You would probably save me from some horror or another. I always love seeing a friendly face."

"Next time I will, I promise."

"Mrs. B., I'm sorry I haven't had a chance to offer my condolences."

"Thank you, Edwina." I winced. She was the only person who still called me Edwina and got away with it. "He was a difficult man to be sure. But he treated me well for a lot of years. I'll miss him."

"At least he and his Emily are together again," I offered by way of rote comfort, channeling my mother for a moment.

Mrs. Bridges laughed. "Now surely you don't believe that, do you? Now really, darlin', we both know Mr. Whitehall has some warm days in front of him before he's allowed to see his sainted wife, may God rest her soul."

"Maybe she put in a good word for him ... "

"And your father would have waited until she left, and then he'd have set Saint Peter straight. No, Peter Whitehall has some penance to do before he rests."

"You don't think my father did?"

"I know he didn't, and so do you. He was a good man, Bryan Sullivan. A very good man. I'd have to say there probably isn't a man or woman alive who'd blame him for that situation with Mr. Whitehall. In retrospect, not even Mr. Whitehall himself."

When my father was dying and in the hospital, Mrs. Bridges would sit with me for a few hours every day. I'm not sure how she knew what was happening, that he was dying. What I do know is that a lot of people disappear at the very end, when the dying starts in earnest. The hours stretch into days, and it's incredibly lonely. I didn't reach out to anyone, and didn't realize that I needed someone, until this lovely lady from my childhood took it upon herself to come and sit with me while I watched my father die. She would bring a thermos of tea and some sandwiches. After a bit she'd say, "Why don't you go for a walk, Edwina? I'll sit with your dad until you come back." And I'd go, knowing that he was in good hands. Other times she'd tell me stories about my mother and her cousin Emily, but only the happy ones. Not about them dying. Not about the feud between my father and Peter Whitehall that ripped the family apart. Only the happy stories.

She wasn't there when my father died, and I thought about waiting at the hospital until she arrived, but Gus had come to be with me and took me home. I didn't shed a tear. I finally sent Gus away. I couldn't bear his kindness on top of my grief. Later that afternoon the doorbell rang. It was Mrs. Bridges. "I'm so sorry, darlin'" was all she said, and then she took me in her arms. I cried like I'd never cried before or since.

By now we were in the kitchen and she fixed tea. She didn't ask if I preferred coffee, or what kind of tea I wanted, or if I wanted decaf. She made tea, and I let her. Though I normally prefer coffee, I knew her tea would prove to be exactly what I wanted. It always was.

"You take milk, don't you?" She put the pot in front of me and began to pour.

"Sure, that would be lovely."

"Emma let me know you might be stopping by. We worried it was an imposition, but Emma insisted that getting you involved in our troubles was our best avenue."

"I'll do what I can—"

"We need to find out what happened," Mrs. Bridges said, sitting down and putting her cup in front of her.

"No matter what that means?" I asked. Mrs. Bridges stirred her tea with great concentration. I reached my hand across the table and put it on top of hers, squeezing it gently. "How do you feel about that?"

"Feel? That's a difficult one. I still can't believe he's gone. There wasn't time to ... "

"To what?"

"Never mind. Just the musings of an old woman. There'll be a lot of people looking into Mr. Whitehall's death. It might be good for family to take part as well, just in case."

"In case what?"

"In case it's family that did it."

I met her gaze and didn't blink. "Do you think it was the family?"

"The suspects, as you'd call them, are few, but you probably know that already. There weren't many of us in the house. Security cameras are around the house. The guard at the front gate—"

"Is the guard there all the time?"

"He's more of a caretaker, really. Lives out at the gatehouse. Not always on duty, and we can control the gate from inside the house too."

"Is the gate always closed?"

"Normally, yes. Days like Saturday, when we're expecting a crowd, those days we leave the gate open. We hire extra security for the grounds."

"On the night Mr. Whitehall was—on the night of the incident, was the gate closed?"

"Yes, and the guard was on duty to let folks in and out. He didn't see anyone else come in."

"Do you trust him?

"Russell? Yes, he's worked here for years."

"I suppose it's still possible that someone got by the cameras and the front gate," I said. It wasn't likely, though. More and more, it looked like the killer had been in the house already. I'd need to confirm my gut feeling that the window in Peter's study was broken from the inside. I always tried to confirm suppositions with facts. It made the puzzle easier to solve the right way, later.

"I keep hoping that's true, but I don't honestly know," she said. "It would be tough to get past it all. But maybe you'll find a way."

"One thing I hope you and Emma understand—I'm not here to find an alibi or cover anything up. It's not how I'm built. I'm here to see if I can figure out what happened."

"Of course, of course. We both understand that. I didn't mean to impugn your integrity—"

"You didn't. I just want to be clear from the outset. I'm going to follow the evidence where it takes me."

"You are your father's daughter," Mrs. Bridges said, smiling. She took a sip of tea, and I followed suit.

"Great tea," I said. "I am his daughter. I'd like to think a bit of my mother rubbed off as well."

"You are the best of both," she said. Her compliment made me smile. It was likely a pile of malarkey, but I was fine with that. "I suppose you'll be wanting to see the scene of the crime, as it were," she said, standing up.

"If it isn't too painful." I took another sip of tea and stood.

"Too painful?" She thought about it for a moment. "Not too painful. Almost, but your work is too important to the family."

∞

Mrs. Bridges stood at the threshold as I looked around. I was careful not to touch anything. The room had been released back to the family by the investigating officers, but you never knew when they'd need to come back in for whatever reason. Next time I'd bring gloves. For now, I put my hands in my pockets to make sure I didn't inadvertently reach out and leave prints.

I'd never been in the study before. Peter Whitehall's private sanctum had not been open to visitors. The room was good-sized but not huge. The wall that connected to the rest of the house was lined with bookshelves. The two walls perpendicular had as much glass as the architecture of the room allowed. On the left wall, which faced the driveway, there was a stone fireplace, with dark paneling running behind it about seven feet high. The remainder of the wall consisted of transom windows. I recalled from my walk around the house that the stone from the fireplace was part of the outside of the house, looking like a natural formation that had intruded into the addition. An interesting architectural detail. The right wall had low cabinetry that matched the bookshelves and paneling, with larger windows providing an impressive view of the side yard and the Trevorton harbor in the background. The back wall was entirely made of glass, and literally sat out over the cliff's edge.

Peter's desk was L shaped, with one side facing the hall door, the other facing the fireplace. His computer and chair were at the part facing the fireplace. Two guest chairs were stationed with their backs to the door, facing the desk; he'd probably used the L part of the desk with visitors. His desk and chair were significantly higher than the visitors'. The other furniture in the room was minimal and very much in keeping with the men's club feel of the room. A beautiful globe stood by the back wall. Next to it was a telescope. The room had the definite appearance of being well used. It gave me a strong sense of Peter, stronger than the man himself had ever given me. I ached to read the titles of the books on his shelves to gain more insight into him, but that would have to wait.

There was a layer of dust on everything, some of it from fingerprint powder and the rest from a few days of neglect. A large leather club chair flanked the fireplace, facing the door to the room. There wasn't a rug on the floor, but I could see where it had been by the different color and use of the floor within a large circle.

"Did they take the rug that was in here?" I asked.

"Yes. They took the matching club chair as well."

"Was it here?" I positioned myself next to the club chair, angling myself toward it but facing the fireplace. Mrs. Bridges nodded. I looked at the chair, and then over at the boarded-up window. Peter would have been angled toward the broken window. But still, I didn't see it.

"Did you come into the room that morning?"

Mrs. Bridges pulled her jacket around herself and folded her arms against her chest. "Yes. I was in the kitchen with Eric. I heard Amelia scream, and ran. I could see Mr. Whitehall lying on the floor. Amelia was beside him. I thought he'd had a heart attack or something. She'd pulled his head into her lap and was stroking his hair. I pulled her up and saw the blood. So much blood. The chair was covered. I checked to make sure he was … gone. I took Amelia and left. I closed the door and told Eric to call the police."

"Who else was here?"

"In the hall, you mean? No one, right then. But it's hard to hear from one end of this house to another, unless you're in the hallway at the right time and the right doors are open."

"Who else was in the house?"

"Terry, Emma, Brooke … Amelia and Eric, of course. Mr. Willis hadn't come down yet. That's it."

"I know this is hard, Mrs. Bridges, but I'm going to ask you to think about the room that morning. Was anything out of—"

"The police already asked me. Everything was as it should have been. Except for poor Mr. Whitehall."

"Okay then, can you tell me what's different now?" I walked over and put my hand out to her. Her hand was freezing. We walked into the room.

"Well, the chair was there, of course. And there was a book next to him on the floor. There." She pointed to a space near the small side table the two chairs had shared. "And there were a lot of ashes in the fireplace ... "

"More than normal?"

"More than I would have expected."

"Did you clean the ashes up?"

"No, the police took them. And the book. And a few other things."

"Like?"

"A decanter with some scotch in it, some glasses ... I'm not sure what else. Emma may know."

"Do you know how Amelia found him?"

"Lying there."

"Facing the door?"

"No. Facing the fireplace, as if he'd fallen forward out of the chair. He may have tried to get up ... " She shuddered. "Have you seen enough? I don't want to rush you, but our tea is probably getting cold."

I looked around and tried to picture the scene with the details she'd provided. "Of course, that's fine." I would have preferred to stay and examine things more thoroughly, but I could tell she couldn't bear to be in the room. I couldn't blame her. If there was a space ripe for haunting, Peter Whitehall's study was it.

I turned for one last glance around the room.

"What the hell are you doing in my husband's study?" Brooke Whitehall asked as she lunged.

Mrs. Bridges sidestepped me and caught the younger woman by her waist, holding her up in the doorway. Brooke looked like a worn-down version of herself. Her eyes had makeup smudges around them. Her hair was pulled back in a tight chignon, but several strands had escaped, and not in an artful, fashionable way. Her clothes were desperate for an iron.

"Edwina is a guest of mine, Brooke." Although Mrs. Bridges still called Peter "Mr. Whitehall" after forty years with the family, Brooke was Brooke after less than a decade as his wife.

"I said, what the hell is she doing?"

"She wanted to borrow a book." Mrs. Bridges steered us both toward the hallway. She locked the door behind her.

"Who said she could go in there?"

"Emma."

"Emma." Brooke said the name in that bratty singsong tone that kids use to make life hell on the playground. It suited her well. "Queen Emma the bitch."

"That's enough now."

"She's a bitch, and you know it. She treats me horribly, horribly." Brooke leaned into me, pressing her nails into my forearm while she complained, and I got a waft of the sour stench of alcohol. "Do you know she took my car keys away from me? Can you believe the gall? She's leaving me stranded. If I didn't have Terry, I don't know what I'd do. He takes such good care of me. Terry. He'd do anything for me. Just ask him. I don't know what I'd do if I didn't have him. If it was up to the bitch, I'd be out on the street."

Mrs. Bridges declawed my arm and moved Brooke toward the front staircase. "I'll bring you up some tea, would you like that? Of course you would. You go on now. I'm going to say goodbye to Edwina."

"Edwina?" She said it in the same singsongy, bitchy tone she'd used for Emma's name. "So your name is Edwina? What a horrible name! You poor thing." She kept saying my name over and over again and laughing as she went up the stairs, bouncing from one banister to another as she cackled.

We watched her slow, unsteady progress. "I'm sorry, Edwina," Mrs. Bridges said.

"Don't be. It's a horrible name. Nice sentiment by my mother to honor her grandfather, but tough execution on a kid. Not the first time someone has made fun." I smiled and patted her arm. "Has Brooke been like that since the funeral?"

"No, not really. Mind you, she was drinking after the funeral, but that's nothing new." Mrs. Bridges gave me a look that spoke volumes. "But she wasn't … she's never been so out of control before. This only really started in the last day or so. I should go up and look after her."

"The shock probably got to her. Delayed reaction. Look," I said, pulling a card out of my pocket and handing it to her, "here's my phone number and email address. Get in touch if you remember anything unusual."

"I will."

"I'll probably come back later in the week, if that's okay?" I asked. Mrs. Bridges nodded and smiled. "Thanks for the tea."

"Thank you for the company," she said. "And for making me walk into that room. I couldn't before."

"Can I ask you two more quick questions? I noticed you locked the door…"

"Emma's request. She had it re-keyed after … afterward. She gave me the only key."

"Why?"

"You'll have to ask her." Sounds ranging from moans to cackles wafted down the stairs, followed by a loud crash and a string of expletives that would make a sailor blush. "Did you have another question? I really should check on her."

"It can wait." I needed more time to figure out the best way to ask about Terry, and about how accurate Brooke's assessment was that he would do anything for her.

∞

I had just closed the front door behind me when another car drove into the driveway. Regina Roberts got out and stomped toward me. "Sully, what the hell are you doing here?" One thing to be said for Regina, she never beat around the bush. Forthrightness is a valuable tool in a police officer, but I wondered what Regina did when an interrogation took more finesse. Of course, most crime in Trevorton did not require finesse.

"Nice to see you too, Regina."

"Sorry. This place makes me forget my manners. Nice to see you, Sully. What the hell are you doing here again?"

"I'm a friend of the family's."

"And your curiosity got the better of you."

"No, not exactly," I said. "Well, maybe a little."

"It's okay, Sully. It's gotten the better of most of this town." Murder, particularly local murder, usually did. Peter Whitehall was famous enough that the interest must have been notched up a level.

"I can only imagine what it's been like," I said. High profile cases were the stuff of my nightmares. "How's the investigation going?"

I recognized the fight that Regina was having with herself. Here I was, an ex-cop and friend of the family. Maybe I could help. But, and it was a big but, this case was huge. She needed to make sure her work, and the force's work, was exemplary. And talking to an outsider, no matter who, was risky. I knew the struggle.

"Sorry, Sully, you know how it is … ongoing investigation and all."

"Of course, sure. I'll let you get to it."

"Who's home?" Regina asked.

"Mrs. Bridges and Brooke. I'm not sure about anyone else."

"Damn. I was supposed to meet Terry Holmes here."

"I didn't see him, but it is a big house."

"So I take it he's not the part of the family you count as a friend."

"Nope, only officially met him Saturday, after the funeral." She was dying to know more, I could tell, but I wasn't volunteering information. "Regina, can I ask you one question?"

"I can't—"

"I was wondering where Peter was shot."

"In his study."

Cute. "I mean, where was he shot on his body?"

"Heart."

"Front or back?"

"Front."

I tried to remember the room. Mrs. Bridges said the police had removed the chair. I assumed it had a bullet in it.

Regina and I played chicken for a couple of seconds, and I gave up. She was doing her job.

"Good to see you, Regina. I guess I'll see Gabe at run-through later this week."

"That's it? The great detective is only going to ask questions that most people already know the answer to?" I attributed her snide tone to fatigue, though the great detective line rankled me a little.

"'Great detective'?"

"Surely you know that your reputation lives on that, right?" I fought to keep my face neutral. There was no longer any hint of a smile. "Yeah, well, sorry," she added. "Bitchy thing to say ..."

"Not really. The tone was bitchy. The statement itself, well, it depends on who its source is."

"Never mind, Sully. I'll talk to you later." Regina turned toward the house. She was a few feet from the front door when it swung open and Terry Holmes stepped onto the threshold to welcome her. He'd been home after all. And he hadn't bothered to say hi.

· Six ·

I was going to go back to the high school, but decided to take a side trip to Salem. Actually, Salem wasn't a side trip. It required a conscious decision to wind my way over to Route 1 and head south. But to Salem I went, to pay a visit to Jack Megan's PI office. I wasn't even sure he'd be there, but I'd rather surprise him than call and give him a heads-up.

In the old days, private investigators spent a lot of time out of the office, sitting on surveillance, looking up financial information in public records, doing old-fashioned legwork. There was still legwork on the job, but now, with the advent of computers, specialized software, and access (authorized or not) to a variety of databases, private investigators did a significant portion of their work online and still caught the bad guys.

Like me, Jack used to be a cop. He'd been retired a few years earlier, with a number of working years left and a family, so he got his PI license. I never knew why Jack left the force, only rumors. Some good, some bad. Hell, it was the same with me. Officially, I left because injuries precluded me from doing the job. But had I not pissed off certain people during my tenure with the State Police, I probably would have been reassigned to desk duty, or even promoted into computer work, where my injuries wouldn't have mattered. But I ticked off the wrong people and they took the first opportunity to get me out. They tried to do it without a pension, but they were only partially successful.

My descent into the unfavored taught me some valuable lessons. The most important: if you go after the bad guys, make sure you get them all. If even one is left standing, their power remains. I'd been assigned to a task force looking into corruption in the state penal system. I didn't have to look too hard; none of us did. We'd started to issue the indictments when all hell broke loose. The man heading up the task force started to have mud slung at him. The problem was, a lot of it stuck. It didn't mean the indictments weren't valid. But clever lawyers got a lot of them thrown out, and the task force imploded.

I went back to my regular job, knowing what I knew, working with people who'd abdicated the honor of carrying the badge. I didn't make trouble, but I also didn't make nice. The minute the injury happened, I knew my days were numbered.

I wish I could say that I'd had a heroic injury in the line of duty. But it wasn't. I was walking through the office and slipped in a puddle of water, fracturing my back. I don't know if the puddle was left there on purpose, and I don't dwell on that possibility. I do know that there weren't any warning signs, and my then-husband the lawyer hinted that we had a case unless they did right by me.

Even thinking about it made my back hurt. I pulled into the first open meter I could find and headed toward Jack's office. Sure enough, he was there.

Jack Megan was in his mid-forties, still physically fit though not as buff as when I first met him. But then, who amongst us was? He had coffee-colored eyes and a great smile with perfect teeth.

"So, what brings you out on this fine day?" he asked, after he got me settled into a chair with a big mug of coffee. Jack thought like me: straightforward worked much better than bullshit.

"Did you hear about Peter Whitehall?" I asked, taking a sip of coffee. I almost moaned aloud. Jack made a great cup of coffee.

"Of course, who hasn't?" he said. "You working the case? I thought you'd gone into theater."

"No. Yes. I am in theater. And no, I'm not working the case. Emma Whitehall called me this morning."

"Ah, so that's why you're here. Emma."

"Yeah. Thought I'd pick your brain a little."

"About?"

"She hired you earlier this year, right?" I asked. He shrugged. This was karmic retribution. I'd done it to Regina, now Jack was doing it to me. "Jack, I recommended you to her, remember? I wondered if there was anything hinky—"

"Ask Emma."

"I'd rather not."

"Sully, you know that I can't tell you anything, even if there was something to tell. Client confidentiality."

"C'mon, I won't tell anyone." He laughed, and I had to join him. What was I doing? "Sorry, Jack. I'm trying to get a handle on the family dynamics, and I figured you've spent some time working them out."

"Not the whole family," he said. He got up and grabbed the coffee pot. "Just one part. Not even a blood relation to the recently deceased." He looked at me carefully, and then topped off my coffee cup. After he put the pot back on the burner, he went and made sure the door was closed. "There's not much to tell. She hired me to figure out if her husband was stepping out."

"Right." That I knew.

"And as far as I could tell, he wasn't."

"As far as you could tell."

"He never went anywhere except home and office. But maybe his mistress was at the office, though that was unlikely since Emma was usually there."

"That's it?"

"That's it. I had a guy on him for two weeks, and he had nothing to report. So she thanked me and pulled the plug."

There was something else, I could tell. The air between us was quiet but charged.

"What did you do for those two weeks?"

"Just some background stuff ... "

"C'mon, Jack. Don't make me beg."

"Listen, I really can't tell you any more without Emma's consent."

I put my mug down. "You're killing me."

"Or possibly with the consent of her lawyer. To whom I forwarded a copy of the report. Including some interesting financial documents. Very recently."

"Her lawyer?"

"Yeah, I think you might have met him at some point. Gus Knight, your ex."

Well. Gus was part of the picture. That was too close for comfort. I was having enough qualms about getting involved, and this cinched it. I decided to just wait till the evening news to hear more details about the case. As curious as I was, I needed to avoid Gus. I couldn't stand the guilt.

I'd inherited a lot of things from my father, most of them good. A sense of humor. A quest for justice. A terrific work ethic. But with the good came the bad. A temper. An inability to let anyone help. A stubborn streak a mile wide. Sometimes, when used in context, the bad could be made good. Stubbornness partnered with my work ethic made me a terrific cop. But I frequently lost perspective and that, coupled with an Irish temper and fierce independence, became a catastrophic combination when my world imploded.

Not that Gus was a completely innocent bystander in the demolition of our marriage. When we were first married, I tried to let him in, to tell him the good, the bad, and the ugly of the job. But—and I know this is a cliché, but I've always found it to be true—being male, he had trouble just listening. He felt obligated to offer advice to try and fix it, whatever "it" was at the moment. Sometimes his advice was helpful. A lot of times it pissed me off. So I stopped sharing my work problems with him. After a while, he stopped asking. Not long afterward, we stopped talking.

After the penal system investigation collapsed, Gus tried to offer advice, tried to warn me. But I shut him out. Things got worse when I found out he was having an affair with someone from his office, Kate something. I couldn't remember her last name, how crazy is that? I'd spent hours cursing it, screaming it, blaming it. Now I couldn't even remember it.

I used Gus's affair to feel completely vindicated and in the right about everything wrong with our marriage. Gus apologized, begged for forgiveness. I told him I'd think about it. And I probably would have, but then the rest of my life went in the dumper, so I threw the marriage on the pile.

When I fractured my back I needed steady nursing, so I told Gus I would stay with my dad to convalesce. Besides, I thought time away was a good idea. He didn't fight me.

Eventually, Dad got the whole story. He was furious with Gus, which made me feel great. Then, as I was getting back on my feet, Dad's doctor called with the news. Cancer. It was a matter of weeks. Dad and I talked a lot, cried a little, and argued some. Mostly about Gus.

Gus came to visit Dad regularly. I was peeved when Dad forgave him so easily. I was more peeved when Dad wanted me to do the same. Sick as he was, we still fought about it until I gave in, a little.

"Dad, I'll figure out this Gus thing." I settled him into the recliner and pulled the TV tray over beside him.

"Sweetheart, he's a good man. He made a mistake."

"A mistake?" I'd brought a large bag from the Beef and Ale with me. Gene was putting a little bit of everything in the bag these days, trying desperately to tempt my father to eat. I always called him back to relay what Dad had liked best, so Gene could adjust the next delivery.

"A mistake. For which, if you don't mind me saying, you aren't exactly blameless."

"What? Dad, he had an affair!"

"Look at it from his point of view. His wife, whom he loves—"

"Loved."

"Loves, shut him out of her life entirely. She was going through hell and only wanted him to watch." Dad unwrapped his sandwich and pulled a piece of turkey out to eat. "A man needs to be needed, sweetheart. You stopped needing him, so he found someone who did."

"What a cliché, Dad."

"She means nothing to him, Sully. It's over."

"Why are you taking his side? You're *my* father." And all I have left, I thought.

"I'm on your side," he said. He reached his hand out and I took it in mine. "I always have been, always will be. No matter what. Thing is, I don't want to leave you like this. You like being right so much that

71

you lose perspective. No one in this world is good enough for you, darlin', but Gus comes damn close. I'm asking you, begging you, to forgive him. Get your life back on track. Go back to Boston, call that friend of yours, become a PI. There's nothing for you here."

"Except you."

"Except me," he said, squeezing my hand and then letting it go. "Promise me you'll go back to your life. Please, Sully."

I promised Dad that I would, mostly to give him peace. Gus and I put on a good front for him, but after the funeral I told Gus I wanted a divorce. Eventually he agreed.

I felt good about being in the right, and convinced myself I was better off. It worked for a while. Then time, and Dr. Melvin, helped me see the gray tones of life instead of black and white. I looked at my past through a different lens. Instead of a wronged wife, I saw a vitriolic woman who didn't trust her husband to love her once she was no longer the tough career woman he'd married. He might have loved me anyway. Not finding out for sure was one thing I truly regret.

I work very hard at keeping myself tightly wound. It's part of my charming persona, the cranky Yankee. Because the thing is, I was and probably still am crazy about Gus. Just seeing him at the funeral made me feel like the spring might let go. My shrink would call that a step forward. I'd call it a disaster.

I did wonder what Gus was up to, and I was tempted to call Emma for clarification. He must have had Emma's consent to get the files on Terry from Jack. And Emma and Gus must be fairly close for her to have told him anything about Jack's investigation. A part of me wondered how close.

· Seven ·

As I drove back to the high school, I did my best to convince myself that stepping away from the case was the best thing for everybody. It wasn't as if the murder was going to go unsolved. Peter was too important. And though I'd spent very little time with her, Amelia hardly struck me as a likely suspect. No, really, it was best to let it go, tempting as it might be to get involved.

I drove by the Beef and Ale and slowed down. Harry, aka Bob Cratchit, was sitting on the patio, smoking. This was problematic on several fronts. First, wearing your costume outside was a no-no. They were too old, and our budget was too tight, to put them through anything but the most vital tasks. The second problem was that Harry was outside the Beef and Ale, and not at the theater at tech for *A Christmas Carol*. The third problem was that Harry was smoking. Harry didn't smoke.

"What horror at the theater brings you here, Harry? Please don't tell me you're waiting for your liquid lunch," I asked, bracing for the worst. Things were already so bad that I couldn't even fathom what could be wrong.

"I was hoping to catch you before you arrived. They've made an arrest for Peter's murder."

"Amelia?"

"No, not Amelia."

"Well, that's good then."

"They've arrested Eric. They think he killed his father."

"That's ridiculous. What evidence could they possible have? He couldn't have done it, could he? Even if he was pushed, I don't see Eric as a killer."

"Neither do I. Otherwise, I never really knew him at all."

∞

So much for remaining uninvolved. Harry piled into my car, and I drove him back to the theater. I refused to let him smoke, and he was not happy.

"I didn't even know you smoked."

"I don't. I used to, though. It's been such a nightmare lately, what with the show and the ... "

"Murder."

"Yeah, that. And Eric's been staying at the Anchorage. I haven't seen him since his father died."

"Well, it's understandable, him wanting to be with his sisters."

"It's completely understandable. I wish he'd let me see him, though. Even if we aren't together, I'm his friend. I thought he knew that."

"He's still shutting you out?"

"Yup."

"Must be a family trait on my mother's side. I always thought I got it from my dad."

"What are you talking about?"

"When things go bad, I tend to shut down and out. I don't let anyone in, even when it would help."

"Really? You strike me as someone who is pretty open ... "

"That's because things have been status quo since we've met. If the shit hits the fan, watch out. I go right back into my shell. My dad called it turtle time."

I looked over at Harry, pleased to see him smile. "I need to talk to Dimitri and Connie. Then I'll go and check in with Eric. No buts," I said before he could object. "As the general manager, I need this show to be ready in four days. You going AWOL from rehearsal doesn't help. And I don't know how you can help Eric right now."

"And you can? Sorry, I'm being bitchy. And I wasn't going AWOL. Connie gave me permission to take a break. I'll go back to rehearsal, but keep me posted, okay?"

"I'll leave a message on your cell as soon as I find anything out. I promise. Let me check in here first." I pulled up by the side entrance to the school, which led into the gym. Usually. Now it contained a half-dozen road boxes full of costumes and props. That alone was concerning, since they should have been downstairs in the dressing room area. More concerning was the rest of the scene, which was chaos. Dimitri was pacing up and down; our stage manager, Connie, was sitting on a folding chair, furiously scribbling down his diatribe, occasionally rubbing her hands together for warmth.

Patrick King was leaning against the basketball hoop, holding court with a few of the other actors, drinking his "coffee." I'd once made the mistake of getting too close to Patrick's mug and learned the coffee was for color only. The majority of the liquid was rocket fuel of some sort. Apparently being a little soused was part of his process.

"Where the hell have you been?" Dimitri roared.

"I've been running some errands," I said.

"Not you, Ms. Sullivan. Our errant actor."

"He had to run a couple of errands too."

"Sorry, Dimitri," Harry said. "I should have let you know—"

"You sure as hell should have. I'm trying to get some work done here."

"Dimitri, I thought he could take a break to get some cigarettes," Connie said. Dimitri swung around at her, but his tirade was interrupted by Patrick King.

"Sorry, old boy. I'm spent for the day. My concentration is gone. I really should be heading back to my flat." Patrick unbuttoned his waistcoat. To his surprise, and everyone else's, Dimitri put his hands on both of Patrick's shoulders and pushed him back slightly.

"You are not spent," Dimitri said quietly. Too quietly. I'd never heard this tone before. I stepped closer so I could intervene if necessary. "You've only just gotten here yourself."

"I assure you—"

"I assure you that if you don't get your bony English ass on that stage right now, I'll kill you and stuff you and use you that way. You'd probably give a better performance." Dimitri let go of his shoulders and turned away from him.

There was dead silence. It was clear that Dimitri had won. At least this time. Patrick slunk toward the door that led to the theater. Dimitri pointed at Harry and the rest of the actors, and then pointed to the door. For once they followed directions. Before Harry went in he looked back at me, making a "call me" gesture with his hand. I nodded.

When the actors were out of sight, Dimitri's bravado deflated. I'd learned early on that Dimitri was not incapable of high drama in order to get his way, and I'd become fairly immune to his scenes. But something about this one was different. He didn't follow up his performance with a request or a proclamation. Instead, he folded his body in half and hung there like a rag doll. He slowly stood up and rolled his shoulders back.

"How's it going today, Dimitri?" I asked once his eyes were open again. Never interrupt a man in the middle of a yoga stretch.

He didn't answer, so I looked over at Connie. She shook her head and looked down at her notes. I swear I saw tears in her eyes. This was really bad if it made the stage manager cry. Stage managers are among the toughest breed ever put on the face of this earth.

"Well, maybe this will help. I'm going to call Frank. We added to the lighting budget so we can get those moving lights you were looking for." I'd actually called Frank three days ago. The lights were being delivered today. It was supposed to be a surprise, but these were desperate times.

Dimitri shrugged his shoulders and tried to smile. "At least the end of my career will be well lit."

I wanted to laugh, but he was serious. I'd never seen him this despondent.

"And I found a new Jacob Marley," I said.

"What happened to the old Jacob Marley?"

Oops. I hadn't told him about David. "David got more remunerative employment."

"That ungrateful—"

"Stewart Tracy will be here tonight, tomorrow at the latest," I said. That did make Dimitri smile.

"Should I call the inn and see if there are any more rooms?" Connie asked. She looked thrilled. Stewart was always one of her favorites. Never underestimate the power of a charming man.

"No, he's going to stay at the Wrights'," I said. The Wrights were on our board and made their condo available to us for housing during

A Christmas Carol. "Could you see if someone can go over and get it shaped up? The key is upstairs in the mug on my desk. We'll also need to get that bike he always uses out of prop storage."

"I'll get one of the kids working on the details. Could you email me his info? Let me know if you need me to have someone pick him up. Or will you be doing it?" Connie wiggled her eyebrows and gave me a wink. She could never understand why Stewart and I had moved into the friend zone.

"I'll try and get him, but I'll let you know," I said. I hated to admit it, but I was looking forward to seeing Stewart. He'd be a tonic.

Connie stood up and patted Dimitri's arm. "Having Stewart around will be great."

"Jacob Marley is a small role for Stewart," Dimitri said. "Besides, he isn't a fan of the show, if memory serves."

"He knows he may need to play a few others as well. He'll play any role we need him to. He can play his age, younger, older, you know him. He's coming to help us, Dimitri. The way I figure it, you can use him to keep Patrick in line."

"By threatening to replace him?" Dimitri asked, a little lilt in his voice.

"Exactly. Have Stewart run some Scrooge lines with Harry."

"But we can't afford to replace Patrick. He's the reason the box office is so good."

"Dimitri, we've switched roles here. I'm supposed to remind you about the box office. You're supposed to tell me that television killed Patrick's craft, but time and effort could bring it back. Blah, blah, blah. Dimitri, unless Patrick is different from every other actor I've met, we won't need to replace him. We only need him to think we're willing to do it. And Stewart will help with that."

"What did you promise him?"

"A shot at a role in *Long Day's Journey*—whichever one you both agree on."

"Done," Dimitri said. "I was going to call him about it after this show was up, anyway."

This might have been true, or it might have been bravado. I knew that calling Stewart would be Dimitri's idea as soon as it was announced to the board. That was fine with me. I wasn't here to get credit, just to get the job done with as little carnage as possible.

"Do you want me to sit in on the rest of the rehearsal?" I asked, hoping he'd say no. The Cliffside needed to be my top priority, but I wanted to check in on Eric.

"God no, Sully. You'll add to my stress level. We are so behind."

"Okay, call me on my cell if you need me." Before I walked out the door, I texted Eric. No response. I tried to call, but no answer. I left a message and drove over to the police station.

∞

I parked at the Mini Mart and walked over to the Trevorton Police Station. It had been a long time since I'd seen a media circus like this one. The reporters had the scent of a major story and they were going to get it, no matter what. I was trying to figure out the best way to traverse the crowd when it parted a bit. I stopped moving forward and stepped to the side. Fortunately, I was so tall I still had a good view. Terry came out first, flanked by Gus. Emma and Eric followed close behind. Gus stood by the microphones until the crowd hushed.

"I repeat, Mr. Whitehall was not arrested, but instead was asked to come down and answer a few questions."

The questions started flying. Gus dealt with everyone calmly, holding his patience even though the questions were variations of the same theme. Did Eric kill his father? No. What did the police want to know? No comment.

"Isn't it true that your client's boyfriend refused to give him an alibi?"

"No comment," said Gus, quickly.

"I'm sure that Harry Frederick is as concerned about Eric's welfare as we all are." Terry ignored Gus's barbed stare and seemed primed to go on, but the renewed barrage of questions stopped him.

"Harry Frederick?"

"The actor."

"Isn't he ... "

" ... *Christmas Carol* ... "

I saw two local reporters whispering. One pointed at me. I ducked to the side and retreated to my car. Eric didn't need me to come to his rescue. Gus was on the case.

I'd settled into my car when my cell phone sang out its tinny version of "Silver Bells," my only ode to the holiday season until after the show opened. I slunk down in my seat. I saw Eric's face come up on the screen.

"Eric?"

"I saw you outside," he said. "I can't believe you came down."

"I wanted to help, but it seems to be under control."

"Under control? No, not really. I don't feel like going back to the Anchorage, and my apartment is probably under siege. After Terry's remarks, the theater will have press hanging around. I need to regroup."

"Where are you?"

"Getting a ride back—"

"Go over to my place. I'll meet you there. There's a key on the back porch, in the gas grill."

"Isn't that a little dangerous?"

"I move it in the summer. I'll meet you there in a bit." I got back out of the car and headed into the Mini Mart for provisions

∞

The Mini Mart had a name that built up expectations of boiled hotdogs and stale pretzels. The inside of the store blew those expectations away. It was more of a gourmet deli, with a dessert section that made me gain three pounds just walking through it. I knew the layout by heart. This was my go-to grocery store most of the time, when I wasn't eating my meals at the Beef and Ale. I dropped quite a bit of money at the Mini Mart, tempted by the selections of cheeses, olives, and breads.

I juggled my bags and let myself into my house. Though technically a condo, it was a renovated carriage house next to a large Victorian that itself had been converted to several condos. From the driveway, the carriage house looked the same as it had historically. When I bought it, the downstairs consisted of a large kitchen, a half bath, and a separate living room; the upstairs had been parsed out into two bedrooms, a small office, and a bathroom. But the back wall on the second floor, which butted up to a marsh that led, eventually, to the ocean, was made entirely of glass. The thought of looking at that amazing view from a lonely bed didn't seem like a great mental health move. That, and I've always found demo work therapeutic. So the living room downstairs became my bedroom. Upstairs, I took out most of the interior walls and turned it into a sort of great room.

The beautiful round oak table that was the focal point of the room had been left to me by my father, one of his most prized possessions. I wasn't sure how old it was, or whether it was a genuine antique or a reproduction, but its monetary value meant nothing. My memories of the table meant everything. I remembered sitting under it for hours, believing the claw feet belonged to a lion named Charlie I'd befriended during one of my imaginings. "Charlie" saw me through some tough times. Some mornings I still kicked my slipper off and ran my foot along the familiar lines of the table legs while I sat eating my oatmeal.

I heard two voices as I stepped inside, and I wondered how Harry had gotten out of rehearsal. I was at the top of the stairs when I realized it wasn't Harry—it was Gus. I hoped I didn't look as stunned as I felt.

"Hi, Sully." Eric took a tentative step toward me. "I didn't do it," he whispered.

"Of course you didn't do it. I never thought for a second that you did." I gathered him in a big hug. He paused, and then buried his head on my shoulder. He began to cry.

Crying for Eric was as foreign a concept as it was for me. Though tempted to join him, I was acutely aware of Gus watching us. So instead I did my best to comfort him. Good Yankee that he was, the moment passed quickly and he stepped back to regroup, staying in my arms.

"Have you called Harry?" I asked.

"No, I didn't think … we haven't … "

"He's worried sick, Eric. I promised I'd text him. Why don't you call him? I'll go down and get us some nosh."

"I'll help," Gus said. He followed me down the stairs.

"Pick out a bottle of wine," I said. "I hope you don't think less of me because of my wine selection. It's gotten a little pedestrian since … "

"I'm sure it's fine," he said. He moved past the cheapest but didn't settle on the most expensive. He pulled out a decent Malbec and took the wine opener off the table. I was slicing some cheese, and Gus came and leaned on the counter, looking at me pretty thoroughly. I felt my toes start to curl, which wasn't a good sign.

"What?" I finally asked. I sounded pretty churlish.

He smiled. "Sorry, didn't mean to stare." He looked around the tiny kitchen, and then back at me. "I like your place."

"It's a little small, but it's good for us."

"Us?"

"Max and me." Max was my cat. He used to be our cat—Gus's and mine—but I got him in the divorce. Actually, it was one of the only things we'd argued about through the proceedings.

"How is Max? When I didn't see him, I wondered if … "

"He's good. Spoiled, but good. He's probably on the bed."

"Who's on the bed?" Eric came down the stairs into the kitchen. He sounded better.

"Max."

"Damn cat." Eric insisted he wasn't a cat guy. Max knew it, and in typical cat fashion, always paid Eric extra attention. As if to prove a point, my beautiful gray roommate came out and rubbed against Eric's legs. Eric bent over to pick the fur off his trousers, but I caught him rubbing Max behind the ears. Softie.

Max took one look at Gus, turned, and walked back into the bedroom.

"Guess he's still pissed at me," Gus said. He looked at Eric and explained. "For leaving." The uncomfortable pause went on a little too long.

"Okay, boys, why don't you bring some of this upstairs and tell me what the hell happened."

"Yes ma'am," Gus said.

I put the repast in the middle of my oak table. Eric went over to the bar and grabbed three glasses. Gus poured us each a small glass. Since neither of them was going to start, I jumped in. "So they didn't arrest you, but brought you in because...?"

"They were going to arrest him, but I pointed out that arresting someone was a serious step and they needed to make damn sure of the evidence," Gus said.

"And they blinked."

"They blinked," Gus agreed, "but they won't blink next time. They apparently have two pieces of evidence. One is a recording that reportedly shows Eric going into Peter's study the night of the murder. Impossible to identify conclusively. There was a lot of foot traffic that night. No one else went in or came out until Amelia found the body the next day."

"Okay, sorry, Gus, but I've got to say it again. He was alive when I left him. I swear to you. Then I went up to the guest room and passed out."

"Passed out?" I asked.

Eric ignored me.

"Do you have all of the recordings?" I asked Gus.

"No, and they took the servers. If they arrest him we'll get copies, but until then we're flying a little blind. Trying to see what, if anything, got saved onto a backup system."

"There are lots of cameras?"

"All on different systems," Gus said. "Apparently Peter liked trying out new surveillance systems, but he didn't bother tying them all together."

"Did he use a specific firm?" I asked. "I might know someone—"

"You do," Eric said. "He uses Frank as his IT guru."

"Frank," Gus said. He pulled out his phone and tapped in some notes.

"Augustine," I said. "He's our tech director at the theater."

"Tech director and IT guru?"

"Most people in theater wear more than one hat to make a living. His brain is very IT, his heart is backstage at the theater. It works for everyone. What's the second piece of evidence?" I asked.

"The gun."

"They found *the* gun? Where?"

"I found it in my apartment." Eric sounded miserable.

"Finding it wasn't the only problem," Gus said. "Moving it was. Eric was just going to explain that part of the story to me when you came in."

"Shall I go back downstairs?"

"No, I'd like you to stay," Eric said. "Is that okay, Gus?"

"Sure, what the hell. You'll probably tell her anyway."

Eric hesitated, taking more cheese from the plate and carefully arranging it on a cracker. It was all I could do not to slap it out of his hand.

"Eric," I finally said. "Tell Gus. He needs to know everything, and I mean everything, if he's going to help you. Don't leave anything out, no matter how unimportant it seems. And I should leave, because I can be forced to testify, which wouldn't be good."

"Please stay. I swear I didn't do it. Okay, I did touch the gun. I found it in my dresser drawer, and I panicked. So I took it with me, wiped it down, and I threw it in a dumpster out on Route 1."

I was stunned. "Did you know if that was *the* gun?"

"The police had asked if we had a small caliber gun in the house. Dad kept one in his desk. Everyone knew."

"Registered?" I looked at Gus.

"No, not registered. Apparently it was part of a set of dueling pistols Peter had bought a while back and restored."

"It was a little gun," Eric said. "It looked like a toy, for God's sake. He got it from some antique dealer. I don't even know that it worked. Or if it was the gun that was used to, you know."

"Ballistics match?" I asked Gus.

"Same caliber. The bullet from Peter's body was in pretty good shape. We'll know in the next couple of days."

"Were the police following Eric?" I asked.

"No," Gus said. "That's the interesting part. A citizen called the tip in."

"A citizen named?"

"Anonymous."

"Jeez, I hate that guy," I said. Gus and Eric chuckled politely, but I wasn't joking. Anonymous tips could be a wild goose chase or someone with an ax to grind.

"By the time the police got to the dumpster, a few other people could, and did, identify Eric's car." Gus must have read my mind. "Handy to have witnesses like that, don't you think?"

"Are you following up on them?"

"Trying to. The police aren't sharing names yet."

"Pretty neat little package," I said."

"Delivered signed, sealed, and with a nice neat bow," Gus agreed.

"Any ideas?"

"No. Probably the same person."

"Hey." Eric interrupted my conversation with Gus. "Could you two clue me in on the shorthand?"

"Sorry. Sully and I agree that someone set you up. And I think that the person who killed your father was the one who did it."

"But the police ..."

I shook my head and tried to sound as gentle as I could. "Eric, the police have been under incredible strain, and they think they've found their man. They aren't going to keep looking unless Gus gives them something else to consider."

"Do you have any ideas?" Eric asked me the question, but Gus looked pretty interested in the answer.

"More questions than ideas at this point. Gus, you may have some answers, but my questions are pretty gruesome." I looked at Eric.

"I'll go get some more of this cheese," Eric said. We heard him turn on the TV in the kitchen, but Gus still whispered.

"Alone at last. Okay, you have a couple of questions?"

"Have you seen the police report?"

"No, but I've been briefed."

"By?" I wondered if Gus had an in with the Trevorton police.

"I put one of the firm's investigators on it," he said. "We keep a couple of them on retainer to help us with corporate investigations. She's going to get me more information tonight, but I know the basics."

"Peter was shot in the chest, from the front, right?"

"Yes."

"Angle?"

"He was sitting."

"Distance?"

"Hard to say. It's a 25mm, not a huge gun, so it wasn't too far."

"Could someone have fired a shot from the door?"

"No, the angle wouldn't work. Probably within six feet, given the layout of the furniture and the angle of the wound."

"So he was shot by someone who could get close enough to shoot him in the chest and he didn't get up. Was he drugged?"

"There was alcohol in his bloodstream, but he was apparently awake. Reading. The blood spatter indicated the book was semi open. As if he was holding his place."

"So it was someone he knew," I said.

"How do you know that?" Eric asked, coming back in and depositing cheese on the plate.

"You don't hold your place in your book and remain seated unless you know the person and you expect the conversation to be brief. And the police think the person in the room was you," I said.

"Sully, if I didn't know better, I'd think it was Eric," Gus said. "He certainly had motive."

"What motive?" Eric and I asked at the same time.

"Apparently Peter had a new will drawn up a couple of weeks ago," Gus said. "Did you know he was going to do that, Eric?"

"He was always threatening to change his will. We'd had an argument. I told him to go ahead."

"Rumor has it that he cut you off without a cent," Gus said quietly.

"You didn't do the will?" I asked.

"No, Peter used his former lawyer for that. The guy is retired but still does special requests."

"Freddy Sands?"

"You know him?"

"He was friends with my dad."

"Ah, the Sullivan connection. The reading is scheduled for Wednesday. Until then it's all speculation."

"If the will cuts Eric off ... "

"It could be the nail in his coffin," Gus said. I winced. "Sorry, bad phrasing."

"Great. So that gives you two days to figure out who." I took a sip of wine and pondered the cracker and cheese that Eric handed me.

"Gives us. You," Gus said. I went to interrupt but he stopped me. "Sully, we both know, Eric goes to trial, I'm his guy. He needs help getting out of a jam, you're a better fit for the job."

"Gus, I haven't done anything like this for a long time."

"Your friend is up the creek. Help him out. Please. For his sake. For your sake. For my sake. Please."

∞

After being asked so nicely, how could I refuse? Besides, I was more curious than ever. Curiosity drove me. It had made me a good cop. It also didn't allow me to let go even when it was politically expedient to do so. Curiosity also was fueling my increasing love for theater. I'd read a play and wonder how we were going to pull it off. Usually, that journey was a joy. This time, not so much.

From the sound of it, the killer really had to be someone in the family. I knew them all to varying degrees, from very well to not well at all. Still, I had a hard time picturing any one of them as a cold-blooded murderer. It would have to be someone pretty cold-blooded to kill a man while he was sitting in a chair reading.

"Gus, did you get some information from Jack Megan? I went to see him today, and he said he'd released a report to you."

"Yes, I got the records. At Peter's request."

"Peter?"

"Sometime early this summer, Peter discovered that someone was accessing some private accounts using secured passwords on unknown computers. He traced the passwords back to Emma."

"How?"

"To say that Peter Whitehall was a careful man is like saying the Grand Canyon is a pretty good-sized hole. Peter had multiple layers of security wrapped around his businesses. Even his most trusted partners only had limited access, defined by Peter. He used a complicated password system."

"That's an understatement," Eric said. "He made us all change our passwords once a month. He also shut off access to different bits of information on a whim."

"Did that drive you crazy?" I asked.

"I had my own computer and a private email. But the family business was the family business. I was used to it. It's all I know."

"From what I understand, every user had his or her own password," Gus said. "No one except Peter had complete access to everything. Peter tracked all of the user activity, and he had an inventory of computers. So when 'Emma' started requesting information on certain accounts, but from an unfamiliar computer, Peter grew suspicious."

"Did he confront her?"

"Confront, no. But he asked her what the hell was going on, and she told him she'd given Jack access to some of her accounts so he could track a few things, see if he could get proof that Terry was having an affair. She told Peter you'd recommended Jack."

"He was probably thrilled about that," I said. "Eric, did you know about any of this?"

"I knew about all of it," he said. "Emma and I tell each other everything. For what it's worth, I was willing to give Jack my logins too."

"In a roundabout way, you're responsible for my going to work for the family, Sully," Gus said.

"How?"

"Peter found out we'd been married and went on a fishing expedition to find out more about you," Gus said. "He wasn't that obvious.

He pretended that he was going to ask me some business questions. It was an interesting meeting."

"What did he think? That I was setting Emma up by referring her to Jack?"

"He was a paranoid guy. Jack had talked Emma into breaching security. Peter knew she was vulnerable, and he wanted to do some damage control. Simply put, he didn't understand why you would help Emma without expecting something in return."

"Why wouldn't I?"

"He thought that your father's animosity toward him had been passed down."

"The family feud," Eric said. He reached over to give me a fist bump. I returned it, and we both opened our hands afterwards. It was a silly ritual we'd created over the past few years, exploding the family history.

"I don't even know the reason for their feud. And I didn't want to ask, just in case," I said.

"In case it made your father look bad?" Gus asked.

"Maybe? Toward the end, after my mother and Emily had both passed, it didn't seem as important."

"Fair enough. I asked Peter what the feud was about." Eric and I both stared at Gus. "Why do you both look so surprised?" he asked.

Eric and I looked at each other, but neither of us spoke. It was hard to explain. Our fathers' falling-out had happened when we were teenagers. Though our mothers kept in touch, our visits to the Anchorage were over. There was a rapprochement of sorts when Eric's mother got sick, but it didn't last, particularly when Peter married Brooke so soon afterward. Eric and I had lived under the shadow of "the feud" for so long that we were afraid to discover its roots, afraid that it might contaminate our generation as well.

"You both look like scared kids." Gus took a sip of his wine before he continued. He'd always loved drama. "Eric, your father and this man, Larry Colfer, used to run in the same business circles. Peter's was a much bigger company, and for a lot of years he saw the Colfer Consulting Co-Op as more of a nuisance than a threat. Then Larry Colfer became more innovative and started using third-party software. This is back when using computers rather than paper was fairly radical. Anyway, Colfer built a whole new approach based on the software, and started innovating with using a cloud-based system that made it available to companies at a much lower cost. Peter paid attention, took notice, and bought the software company out. Then he removed the rights to the software from Colfer and co-opted his ideas."

"How could he do that? Didn't Colfer have some sort of agreement with the company?" I asked.

"Wouldn't have mattered to Dad," Eric said. "If it was a license, he would have revoked it. If it suited his purposes, he would have put the software company out of business and hired another company to develop the same thing."

"Did Larry Colfer sue?" I asked.

"Sure, but he couldn't afford to wait out the litigation," Gus said. "He'd put himself out on a financial limb, and when it broke, he lost his business."

"What a bastard," I said. I immediately regretted making the remark. Not because of what I'd said but because the timing was tough, considering the man had just died and his son was here in the room.

"You have no idea," Eric said. "So where does Sully's dad come in?"

"Bryan and Larry Colfer were golfing buddies. Bryan had even asked Peter to give Larry a break."

"That couldn't have been easy for my dad." My father disliked asking anyone for a favor.

"I can't imagine it was," Gus agreed. "Anyway, it got worse. Larry Colfer committed suicide. Bryan blamed Peter for Colfer's death, and made no bones about it to anyone who'd listen. Bryan wasn't a power player, but a lot of people thought highly of him, and Peter began to feel a distinct chill in certain circles around here. And so it began."

"At least someone's death is enough to explain the feud," I said. "I was afraid that it was over cheating at bridge or something."

"From what I understand, even that could have been enough. Your father never liked Peter. I don't think he thought a lot of consulting as a way to make a living."

I remembered well what my father thought of Peter's line of work, particularly when he found out how much Peter's company charged per hour. Since I'd already called Peter a bastard, and Larry Colfer was obviously not on the suspect list, I changed the subject.

"Eric, did you speak to Harry?" I asked.

"Texted. He said to tell you that Dimitri announced that Stewart Tracy will be coming in later tonight."

"Good." I checked my phone and noticed a few texts had come in, two from Stewart. My fingers flew as I responded. "Actually, I need to go and get him at the train station."

"Is he staying..." Eric let it hang.

"He's staying at the Wrights' condo. They lent it to us for Patrick, but he didn't like it. No room service."

Eric smirked at me, and I shook my head. Eric loved to tease me about Stewart, but now wasn't the time. I didn't look at Gus.

"I told Harry that I'd go over and watch rehearsal," Eric said. "I called a cab to take me over. Harry said it's going to be a long night, and I want to see him."

"Did he say why it was going to be a long night?"

"They took their dinner break early and they're way behind."

Eric hadn't finished the sentence before I was on the phone to Dimitri's cell. Which he didn't answer, of course. I called Connie next. She didn't answer either, so I called again and texted them both. And called again. She never turned her cell phone off, letting it vibrate during rehearsals,in case her kids needed to get in touch. After the eighth try, she finally picked up.

"About damned time, Connie. What the hell is going on?" I stood up and walked over to the window. My back was to Gus and Eric. The view did what it always did: washed over me. Unlike normal, though, it wasn't calming my nerves today. Too many reasons for them to be frayed.

"The shit hit the fan again with Dimitri and Patrick, so I called a dinner break to cool everyone down. It worked, for the most part. We're back now, and we're going to finish teching Act One if it kills us all. Which it might." Stage managers can be as dramatic as actors. Maybe it's because they belong to the same union.

"Do you need me?" I asked.

"God, no. Sorry, Sully, I didn't mean it to sound like that. Truth is, we've sort of used you as the 'don't make me call Sully' threat. You shouldn't come down until we need you to crack some heads. I'll call you later and fill you in, okay?"

"Okay, but keep an eye on the time. We've got a lot of union actors in this show, and I'd love to avoid overtime if we can."

"I'm on top of it."

"Call me later." I ended the call and turned around.

"Trouble?" Gus sounded amused, which annoyed me.

"Yes, there's trouble. Where's Eric?"

"He went down to wait for his ride." Gus still had a grin on his face.

"What's so funny?" I admit I sounded a little irritable.

"I don't know. You, I guess."

"Me?"

"I've seen you do that routine before of calling and texting someone over and over until they pick up. But you were contacting an informant or a cop or someone important. Now it's about actors. It seems odd."

I took a long, deep breath and looked directly into Gus's gray eyes. This time my toes didn't curl. "If we're going to work together, we need to get one thing straight. My new life may not seem as significant to you as my old life, but it is to me. I'm not defending truth, justice, and the American way, but I am doing important work."

"I think it's great that you've found a new life. But you can't really expect me to believe that you think it's as vital as what you were doing before."

"Let's drop it." I'd become a vocal arts advocate these past three years and deeply understood the importance of the arts in our society. I could have argued this point easily, but I didn't want to complicate our relationship. "What matters is helping Eric out of this mess."

"I'm sorry if—"

"So Peter called you to check me out?"

Gus recognized my tone and wisely changed the subject. "Okay, where were we? You and Emma spoke last spring about hiring a PI?" I nodded. "I guess it took Emma a while to work up the courage to talk to Jack," Gus went on. "She met with him around Memorial Day. Jack put a tail on Terry, and asked to see Terry and Emma's financial records."

"Pretty standard stuff." I didn't let on that I had already heard this from Jack.

"Very standard. Except that all their financials are tied up with the company. Peter held tight rein on them all. Everyone had generous allowances, but all of the houses and cars were part of the business and used to leverage investments. Peter thought that most expenses were client or company related in one way or another, so all expenses were filtered through the company."

"Is that legal?"

"Sure. Remember, this is a privately owned business, Sully. And Peter is, was, the head of it. He set the rules."

"That must have been tough." Gus and I had kept our own bank accounts while we were married. I couldn't imagine having him scrutinizing how many trips to Target I made in a week when I didn't feel like justifying them. "No privacy."

"I hear you. But Emma, Terry, Eric, they all seemed on board. There was definitely a big brother aspect, but Peter never passed judgment, or so he said."

"In other words, Terry could spend a fortune on Internet porn, and Peter wouldn't have minded."

"Peter would probably have figured out a way to bill it to a client. At least that's the impression I got."

"Hard to believe."

"I agree. But we're getting off track. When Peter found out that Emma was using a different computer to look at account activity, he became suspicious. Peter figured out that Emma had hired Jack Megan."

"What tipped him off?"

"Unknown IP address accessing the network, then a cancelled check from her personal account. Peter confronted Emma, she told him why she hired him, that it was your suggestion. He suggested she fire Jack."

"Which she did."

"After a couple more days. Jack hadn't found anything that showed Terry was cheating, at least not according to the files. Peter decided to bring the investigation in house."

"That's where you came in?"

Gus nodded his head. "Sort of. Peter called me, asked for an appointment. Which I agreed to, of course."

I let the "of course" slide, or tried to, but I must have made a face.

"Sully, I work for a firm now. If Peter Whitehall's going to throw some work our way, I'd be an idiot not to pursue it." He paused, challenging me to say something.

"Finish the story. We can debate our career turns another time, okay? So Peter meets with you, and ...?"

Gus paused. Our détente was in jeopardy; we both knew it. He gave it a longer life span and continued with his story.

"Peter came in to meet with me. He told me he'd found some discrepancies in his company's accounting and might need outside legal help. I told him it wasn't my area, but I could refer him. He cut me off. He told me that the discrepancies had come to light in a roundabout way, partially instigated by you. And he needed to know what your motives were—were you trying to right a wrong for your father, or were you really trying to help Emma when you suggested she hire a private investigator?"

I was seething, but Gus cut me off. "I told him that if you wanted to right a wrong by going after the Whitehall family, you wouldn't sneak around. He'd know you were coming. I told him I thought you probably really wanted to help Emma but didn't want to do the legwork yourself."

"Right on all counts," I said.

"We talked for a while, and he left. He called me a few days later and put me on a retainer. He gave me some work to do on this new Century Project idea. That kept me busy for a while. Huge project, another story for another time. He asked that I get the files from Jack, which I did, after getting Emma to sign a release. Apparently Jack's investigation triggered something for Peter, and he started exploring different paths on his own. We spoke, and it was clear something was bothering him. I offered to help, but he declined. Said he wanted me to be available once he had his ducks in a row regarding some other matters. I wanted specifics, but he was vague. He told me he was going to email me some files, and also send over hard copies with his notes. He asked that I look them over in preparation. That was a week ago Friday."

"The day before Peter was killed."

"Right."

"Did you get the files?"

"He emailed them to me that night and had them couriered over the next morning. They track money moving from one account to another. I don't know who did the moving, or what the accounts are, but I do know that Peter was pretty upset about it. If he hadn't been looking for it, he might not have found it. That bothered him."

"I thought you said that he tracked all financial information?"

"Someone circumvented his system."

Given what Gus had told me about Peter's control issues, I realized that wouldn't have been easy.

"And he didn't give you any other information?"

"No. We had a meeting set up for that Monday, but of course he was dead by then. The retainer was significant, so when Emma called me today to tell me Eric needed help, I figured I'd use part of it for that."

"So what are you going to do?"

"What are *we* going to do, Sully."

"Gus, I—"

"Don't. You know some of the players. You have an in with the family. And you're curious, admit it. What I'm guessing is that Peter had figured something out, and he had a plan. I think that probably got him killed. If someone in the family murdered Peter, they must be pretty desperate. We both know that desperate people do stupid things."

Then he gave me that look, and I felt my toes curl. Despite the warning bells going off in my head, I said, "I may be able to free up some time to help you out."

· Eight ·

Gus and I agreed to meet on Tuesday so that he could give me copies of the files from Jack. He was hesitant to give me all the records Peter sent him, but was going to give me what he could without breeching confidentiality. We argued a little about dead clients and confidentiality, but we both knew neither would concede.

I texted Connie and asked if she could send someone to pick up Stewart. *Sure thing, I'll do it. I need a break from here anyway,* she texted back. I sighed with relief. My time with Gus had been taxing enough, and Stewart required a whole different set of avoidance skills. I wasn't sure if I was up to it. Besides, Connie wanted to catch Stewart up, give him his script, and talk him through the blocking of his scenes. He was going to have to hit the ground running and needed to know where to go, what props to pick up or put down, and where everyone else was so that the technical rehearsals could continue.

I needed to orient myself to the Peter Whitehall case, so I made a list of all the names that had come up in my conversations and did Google searches for information. I wrote things on Post-its and took notes. None of the information I found was earth-shattering, at least not at first. Basic biographical information. A lot of the family stuff I already knew, but there were a few new morsels of information that provided food for thought.

For example, I learned that Terry had gone to Cleaver Business School and graduated in 1982. I learned that Brooke's maiden name wasn't Gooding; it was Goodowski. Her family came from Western Massachusetts, an area of the state with a large Polish population. I also learned that she'd been married before, to a Kent Mackay. The divorce seemed to coincide with her marriage to Peter by a very slim margin.

On a whim, I looked up Kent Mackay. His name came up in a 2004 newspaper article about the guy who tried to ram the gates of the Anchorage. The article named him as a business associate of Peter Whitehall. I wondered what business, aside from Brooke, Mr. Mackey and Peter had in common. Particularly in 2004, the divorce and marriage year in question. Interesting.

I did some research on Larry Colfer as well. Among other things, he'd been adjunct faculty at Cleaver Business School. I double checked my information on Terry. He'd been a student there at the same time. I wondered if they knew each other. I decided to add that to my list of questions for Terry. Questions that I planned to ask in the morning.

I was still making lists when the phone rang. "Hello Stewart."

"Sully, my love, I thought you were going to pick me up. Not that I wasn't happy to see Connie," he quickly added, and I heard her in the background along with a number of other people. "Come have a drink with us."

"Sorry, I'm in the middle of a project and getting ready for bed."

"I could come over there."

"A lovely thought, but I need to rain-check on both. See you tomorrow?"

"Promise?"

"Absolutely."

"Then I'll have to make do with the lovely Connie as my companion tonight."

∞

I ended up spending longer than I intended on the computer, and didn't get to bed until three a.m. When I was younger, staying up later meant sleeping later. These days, once the clock hit seven I was up. I didn't know if it was age or routine, but on mornings with four hours of sleep under my belt, it was damned annoying.

I was on my second cup of coffee when Gus came by. He looked as tired as I felt. I handed him a cup of coffee—black, two sugars. He took a long, slow sip, closed his eyes, and smiled.

"I wasn't sure if you still took it the same way," I said.

"I do. Considered fake sugar for a while, but the hell with it. This hits the spot. I need it this morning. My car's engine light came on last night. I brought it to the dealership, and they're stumped. What a pain in the ass."

"How did you get here?" I asked.

"Took the commuter rail and walked."

"With the files?" Gus had hauled in an impressive canvas bag filled with brown expanding files.

"And the doughnuts. It isn't a bad walk, but in this cold it isn't a good walk either. I'll be bumming a ride to the station later today. Anyway, the coffee's great."

Not as good as you used to make, I wanted to say, but refrained. "There's plenty of it. Let's take this upstairs and look at what you brought."

I'm sure I seem a little off to most people. Conversations are always on two tracks with me. One of them is aloud, with the people in the room. The other one is internal, with myself. The internal conversation tends to move at a more breakneck speed, so I take shortcuts with the external conversations. The thing is, I think Gus works the same way. When we were married, we would be in the middle of a conversation and I'd jump in with a suggestion for our summer vacation, and he'd take it in stride and go with it. I'd never been so in synch with anyone in my life. I wondered if that connection had been broken with the divorce, but Gus's first question helped me realize it hadn't.

"Larry Colfer taught at Terry's alma mater." Okay, it wasn't a question, but Gus had obviously spent some time on his own computer.

"Yes, at the same time. I wonder if Peter knew that?"

"I'd think so. He seemed to know everything there was to know about me, and I didn't marry one of his daughters."

"What do you mean?"

"One day he asked me if I had the recipe for the Blue Pearl's chowder. He said he'd never tasted any that could compare."

Gus's grandfather had owned a pub in Woods Hole called the Blue Pearl. Grandpa Lowe was the black sheep of his blue-blood family and Gus's mother allowed Gus to visit his grandfather two weeks a year, but only because he was her father. Gus's mother was, and probably still is, socially conscious. Being a barkeep's daughter didn't suit her. Being a lawyer's wife, and mother, did. But Gus loved his grandfather, even after the Pearl was shut down due to gaming activities, which sent Grandpa Lowe to jail for a year when Gus was in high school. Although Gus wasn't ashamed of his grandfather, he didn't go out of his way to advertise their connection. He was enough of his mother's son to be mindful of appearances.

"What did you say?"

"I told him the recipe was a family secret, but next time I made a batch I'd save him some. He never mentioned it again."

"You passed the test."

"Yeah, I guess I did. Back to Terry. Peter had to have known about the connection. We'll have to ask Terry about it. I rearranged my schedule to be here today."

"I was planning to go over—

"Terry can meet with us at three this afternoon. I've had a meeting with Terry and Emma to talk about the Century Project, so he knows me. He might be more willing to answer questions with me in the room. Not that you couldn't get him to answer questions on your own."

"No, you're right. I think it would be better if you were there," I said, cutting Gus off. I wanted him there for a couple of reasons, getting answers from Terry only being one of them. "Kent Mackay."

"I know the name ... " Gus picked up his phone and started tapping.

I didn't wait. "He tried to drive his car through the Anchorage gates in 2004. He had a gun with him. I'm guessing he was planning on using that as his calling card. At the time, the press listed him as a business acquaintance of Peter's. I remember the incident mostly because it tickled my father to no end. He even joked about setting up a defense fund."

"Bryan was always so shy about his opinions."

"And sharing them. Anyway, I was researching Brooke last night, and she was married to Kent Mackay until 2004, the same year she married Peter."

"Okay," Gus said, reading from the small screen in front of him. "I know the name Kent Mackay because he's one of the players on this Century Project. A minor player, but involved."

"Did Peter know that?"

"I just found out myself. Peter asked me to research the other interests in the Project. I emailed him that information the Friday before he was killed. I don't know if he saw the email or not."

"Hmm. This is turning out to be quite the tangled web." I tried to keep my tone appropriately somber, but I didn't completely succeed. My brain was firing on all pistons, like it hadn't for years. I'd always loved the fact-finding part of an investigation, when an open mind allowed for all possibilities until the truth emerged from the ether. Then I was always a little disappointed when it was over, particularly when truth and justice didn't work in tandem. It may be the cynical view of an ex-cop, but it repeatedly blew my mind when the bad guys didn't get their due because of some random loophole that lawyers like Gus exploited.

I piled the plethora of papers I'd printed out into a semblance of order and put them on one of the chairs to make room for the files Gus had brought. I booted up my laptop and moved it to one side of the table.

"Okay, here's some more fuel to put in that brain of yours." Gus smiled as he started pulling files out of the canvas bag. Each file was in an expandable folder with accordion sides that were stretched. Jack must have been busy; there were four full jackets total.

Gus read my mind. "It's not all from Jack. See the yellow paper? That's from Peter. He always used yellow paper to print stuff. Yellow pads to write. That's why I brought the hard copies. If nothing else, it might help you figure out how Peter thought."

The yellow paper outweighed the white two to one. I picked up one of the files, pulled the stack out, and began to fan through the papers, looking at headings and not getting mired down in detail. Yet. I looked back into the file to make sure I hadn't left anything behind and noticed a plastic sleeve adhered to the inside of the jacket. I pulled out a flash drive and held it up to Gus.

"What's this?" I asked.

"No idea. Where did you find it?"

"Inside the jacket."

Gus checked the two jackets next to him and I checked my second jacket. Each had a flash drive. Someone had written a series of numbers on each one, and then labeled them 1.1, 1.2, 1.3, 1.4. I put the flash drive numbered 1.1 into my computer and opened it. Gus moved his chair close to mine and looked over my shoulder. I felt his breath on my neck and had a lot of trouble concentrating.

"Can you pull the papers out of the coordinating file jacket?" I asked Gus, partly to distract him, partly for illumination.

"Sure." He moved his chair back and grabbed the file. "What are we looking for?"

"I'm not sure. I wonder if this is the same information or different from the papers. And also from the files he sent you. Can you pull them up too?"

"Sure. I brought my laptop. Can you give me your Wi-Fi password? I'll send them to you. They're all PDFs," Gus said.

"So are these. At least the spreadsheets are. The notes from Peter are in a Word document. Interesting. He gave you insight to his process, but he's controlling what you can see."

"What do you mean?" Gus asked.

"I bet these spreadsheets pulled data from other spreadsheets, and that would give us a lot more insight."

I opened up the first of a series of electronic documents. They appeared to be case notes from Jack Megan. Gus read the first few paragraphs aloud while I confirmed that they were identical to the printouts in the jacket. I looked at the other documents on the flash drive. They seemed to have some sort of naming structure, which must have been a code Peter devised or understood. I certainly didn't. One of the files was called 0317T, another called 0318B, a third called 0319A. Gus searched through the jacket until he found the papers. Again, the papers seemed identical to what was on the flash drive, but unlike Jack's notes, which were dated, there didn't seem to be any correlation between the naming of the electronic documents and where they appeared within the physical documentation.

"Sully, the flash drives must be backups of these papers..."

"Um, yeah, they look like it. But I'd love to know what Peter's system is. Was."

"Because?"

I looked away from the screen and back toward Gus. "Because of the detail. It makes no sense to me, but it obviously did to Peter."

"I agree. I think it's worth looking into, but maybe it should be a project for later? I mean, isn't it interesting to see what he clipped to Jack's notes? And shouldn't we look this over before we see Terry?"

"Okay," I agreed with disappointment. "How about if I copy the flash drive documents onto my computer and you keep the originals? Won't take any time..." I worked quickly, creating folders on my computer that duplicated the numbers Peter had put on each flash drive, and then copying the contents of each flash drive into the correct folder. Gus read Jack's notes aloud while I worked, and then read the corresponding yellow paper. Sometimes there was a clear correlation, and most of the yellow notes were about money. Jack's notes would say something about the movement of funds from one account to another. Peter's notes would include more detailed banking information and some general ledger coding. The yellow papers frequently had cryptic handwritten notes in the margins.

Gus had started making notes on a pad. I had long since finished my copying and replaced the flash drives, so I started to read Gus's notes over his shoulder. He finally looked up and grinned.

"This is what I think this means," he said. "Jack noted some initial transfers from one account to another, probably trying to see if Terry was hiding assets." I nodded. "But in almost every case, the transfers were moved back to another company account within a day or two. This didn't seem to trigger anything for Jack, since the money in and the money out was the same."

"Right. But Peter noticed something?" I asked.

"Yeah. The second transfer was minus the interest."

"On one day? Or two? How much interest?"

"Enough for Peter to try and track it. See the numbers he uses? I think that must be the missing interest. Looks like a few hundred per transaction. You're right about wanting the spreadsheet. I could track it better if he'd sent the entire spreadsheet, or told us where he was pulling the numbers from. That interest could really add up after a while."

"Finding the spreadsheets goes on the list," I said. "Can you see where the interest went?"

"To a different account. From what I can see here, Peter hadn't tracked it. Part of his notes seem to be questions ... "

Gus's voice trailed off, and I knew that he needed to work something out on his own. He began to look back and forth through the papers, occasionally stopping to scribble a note or two. I picked up the fourth jacket and perused the contents. Presuming that 1.4 was akin to the fourth section of files, I decided to skip to the end. Peter's notes were scrawled all over the yellow paper. On the final page he seemed to sum it up with a note, presumably to himself:

TO GK ice 11/28

· Nine ·

Rehearsal began at ten. By eleven I hadn't heard from Connie, and Gus and I needed a break, so I decided to stop in at the high school. Gus volunteered to come with me, and I reluctantly agreed. I didn't like the idea of him seeping into this part of my life, the part that was a Gus-free zone, but I couldn't figure out how to prevent it without seeming like a jerk.

We stopped by a deli on our way to the theater to get sandwiches. I also bought a quart of peach cobbler and a pint of rice pudding.

"Carbo loading?" Gus asked.

"You have no idea," I replied.

The theater seemed to be a scene of controlled but palatable chaos. I ensconced Gus in the back row, put a couple of spoons in my jacket pocket, grabbed the cobbler and pudding, and walked toward the stage where Dimitri was holding court. Apparently the chaos wasn't as controlled as it appeared from the back of the house. The veins on the sides of Dimitri's neck were popping, his color was a frightening hue somewhere between gray and red, and his teeth were clenched. His words hissed from between his teeth. Connie, Patrick, and Harry were standing as far back from him as they could, leaning in slightly in order to listen. Before I could hear what he was saying the group disbursed, the actors practically running backstage, and Connie put her hand on Dimitri's arm either to comfort or restrain him. Probably both.

"We're canceling the show." Dimitri's tone dared me to disagree. I often heard yelling, screaming, ranting, and raving from Dimitri; I seldom heard this flat, resigned defiance. I chose not to take the bait.

"Why are we canceling?"

When Dimitri didn't answer, Connie jumped in. "Patrick is still having trouble with his lines. So we're trying to have some of the other actors ready to step in when they're needed. And to create opportunities for Patrick to go offstage so he can look at the script or pull himself together."

"Have you ever heard of such bullshit? Scrooge leaving the stage? The play is about Scrooge's journey," Dimitri snapped. "The whole point is that the audience sees the transformation. Okay, I was willing to create a moment here and there—during the Fezziwig scene, who'd miss him? But now he needs more time, more breaks. He's having trouble with the fourth scene—the Ghost of Christmas Future. He needs prompts. The ghost doesn't even speak, for the love of Mike, but he wants the kid to prompt him."

"Dimitri, we'll figure this out." I handed him a container. He lifted the corner of the lid, ascertained what it was, and grunted his gratitude. I handed Connie her pudding, pulled the spoons out of my pocket, and passed them out.

Dimitri sat in the front row with his cobbler. Connie called a break, and then sat down beside him to eat. I leaned on the edge of the stage.

"Stewart could take over Scrooge," I said.

"And who would play Marley?" Dimitri and Connie had obviously had this discussion before. They looked at me, expecting me to get them past the point where they'd gotten stuck.

"You, Dimitri. You'll play Marley."

Dimitri paled. His performance anxiety, onstage at least, was his Achilles' heel. I'd always respected this issue as out of bounds, but not today. Not with this much at stake. "Yes, you. People will love to see you on stage, Dimitri. It might even convince some of them not to demand refunds. Which they can, you know, since Patrick King is above the title." I reminded him of this fact mostly because I'd argued so hard about *not* putting Patrick's name above the title. *"We're sold out for a four-week run.* Three of those weeks are needed just to cover our expenses. The only reason we could sell that extra week, the week after Christmas, was because of Patrick's name. And that's our week of pure profit. Not a lot, not as much as I would have hoped, but there you go. So there will be a show. We aren't canceling."

Neither one of them spoke. Dimitri put his spoon back in his cobbler, and then threw his head back and roared. Roared in frustration. I'd heard it before, but was still impressed. Connie didn't stop eating, and I didn't blink.

"Where is Stewart?" I asked, changing the subject.

"Over at the shop for a fitting. He should be back soon."

"Well, let's see how the Stewart factor plays out before we do anything rash like recast the show, okay?"

When I saw Patrick King I took him aside to talk, privately but in full view of the cast. Then I went back to sit next to Gus and watch the Christmas Past scene rehearsal. Harry was sitting near him, my deli sandwich on his lap, half of it gone. He handed me the rest as I sat down.

"Everything okay?" Harry asked.

I nodded while I took a big bite. "You couldn't hear me, could you?"

"No," he assured me.

"Good. Do you two know each other?"

"No, we just met," Harry said. "I wanted to thank him for helping Eric."

"Only doing my job," Gus said. "Sully, that guy you were just threatening? Hasn't he been on TV?"

"I didn't threaten him."

"Sully, I saw you. I saw him. You threatened him."

He was right, of course. I did threaten Patrick. I told him that this show might be a blip on the course of his career, but if he screwed it up, I would make it my life goal to make his life miserable. I would create an anonymous website that talked about what a hack Patrick King was, and I would email everyone I knew and have them hit on the website over and over until it was in the top ten Google searches under the name Patrick King. But I didn't want to tell Gus I was strong-arming a TV star these days.

"I think there might be something wrong with him," Harry said. "He's trying to remember his lines, but he can't. I've been working with him, but they just don't stick. It's heartbreaking in a way, though a lot of it may have to do with the drinking."

"Gee, you think?" I said.

"And the partying till all hours. And the womanizing."

"Harry, this isn't funny."

"I know it isn't, Sully. Sorry."

"He really can't remember?"

Harry shook his head. "I think he's scared to death. He hasn't had this big a stage role in years."

"Great."

"Maybe we should get a teleprompter. Or he could wear an earpiece and we could feed him his lines." Frank Augustine had sat down behind us. I hadn't heard him and was startled by the sound of his voice. Frank was our sound designer as well as the all-around tech director for our shows. Like a lot of people who found themselves out of step with society, Frank found his tribe in theater and was an institution at the Cliffside. His real job, of course, was as an IT tech, consulting with most of the businesses around town. I had no idea when he actually worked because he was always available when we needed him.

"Damn, Frank. You scared me."

"Sorry." He sounded bereft, and I felt instant guilt. I suspected he had a little crush on me. I turned around to face him and gave him a smile. I could never figure out how old he was. He had that generic computer-geek look that could put him anywhere between twenty-five and forty: stringy hair pulled back into a ponytail that enhanced a slightly receding hairline. Dirty jeans slung low on his hips, not by fashion but by an ill fit. An oversized, stretched-out, grayish-green crewneck sweater worn over a black T-shirt. The T-shirt probably had something with a skull on it. Frank wore a lot of skull T-shirts. White, or formerly white, athletic shoes completed the ensemble.

Looking past the clothes, Frank had potential. He had clear blue eyes and a nice smile. If he trimmed his beard, cut his hair, and got a fashion makeover, he could be quite the package. And undoubtedly would be, with the right woman running the show. He probably wouldn't put up much resistance to that. Me, I preferred my men to already have those skills. I wasn't swift enough with my own wardrobe to give advice to others.

"It's okay," I told him. "Let's go out into the lobby so we can talk."

"I have to go backstage. Can I take the chips?" Harry asked.

"Please do," I said.

"I'll get the trash. You go talk to Frank," Gus said. He shot me a look that said "find out what he knows about the Whitehall security system." I was way ahead of him, but knew Frank well enough that jumping right into the conversation would scare him off.

Once we were out in the lobby I turned to Frank. "What's this about an earpiece?"

"An idea—we could put an earpiece on him and feed him his lines off stage."

"Expensive?"

"No, not at all. I can probably throw something together from stuff I've got back at the house." Frank's eyes wandered toward Gus as he joined us, looking for a trash can.

"As long as it doesn't take you too long, let's give it a shot. Oh, and Frank, this is Gus Knight. Gus, Frank Augustine."

"Aren't you Eric Whitehall's lawyer?"

"Yes, I am."

"He's a good guy. I can't imagine he could kill his father. His dad was a good guy too. I still can't believe I won't see him again."

"You knew Peter Whitehall?" Gus asked casually. He was smooth.

"I did some work for him, on and off. Setting up a home network. Keeping up with the security stuff. Plus he was testing out new camera systems, adding a backup system, looking at web browsers."

"Did everything the cameras recorded get saved?"

"Not yet," Frank said. "Like I said, he was testing out systems. He loved playing with new technology. It took him a long time to commit to changing over systems. He was moving toward a motion-activated system with infrared cameras."

"Did he need to be that worried about security?" Gus asked.

"You wouldn't think so, but lately he'd really stepped things up. He was moving fast."

"Had you switched the system over yet?"

Frank paused, and then said, "No, not yet," without looking either of us in the eye.

He was lying. I knew it, but I didn't think that Gus had caught on. I could call Frank out on it now, or talk to him privately later. I decided on later.

"That's a shame, Frank. Ah well, we all knew it wasn't going to be that easy. I've got to run, but I'll be on my cell. Let Connie know, will you?"

"Sure thing. See you later."

Gus and I were bundling up for the walk to the car when I stopped for a minute.

"Damn, I need to tell Connie that I've okay'd the earpiece Frank suggested."

"Can't you call her later?"

"I could, but by then Frank will have already told her and I'll have to deal with her nose out of joint. It's much better if I run it by her now. I'll be there in a tic—maybe you can go get the car?" I tossed him my keys and gave him a grin.

"You want me to warm up that box of yours for you."

"Well, there is that. But you've little room to be critical, since your car is conveniently at the shop. Seriously, I'll only be a second."

Gus hesitated for a moment, but seemed satisfied about something. He tossed the keys in the air and grabbed them in his fist. "I'll go get the car."

· Jen ·

*J*found Frank at the top of the center aisle, talking to Connie. They didn't bother to stop their conversation when I approached, instead turning slightly toward me to include me in the discussion.

"It won't screw up any of the other frequencies?" Connie was asking. "Remember what happened last year?"

Last year we'd had a few technical glitches the first weekend of the run. Well, more than a few. The Ghost of Christmas Present makes a grand entrance by flying in from the catwalk on an invisible wire, but he'd lost his balance a little while getting onto the swing. The arc from his readjustment had gotten progressively worse as he descended. By the time he was about twelve feet from the stage, he hit the side of the set. It was frightening.

The other disaster had fallen into Frank's purview, though it wasn't his fault. Our regular sound board op wasn't available, so we'd hired a substitute, thinking that his resume indicated a level of competence. We were wrong. He didn't understand the channels and the sound design of the show, and he kept forgetting to turn the actor's microphones off when they went off stage. A couple of times he left Connie's mic on, and the audience was treated to her hissing as quietly as possible, "Cue the Cratchit kids, cue the Cratchit kids, CUE THE CRATCHIT KIDS" in a desperate manner. For most of last summer, "cue the Cratchit kids" was the "in" phrase at the theater, a kind of "where's the beef" for the nonprofit set. Even though it wasn't Frank's doing, it was a technical foul-up, so he fell on his sword. He actually ended up running the sound board when Dimitri fired the sub after that show.

"It won't screw up—" Frank began.

"Because this is bad enough, but if Patrick starts spouting off lighting cues—"

"He won't, I promise."

They both looked at me. If it turned out to be a disaster, I would be the one blamed. Connie wasn't going there this year.

"Connie, I think we should give it a shot. I'm sure Frank can figure this out."

"Okay," she said, her look clearly indicating that my head was on the block. "Go ahead, Frank. Let's get it ready and test it out ASAP. I'll find one of the students to feed Patrick his lines."

"We can try it out tonight, after dinner break."

Connie walked down the aisle toward Dimitri, who was having a loud discussion with Cassandra Ryan, the costume designer, at the foot of the stage. Cassandra was the only person I knew who took up more space than Dimitri did. She was tall already, and wore perilously high-heeled boots. Her braided hair was piled on top of her head, giving her another few inches of height. It wasn't only her physicality, it was her personality. I didn't need to worry about Cassandra holding her own with Dimitri. I only had to worry if they decided to gang up on me.

"Thanks for the backup, Sully," Frank said. "Sometimes Connie doesn't trust me..."

"Not true. She's cautious. It's her job to be the resident naysayer. That way she's run it through the system so that any possible resistance will have been vetted. Are you sure you'll have it ready by tonight? That's pretty short notice."

"I thought of it a few days ago and started to rig it."

"Really?" I was impressed by Frank's entrepreneurship. I hadn't been giving him enough credit. I looked at my watch and realized that the praise would need to wait. "That's great, Frank. I don't know what we would do without you. I don't want to think about what we'd do without you."

"Don't worry, I'm not going anywhere. I like helping out. My job can get pretty lonely … it's nice to be around people, to be part of all this."

"Yeah, I know," I said. "It's a crazy group, but it's our crazy group." Frank nodded and smiled.

"I need to run, but I have a question," I said. "It's about Peter Whitehall's house. How far were you on the setup? It's okay, you can tell me."

"I know it's weird, but he'd told me not to tell anyone and I feel like I owe it to him—"

"I'm sorry I didn't realize you were friends," I said. "I don't think that he had many of those."

"I wouldn't say we were friends," Frank said. "But he was good to me … "

"Frank, someone killed him. His son isn't that someone, but I'm afraid that since everyone thinks Eric did it, people will stop looking. I haven't stopped looking. In fact, I just started. Anything you can tell me that might help would be great."

Frank let that hang in the air for a moment. He looked around and moved closer, lowering his voice from its already quiet pitch. I had to lean in further to hear him.

"I started to work on it, but I wasn't completely finished." Frank seemed to consider what he was saying. "Mr. Whitehall kept adding stuff to the system, and he hadn't finished yet. He was putting some of the cameras up himself. They were infrared, so they didn't need to be wired, just tracked for the software. He was going a little nuts. I don't even know why he was doing it … he was, well, playing it pretty close to the vest. He didn't want people to know where all the cameras were, so I had to do the software install when no one was home. Kinda made it tricky, but I have a pretty flexible schedule. And he made it worthwhile."

"Had you done the hallway camera yet?"

"We'd tried, but we kept running into problems, some kind of interference. But the feed from there was available live on a website. All the cameras were. It would be easier for the guard to keep up that way."

"Did anything get recorded?"

"I gave the police all the passwords. Mr. Whitehall was still playing with the system, so I'm not sure if anything was saved. I can try and find out if you'd like."

"That would be great. Call me if you find anything, okay?"

"You can count on me."

∞

I was leaving the high school as Stewart was chaining up his bike. He swept me up in a big hug and kissed me. The kiss lasted a few seconds longer than was strictly friendly, but I didn't mind.

"You look great, Stewart."

"Thanks, liar." He rubbed his hand over his stubbled chin and then through his helmet-crushed hair. "You look good."

Keenly aware of my lack of makeup and tired eyes, I laughed. "Okay, so we're both full of crap. But it's wonderful to see you. And that isn't a lie. Now get in there before Connie has a fit."

With another quick kiss, Stewart hurried into the building. Turning toward the car, I saw Gus break his gaze and look quickly down at his phone. My social life had gotten complicated. But I kind of liked it.

· Eleven ·

Gus and I drove to the Anchorage in the same car I owned when we were married. He had the good grace not to mention the ice puddle on the bottom of the passenger-side floor. I had an unknown and heretofore undetectable leak on the passenger side that had proved a considerable problem during rainstorms. If I didn't mop up the puddle, it would freeze up until the heater kicked in. Fortunately, it didn't smell, yet. But I would need to buy a new car in the spring. One more winter was all I asked.

We spent the short ride discussing our strategy for talking to Terry. Gus didn't mention Stewart—or our kiss—and I didn't bring the subject up. Gus had said that Terry seemed willing to do whatever was necessary to help Eric. Of course, Gus also said that Terry seemed pathological in his ability to say whatever needed to be said in any given situation, so he couldn't read him. We decided that he would take the lead, and I'd add to the conversation if needed. Actually, this was more Gus's idea, but I concurred. For the time being.

The guard at the gate waved us in. He must have then called the house, because Terry was waiting at the open front door. He shook

Gus's hand, turned to me, and took my hand in his. "Edwina, so good to see you again so soon."

"Sully, please." I shook his hand.

"But Mrs. Bridges refers to you as Edwina—"

"Mrs. Bridges used to change my diapers, so she can call me whatever she wants." I hoped that would put an end to the conversation. How much do I hate my first name? We had a momentary staredown, and then he turned to lead us into the house.

"Sorry for the confusion," he said over his shoulder as he pushed the big door open, "but I heard Mrs. Bridges call you Edwina and thought it was optional."

I tried to remember back to my visit yesterday morning. Did she call me Edwina? I couldn't remember, but she probably did. I wondered when it happened, and what else we were discussing at the time. And where Terry had been. And how much he'd heard. And how he'd heard it. Maybe Peter wasn't the only survcillance fan?

As we crossed the threshold, Gus leaned in and whispered, "Edwina, the game's afoot!" Problem was, I didn't know which game we were playing or the rules. I felt a rush of adrenaline kick in and realized that I needed to focus. Why, on whom, and on what—these details weren't clear—but focus nonetheless.

I tried to look nonchalant as I surveyed the entrance area of the house for hidden cameras. They were very small these days, but I thought I picked one out below the bottom railing of the staircase.

Someone had added a few Christmas decorations to the hallway. The house was still far from festive, appropriately in mourning, but a few sprigs of holly, greens on the staircase, and red candles were faint reminders of the season. I ran my fingers along the greens on the table and smelled my fingertips. What memories were encased in that smell. When I was a little girl it was all happiness. Now, the memories

123

were as bittersweet as happy; I could remember the first Christmas without my mother. I'd wanted to forget the whole holiday, but Dad went out and bought a small tree, put a wreath on the door. Nothing more, but enough to give us permission to celebrate the season. "Your mother would be very upset if we skipped Christmas, Sully. She loved Christmas." He was right, of course. After he died, I bought one of those fake trees in a box: two-foot high, lights on, paper decorations. It was all I did, but I made the effort. Funny how that time, it didn't make me feel better. Maybe I missed the smell.

Gus had stopped to wait for me, a strange look on his face. I smiled and followed Terry toward the back of the house, counting two more cameras on the way. He led us into the library, the room closest to Peter's study. The old library was originally a huge room that took up the back of the house. But when Peter put on his addition, some hallways were added and the library became a series of smaller but still grand rooms along the side of the house. I looked around. Was that another camera outside the study? I couldn't tell, but I didn't want to stare too long. Terry noticed my glance and seemed to mistake it for something else. He sighed heavily and opened the door to the library.

"We can talk in here, if that's okay. The fire is already started."

Once we entered, I realized that the library also served as an office, presumably Terry's. The desk had a computer like the one I'd seen on Peter's desk. Settled on top of it, in a docking station, was a laptop. At the other end of the desk was a second laptop. Three monitors lined the desk, each tracking a different program. I couldn't see specifics on the screen, and couldn't imagine trying to keep track of all that information at once. I glanced around the room quickly but didn't see any cameras.

We'd just settled into the chairs when the door opened. Mrs. Bridges entered, carrying a large tray with tea things on it. Gus jumped up to take the tray from her. Terry didn't move.

"Will that be all, Mr. Holmes?" she asked.

"Yes, thank you, Mrs. Bridges."

"Call if you need anything else." She gave a short bow toward Terry and I saw him clench his jaw. She turned to walk out and gave me a quick wink. I stifled a smile. No love lost between the two of them.

"Well, Gus, you said that you wanted to talk, but you didn't say what you wanted to talk about. I thought it was probably business, but since you've brought Sully, I must have been wrong."

"Sully is here to help give me some perspective about the case against Eric..." Gus started to use the explanation we'd rehearsed in the car.

"But surely your years as a defense attorney would be sufficient to—"

"Defense attorneys react to a case and its evidence," I said. "Cops find the evidence. Gus thought that perhaps I could help figure out how strong the case is. And to see if any evidence could be interpreted differently."

"Differently?"

"I don't believe Eric is guilty."

"No one does," Terry said. He made no move to pour the tea. Nor did I. Another stalemate.

"So I have to wonder if the evidence could be reinterpreted to point in another direction."

"Another direction?" he asked.

"Toward the truth," Gus said.

Terry paused. "And I can help how, exactly?"

"Eric told me what happened that night, as best he can remember," Gus said.

"Which probably isn't much, am I correct?"

"You're right, it's not much."

"He was pretty drunk," Terry said. "Started early and kept on going. It was embarrassing, though there weren't too many people there. Just family, really—"

"Eric remembers Emma, Amelia, Mrs. Bridges, Brooke ... "

"Clive Willis was there as well. The Cunninghams came with Hal Maxwell, but they left early because of the storm. You were going to come, weren't you Gus? You and your friend there, Kathy, isn't that her name?"

"Kate. The storm really buried us in the city, so we decided to stay put. I was planning on coming up on Sunday."

Gus said my name twice before I realized he was offering me a cup of tea. Kate. Bah.

"We didn't get as much snow up here, but we usually don't," Terry said. "Too close to the ocean. Anyway, we had dinner. Russell went home early—"

"Russell?" I asked.

"The guard," Terry explained. "Clive decided to stay over. Peter went into his study around ten. We had our conference call at midnight—"

"Were you all in the same room?" Gus asked.

"Eric and Emma were in the kitchen. I was in here, Peter was in his study."

"Once Russell left, how was the house secured?"

"Peter had an intercom system put in. It's tied into the security system. Aside from that, the house has an alarm system that was on all night."

"What happens if the power goes out? Does the system reset itself?"

"The generator keeps the power running at an even level, no matter what. Why all the questions?"

"I'm wondering if there was an opportunity for someone outside to come in during the storm," Gus said.

Terry shook his head. "I wish there was, but no. Besides, the recordings…" He shook his head again and looked down into his teacup.

"What about the other cameras?"

"The system only records one camera at a time, and it switches views. This was the first time we even had to look at one of the recordings."

I decided to go for the role of good cop. "Does it ever creep you out, the idea of being taped all the time? I always wondered about that. It would give me the creeps, that's for sure."

"Peter loved high tech toys, did you know that? The family was concerned about the camera locations, so Peter agreed to put most of them outside. The only cameras in the house are in this area, the business area as it were. It shows this hallway. Peter's study is at the end. Mostly the cameras are for monitoring."

"Monitoring what?" Gus asked.

"Who was where when," Terry said. "Peter ran a tight ship. He liked to know all. What the hell is that racket?"

Racket it was, and what it was became apparent in the next moment. Like her auspicious entrance yesterday, Brooke Whitehall's entrance was on none-too-steady legs.

"Terry, I can't find my… oh Gus, you're here! Terry, why didn't you tell me Gus was here? You know how much I enjoy seeing Gus… and Sally, isn't it? What is this, a party? Why wasn't I invited?" She sat on the edge of Gus's chair, leaning in toward him. He deftly got up and offered her his seat, moving to an armless chair closer to me. She slid down into the seat and leaned toward the tea set, rattling the cups on the tray.

"Here, let me." Terry poured her a cup of tea, adding three sugars and a twist of lemon. He put the cup and saucer on the coffee table in front of her, easily within her reach. She reached into the pocket of her jacket and pulled out a small flask, pouring amber liquid into her cup.

"Honestly, Brooke." Terry sounded annoyed. Really annoyed.

"I told you before, leave me alone, Terry. I've been through a lot this past week. This helps steady my nerves. That's okay with you, isn't it? You want me to have steady nerves, don't you? Maybe you should have some."

"No, thank you."

"How about you, Gus? Or Sally, would you like some?" As she turned to offer us the flask, Brooke gestured with her hand and the liquid came flying out all over me. The aroma was strong, like very strong cough syrup.

"Oops," was all she said.

"Honestly, Brooke..."

"It's fine, it barely hit me," I said.

"It doesn't stain anyway," Brooke said.

"That's good. Usually brandy stains." I took a sniff of it. Wow. I hoped it didn't burn a hole through my pants.

"S'not brandy. It's an old family recipe—my father sent me a case last Christmas. He makes it every year. So why are you here, Gus? I thought the business was shut down this week? Isn't that what you said, Terry? That the business was shut down, that's why you're staying home?"

"The business isn't shut down; I'm working from home this week. Gus isn't here on business. They came to talk about Eric, and the evidence against him."

"Poor Eric. I wonder why he did it?"

"We don't think he did it, Brooke," Gus said. "That's why Sully and I are here, to follow the evidence, see if there are other solutions."

Brooke looked like she was going to say something, but Terry put his hand on her knee and she stopped. "Brooke, drink your tea." She put her hand on top of his very briefly, and then took her tea cup and sat back in the chair.

"Gus, I don't know what to say," Terry said. "I don't think that Eric did it, but I don't have any information that can help you get him off. I wish I did, but I don't." He didn't sound that sorry to me.

I could see Gus trying to formulate his next question, but I decided to dive in. I'd lied to Brooke; a lot of her drink had landed on my sleeve, and the smell in combination with the fire and the company was making me nauseous.

"So forgive me, then, Terry, but I think we need to look at everyone else in the house that evening," I said quickly. "Did you know I used to be with the State Police? Old habits die hard—I need to get back in the groove. Do you know what time the police think Peter died?"

Brooke flinched, but Terry stared at me. "Between midnight and eight o'clock in the morning. Why?"

"Do you mind telling me where you were then?"

"I was in bed." Beat.

"With Emma?" This time Brooke spilled some tea.

"That's a pretty personal question, Sully."

"Sorry." He wasn't going to answer, so I moved on. "Can you tell me about Larry Colfer?"

"Larry Colfer?" The color drained from Terry's face, but his smile never wavered. "You've been doing your homework, haven't you?"

"Eric is my friend. So yes, I've been doing my homework. Larry Colfer?"

"Larry Colfer was a college mentor and a friend. Not only my friend, from what I understand—your father's friend as well."

"Yes. My father blamed Peter for Larry's death." I paused, and then leaned forward slightly and lowered my voice. "Did you?"

"No, I didn't." Terry paused and took a sip of tea. I noticed his hands were a little less steady as he put the cup back in the saucer. "Larry was a brilliant man with great ideas, who invested enough in his ideas to protect them until it was too late. Sounds harsh, I know, but I'd already decided that he was missing the wave, so I'd bailed on him. If anything, I blame myself for his suicide. Perhaps if I'd stuck with him, tried to make his dreams more businesslike, maybe then he would have had some more success. Not great success, but success enough to satisfy him."

"What does some dead guy have to do with helping Eric?" Brooke asked.

"Good question." Terry turned toward us. "Sully, Gus, what does Larry Colfer have to do with helping Eric?" He seemed glad for Brooke's interference and gave her a smile. She smiled back, and then looked away.

"Well, Brooke, here's the deal," I said. "I don't think Eric killed his father. Terry told us that there were very few people in the house that night. So if we want to figure out who did it, we need to figure out who else had a motive. This Larry Colfer connection could be seen as a possible motive for Terry. Obviously, it wasn't. So we'll need to see if other people had motives. Brooke, I wonder if … "

At this mention of her name, Brooke dropped her tea cup onto the middle of the table. At first I thought she was being dramatic, but one look at the color of her face and I realized that the swoon was for real. I rushed to the side of the couch as Terry helped her lie down. Her skin felt damp and clammy. Her color was the same shade as the ashes in the fireplace. A fine thread of perspiration peaked out on her upper lip, and she began to tremble. I grabbed the decorative throw on the back of the couch and spread it across her. It barely covered her legs.

"Tell Mrs. Bridges to get a blanket. And call the doctor," Terry barked toward Gus. Gus ran out of the room. I did my best to recall all the first aid I knew, but I wasn't sure what was wrong. Brooke might be having a heart attack, but her breath was smooth and steady. Maybe some sort of reaction…

"Terry, do you have any idea what's wrong with her?"

"She's been under a lot of strain … there, there, Brooke. You're okay. You're okay."

She'd regained consciousness and started clawing at Terry's arm. "Terry, don't let … I can't … "

"Shhh, Brooke, don't say anything, rest. *Sully* and I are *right here*. We won't leave you, I promise." With that subtle reminder of company in the house, Brooke looked at me and wailed. Not cried. Wailed. She sounded so pitiful, I felt sorry for her.

"I'll go check in with Mrs. Bridges and Gus." I closed the library door behind me but didn't latch it. Instead, I counted to ten and peeked through the crack. Terry was sitting on the edge of the couch, holding Brooke down by her shoulders. She was speaking in low tones, so I could only make out snippets: "Shouldn't have … know … not going to … you can't … " Terry looked more concerned than when she'd first collapsed.

"Sully." I couldn't tell if Gus was warning me about something or disgusted that I was eavesdropping. I closed the door quietly and turned toward him. He was followed by Mrs. Bridges and another man, someone I didn't know but recognized from the funeral. He'd sat in the second row.

"I'll go and check in with them while we wait for the doctor." Mrs. Bridges slid beside me, rapped once on the large door, and stepped inside. She kept it partially opened. Terry stood while she entered and started fussing about the room, putting a blanket over Brooke, rearranging the pillows behind her head, patting her hand. Mrs. Bridges said something to him, and he began to collect the tea things and put them on the tray. She reached inside Brooke's pocket and removed the flask I'd seen earlier. She handed it to Terry, who quickly pocketed it and resumed gathering the china.

I became aware of the men talking behind me and turned away from the scene of domesticity in the library.

"I thank God we're not a public company. This kind of story doesn't go over well with stockholders, let me tell you."

"The company will be fine, Clive, you know that. Emma's been a major figure for years—"

"Still, I don't know what he was thinking. But I'm glad to have seen you—you saved me a phone call." He turned to me and held out his hand. "Clive Willis." His handshake matched the rest of him. Solid, hearty, and businesslike. Clive Willis was of an indeterminate age—he was the kind of man who probably looked the same at thirty as he would at seventy. Thinning hair swooshed over a bald spot, gray eyes, pale skin stretched over a large skull, thin lips. The lines on his face seemed chiseled on either side. Absent from around his eyes and mouth were laugh lines.

"Sully Sullivan," I said.

When I was fairly young, twelve or thirteen, my father had given me a long lecture about handshakes and their importance. He warned me about downturned hands, fishy fingers, and nondescript grabs. Grasp, shake, squeeze, let go. We practiced several times that night, and often over the years he'd give me a handshake pop quiz. If Clive

Willis had children, he'd probably given them the same lesson. He seemed to appreciate my technique.

"Ah, I should have seen the resemblance. I knew both of your parents. Good people, both of them."

"Thank you. I thought so."

"Of course, your father was one of the most pig-headed bastards I've ever met, but you probably knew that about him already, didn't you?" He didn't wait for an answer and turned to Gus. "Did you know Bryan?"

"Very well."

"And was he, or was he not, a pig-headed bastard?"

"I think I prefer strong-willed..."

"A polite way of saying pig-headed. He wasn't a big fan of Peter Whitehall's, that's for sure." I thought I heard a note of admiration in the man's voice. But that was it. Clearly he didn't plan to elaborate. And I wasn't sure how to.

"Clive, I'm going to run Sully home. Please tell Mrs. Bridges and Terry that I'm on my cell if they need me."

"I'll see both of you tomorrow at the reading."

Gus grabbed me by the elbow and steered me toward the front door as Clive walked into the library.

"Peter's will?" I whispered. "Why would I go to a reading of Peter's will?"

"Because apparently, you're named as one of the beneficiaries."

∞

We were back in the car, passing the front gate before I got the words out. I'll admit, it takes a lot for me to find myself at a loss of words, but news that I was in Peter Whitehall's will did it. I'd barely known the man. Even when our families were on speaking terms, he was never around. "Maybe I'm mentioned because he left something to my mother and since I'm her heir … "

"That's not it. The will is fairly recent, from what I understand. It names you specifically. Not your mother or your father, you. Freddy Sands gave Clive a list of beneficiaries, and Clive's trying to round them up for tomorrow's reading at his office."

"Did Clive tell you anything else?"

"He said he hadn't even known there was a new will. He thought the most recent one was from three years ago, when Terry took over as CEO of the company."

"Didn't you tell me there was a rumor that Eric was cut out of the will?"

"Rumor."

"Do you remember where you heard it from?"

"Terry."

Now that was interesting.

· Twelve ·

woke much earlier than I needed to in order to get ready for Gus to pick me up at eight o'clock. Like, two hours early. I started to fuss over what to wear, but not for the same reasons as on the morning of the funeral. This time it was vanity, pure and simple. Gus was picking me up, and I wanted to look nice. There, I admitted it. It was out in the open. I might have a crush on my ex-husband. Talk about nuts. For the first time in I don't know how long, I cared about how I looked. Really cared, not just "I don't want to scare anyone so my clothes better match" or "I should probably wear a suit since I'm going to ask them for $50,000," but "I think this shirt makes my eyes look blue" and "I think this jacket covers my butt enough to hide the damage a pint of ice cream a day for three years has done." I wasn't quite giddy, but the butterflies were back.

They needed to be squashed. Fast and hard. Gus wasn't going to be in my life for long. Maybe I could make some amends, and we could end up as friends. But nothing more. I wasn't up to it, and he had Kate. Nevertheless, I chose the shirt that brought out the blue in my eyes.

All of this planning took about fifteen minutes, so I decided to burn off my excess energy. I considered a run, which for me meant a slow jog, but decided on a bike ride when I saw the glorious sunrise beginning to peak. Running required me to concentrate too hard on breathing—and on not keeling over—to enjoy the sites, but I could enjoy a bike ride. I decided to do a five-mile loop by the beach. It was uphill the first half of the ride, but I needed to warm up, and what better way than to fight screaming quads?

I'd reached the top of the hill when I thought I heard someone calling my name. I slowed down and looked at the beach. In the haze of the sunrise burning through the morning fog, I saw Stewart Tracy sitting on a piling. Next to him was the bent frame of our loaner bike.

"What the hell happened? Are you okay?"

"Thank God you came by, Sully. I was contemplating which house to wake up."

"You're bleeding."

"Scrapes, that's all. I was coming around the corner and something darted out ... probably a coyote."

"Probably a dog."

"Whose story is this?" he asked. "Anyway, I veered to avoid the werewolf, hit a patch of sand, and wiped out. I'm fine—a couple of scrapes, but most of me is covered. The bike, however, is toast."

"Can you walk? We could get my car."

"I can walk. How far is your house?"

"A half mile or so."

"Really. I was trying to remember, but it seemed much farther that time we went back after the cocktail party. Remember that time?"

I did remember, and blushed. Damn him. I slapped him on the arm and bent over to pull his bike up. On the way to my house I caught him up about Peter Whitehall's death. He'd heard stories, of course, but had been so busy in the past day and a half that he hadn't had a chance to put all the pieces together.

"So Peter Whitehall left you something?"

"I guess so. We'll see in about, oh, three hours or so."

By now we were back at the house, and I stowed both bikes in the carport. I noticed a slight limp when Stewart climbed the stairs, but he shook off my concern.

"Ice, Advil, and coffee are all I need. I'll be fine."

My forays into physical fitness left me with a wide variety of ice packs to choose from, but when I offered to make the coffee, Stewart quickly declined. He knew about my lack of skills. "Please, I'll make the coffee. You go up and get ready. How did you say you were getting to Boston?"

"Gus had to get his car from the dealership, so he said he'd pick me up."

"Gus being the ex? Interesting. Seems a little out of the way, don't you think?"

"Shut up." I was blushing again. "I'm going to take a shower. Why don't you use my car today? Or my bike, whichever you prefer."

"Let me have a cup of coffee first, then I'll see how I feel. Unless you want me gone before Gus gets here?" I didn't answer him.

My shower was brief, but getting dressed took longer than normal. I put on three, count 'em three, colors of eyeshadow and changed my earrings twice before I heard the doorbell ring. Dammit, he was early. I moved as quickly as I could and walked out into the kitchen as Gus was hanging up his coat.

"We met," Stewart said. He went back to the table and settled into his chair, putting his feet up on another and resettling the ice packs on his knees. "Gus, do you want a cup of coffee? I just made it."

"Or should we hit the road?" I asked. My handbag was by the front door. If he wanted to leave, I could go.

"A cup of coffee would be great." Gus smiled and lifted a bag. "I brought some scones, hoping you'd have coffee made. You do still like scones, don't you?"

"I love scones. I have some clotted cream."

"Great. Stewart, will you join us?" Gus asked.

"No thanks. I've got to hit the road before I completely seize up. Sully, the car seems like the best bet. Are you sure that's okay?"

"Of course. Are you going to be all right?"

"The show will go on, have no fear. Good to meet you, Gus. Hopefully we'll see you again soon. I'd love to grab a beer sometime." I shot Stewart a look, which he ignored. He gave me a quick kiss on the cheek and limped to the back door. I wasn't sure if his pain was real or an act until he turned and gave me a pitiful wave followed by a huge wink. He was going to be fine.

I found the clotted cream in the refrigerator and put it, mugs, plates, and knives on a tray and brought them upstairs to the table, Gus following behind. The café table I used for meals was clear enough to set the tray. Gus waited while I started to gather the papers from the dining room table cum desk. I kept the piles as they were, and moved them to the coffee table one by one. Gus smiled while he watched.

"Sorry," I said. "It will take another sec."

"That's okay. I remember the filing system. I didn't realize theater created so much paper."

"The theater does create a ton of paper, but most of this is stuff for Eric."

"Really?"

"Why do you sound so surprised? You asked me to look into it … "

"Whoa, let's not fight. I didn't mean anything. It's only been a couple of days."

I took a deep breath. "Sorry. You're right. It is a lot of paper. But I've been following tangents. You know how I get." We both let that hang. He knew how I was a lifetime ago, but not now. Nor did I know him.

"What sort of tangents?" he asked.

"Larry Colfer was one. So I had to look into it, for my own sake. When I realized that Terry was at the same school as Larry Colfer I looked into it a little while longer, to see if there was anything else."

"And was there?"

"Not that I could find."

"Me either. What's this pile?" Gus pointed to one of the smaller stacks. I glanced at it for show, but I didn't need to. I knew what it was.

"That's the security camera pile. I looked into a few systems. I thought I'd ask Frank some more questions."

"Research for research? But didn't Terry say the new cameras weren't operating?"

"But I got the impression from Frank that they were, at least partially. Anyway, finding out about his camera system tells us a little about Peter, don't you think?"

Gus reached for the clotted cream and slathered more on his scone. "How do you mean?"

"Well, it seems to me that there are a few different types of technology geeks. Some who upgrade because they can afford it and only want the best. Some who upgrade because they feel that they should, though they never completely get the hang of it. And the third type, the type I think Peter was, who upgrade when it's necessary because they want to be able to do something they haven't been able to before. Peter added cameras to the inside of the house. Why? What made him think that he needed more security inside? Was it security or spying? Did he do it because he suspected something? Or because he could?"

I took a sip of coffee and looked out the window at the sea. For a moment I lost myself in the view, which was, after all, why I'd bought the carriage house in the first place. My view. This morning, the clear blue winter sky was peeking above the marsh, where the early morning dew was creating a haze as it dried out. Tomorrow it would look completely different. That was what I loved.

I looked down at my scone and realized it was a little skimpy on the clotted cream. I reached across the table and caught Gus staring.

"Where were you just then?" he asked softly.

I felt the color rise to my cheeks. "Nowhere. Daydreaming."

"I didn't think you were the daydreaming type."

"This view makes it easy."

"It is a beautiful view," Gus said, looking at me. He held my gaze a little longer and then looked down at his phone. "Sadly, I think we should leave it for now and get to the reading. What do you think?"

I thought I wanted to stay put for a while longer, but Gus was right. I needed to go and see what Peter Whitehall had left me in his will.

· Thirteen ·

We drove Gus's car to Clive Willis's office in Boston. Gus had a nice car—sporty but solid, green exterior, tan leather interior. Bells and whistles on the dashboard that I couldn't even begin to fathom. I was warm, really warm, immediately. Odds were good the seats were heated. Heated seats were a fantasy of mine, as yet unrealized.

"Nice car, Gus," I said.

"Thanks. I think it's a mid-life thing … an indulgence." Gus sounded like he felt he needed to justify the opulence of his vehicle to me. Maybe my tone had been a little sarcastic. I decided to try again.

"No, really, it's very nice. I love the leather seats." I patted the seat beside me and then looked out the window. Back to work. "So, I know he's a business associate of Peter's, but who is Clive Willis exactly?"

"Basically, he's a banker."

"What does that mean?"

"He started off as a banker. Then Peter's business started to expand, and Clive hitched his wagon to Peter. He started extending credit to some of Peter's clients. Branched out to venture capitalism in the '90s."

"Isn't that pretty risky? How did he do during the bust?"

"Clive is savvy, and he saw over the horizon in time. He also leaned on Peter a lot for advice. Fiscally, he's pretty conservative. The dot com bust impacted him a little, but he regrouped. Made it through the last recession just fine."

"And?"

"And what?"

"And Clive was there the night Peter died, right? How do you think he stacks up in the suspect department? Were he and Peter on good terms?"

"They were on very good terms. Peter trusted Clive implicitly. More than anyone else. Probably because Clive didn't quake in Peter's presence. He treated him with respect but told him what he thought, not what he thought Peter wanted to hear."

"Unlike Terry."

"Or Emma, or me, I guess. Peter was a great arguer. If you told him something he didn't want to hear, he'd argue. He'd argue so hard it would wear you down. The next time you spoke, he'd usually concede your point of view if, upon reflection, he thought it made sense. But he'd never tell you that you were right or that he was wrong. He'd only mention, in passing, that he'd changed his mind."

"That would drive me nuts."

"It did. I was learning how to deal with it, call him out. Clive was a great example. The few times I saw them together were the times when Peter seemed most at ease. He considered Clive an equal. I'd hoped to reach the same place with Peter at some point."

"You liked Peter, didn't you?"

"I don't know if 'like' is the word," Gus said. "I began to appreciate him. And I looked forward to our meetings. You know I was Bryan's son-in-law for five years." He glanced over at me and smiled. "So I don't know if I could ever *like* him, but I did respect him. Sorry, I know you had issues."

"My father had issues ... " I let the silence hang for a second. Gus didn't rush in to fill the gap. We were getting into rough waters. Discussions of my father's issues, or pigheadedness, would no doubt remind us both that I'd inherited the trait. Back in the day, if I thought something was white, no one and nothing could convince me otherwise. There was little to no gray in my life when Gus and I were married. I wanted to tell him that there were more hues now, but I couldn't find the words. Luckily, we were almost there, and we had more pressing issues to discuss.

"How did Clive know about the will?"

"The executorship was changed. He'd been named executor of the old will, but Freddy Sands called him and told him about some of the changes in the new will."

"Clive wasn't the executor any longer?"

"Not exclusively. A coexecutor had been named."

"Will there be a problem?"

"I guess it depends on what's in it, but Clive said it's pretty foolproof."

Once in the city, we parked the car in a garage in the financial district and walked to Clive's office. The garage was going to cost an arm and a leg, but street parking in Boston, particularly in that area, was a fool's folly. I admit I'd have cruised around for a while, but Gus didn't give it a second thought. Clive's office was in one of the swankiest buildings in Boston. The financial district, which straddles Chinatown, Faneuil Hall, and Downtown Crossing, looks closer to the textbook definition of a major American city, complete with skyscrapers, than the rest of Boston does. With the exception of the Hancock and Prudential towers, most of the city's buildings are well under five stories high. The financial district, which packs a number of tall buildings into a small space, makes it feel more like New York.

While on the force, I'd had occasion to come to this part of town, but I hadn't been here in a while. I marveled at the new construction and mentioned it to Gus.

"There's also a lot of refitting of older spaces. I'm working with a few clients on some major redevelopment—Jerome Cunningham? Have you heard of him?"

Had I heard of him? Yes, I'd heard of him. A rich, handsome, entrepreneurial real estate developer who'd been cutting large swatches throughout the city for about ten years—his PR machine had set him up as a kind of Robin Hood. His projects always had a nonprofit edge to them. He could be altruistic, I supposed, but he was probably just smart. Building a little league field made him a community hero. Never mind that his building next door had made two hundred residents homeless.

"I've heard of him, yes…"

"Don't start."

"I wasn't going to say anything."

Gus ignored me until the elevator stopped and we were on the thirty-fifth floor. A young man was waiting for us.

"Hello, Mr. Knight, Ms. Sullivan. You're in the conference room at the end of the hall on your right." Gus smiled and nodded. I wondered how often he'd been there that they knew who he was. And how they knew who I was.

"The front desk calls up when you sign in downstairs," Gus whispered as we walked down the hall. "It took me a couple of visits to figure the system out."

"It throws you off balance a little, don't you think? I mean, it seems nice, but it's also pretty intimidating to have Super Boy meeting you armed with your name."

Gus laughed as he pushed open the door to the conference room and stepped back to let me enter. We were on time, a couple of minutes early even, but we were the last to arrive.

There was a logjam at the door to the conference room. Coffee was being rolled in, and cups and saucers were being set on the table. The waiter tried to move the cart to let me pass, but I shook my head and walked the long way around, away from the crowd, in order to join it.

"What is she doing here?" Brooke pulled on Terry's arm and pointed toward me with a shaky hand. Everyone stopped talking, and I stopped walking. I couldn't decide whether Brooke looked worse than she did yesterday. She certainly seemed more fragile, but her makeup and hair were perfect. And the look she was giving me was pretty clear, though I couldn't figure out what I'd done to earn such contempt.

Gus squeezed my upper arm and kept walking toward Brooke. I stopped and took a moment to look out of the windows. The view was breathtaking, and the sight of the water did what it always did and calmed me. Suddenly it all hit me. The time spent with Gus, Eric's questioning by the police, my visits to the Anchorage—they'd all been a little surreal. But the reading of a will? That was very real. Peter Whitehall was dead, and he'd left a new will for his family. I wondered how extraordinary that was. How often did he change his will? Soon enough we'd all know his intentions, even if the reasons behind them were still unclear.

A short burst of sound came from the phone on the wall beside me. Clive picked it up.

"Freddy Sands has arrived." Clive ignored Brooke and walked over to the table. He pulled out the chair beside him and offered it to me. "Sit here, Ms. Sullivan."

I thanked him and sat down. Gus had walked over to Emma and was talking to her in a low voice. He turned to sit in the seat beside me, but Eric got there first. He leaned over and gave me a kiss on the cheek. Gus avoided the chair next to Brooke and sat beside Terry.

Freddy Sands walked into the room, escorted to the door by Super Boy. I smiled when I saw him. Though his two-hundred-dollar suit and loafers didn't match the décor, it was obvious from his body language that the room and its inhabitants didn't intimidate him. I hadn't expected them to. My father always said attorney Freddy Sands was as comfortable with paupers as he was with kings. I watched him work the room while Clive introduced him. He seemed unaware of the palatable animosity. He smiled at each person and treated them like a long-lost relative.

I noticed he spent slightly more time speaking with Gus, and I wondered what he said. Then he reached Eric, who stood to shake the older man's hand.

"Freddy, this is Peter's son—" Clive began.

"No need, Clive, no need. Good to see you, son." Freddy wrapped both of his hands around Eric's, and then reached out and squeezed his shoulder.

Clive turned to me. I was still sitting, mainly because all of the standing men didn't allow me a lot of room to maneuver my chair out from the table. "And lastly, this is Edwina Sullivan ... "

"Edwina, what were your parents thinking, God rest their lovely souls. How are you, darlin'?" He gave me a wink. Had we been anywhere else, a hug would have followed, but not there.

"You know each other?" Clive had caught the wink and sounded surprised.

"I've known Sully since she was a baby. It's a small town, Trevorton. We all know each other."

Of course, there was more to it than that. Much more. Freddy and my father had played poker together. His wife Cathy and my mother were great friends. Freddy was a subscriber and donor to the Cliffside, and had helped more than once with contractual issues. For a moment I questioned the familiar "darlin'," but then I thought about it and realized that it was his way of providing full disclosure. Clive let it pass and sat down, with Freddy on his other side.

"Shall we begin?" Clive asked, taking the time to look at each face around the table. Taking the silence for assent, he turned toward Freddy Sands.

∞

Freddy donned his reading glasses, opened the portfolio in front of him, and, without pretext, began to read. "I, Peter F. Whitehall, a resident and citizen of Essex County, Massachusetts, being of sound mind and disposing memory, do hereby make, publish, and declare this instrument to be my last will and testament, hereby revoking any and all wills and codicils by me at any time heretofore made.

"Item I: Debts, Expenses, and Taxes: I direct my Executor, hereinafter named, to pay all of my matured debts and my funeral expenses, as well as the costs and expenses of the administration of my estate, as soon after my death as practicable. I further direct that all estate, inheritance, transfer, and succession taxes which are payable by reason under this will, be paid out of my residuary estate; and I hereby waive on behalf of my estate any right to recover from any person any part of such taxes so paid. My Executor, in his sole discretion, may pay from my domiciliary estate all or any portion of the costs of ancillary administration and similar proceedings in other jurisdictions..."

I was in a great location to watch most of the faces around the table, and all of the faces I was interested in: Terry, Brooke, Mrs. Bridges, Amelia … and Gus. I couldn't tell if people were breathing. I don't think Terry blinked once. Even Gus was transfixed. I was curious, but since the chance that Peter had left his worldly fortune to me was between slim and none, I was able to observe. I caught Mrs. Bridge's eye and smiled. She returned a curious smile, something I'd expect to see on the Cheshire cat. She seemed to be the most relaxed person, next to Freddy, at the table.

Freddy's tone didn't change as he got to the meat of the will, but the air in the room did. Emma was named as Trustee of the Will. Gus was named as Coexecutor, along with Clive. Emma didn't look terribly surprised by this news. I couldn't tell if Gus was surprised or not. I thought not, but Gus had his game face on, which was a tough one to read.

Terry, on the other hand, looked apoplectic, but kept silent and still. The only movement I noticed was a light tapping of the fingers of his right hand on the arm of his chair. Brooke kept glancing over at him, but he never took his eyes off Freddy.

My inheritance was listed right away:

"To Edwina Temple Sullivan, I leave the coin collection and silver tea set owned by her namesake, Edwin Temple." That was it. I looked across at Mrs. Bridges, who smiled back. I couldn't help but wonder if she hadn't nudged this generous gesture in some way.

Mrs. Bridges was next. Her bequest wasn't nearly as clear as mine—she could stay in the family employ if she wished, for as long as she desired. Upon retirement, she would be awarded a monthly stipend and accommodations mutually agreed upon by herself and Emma, as Trustee of the estate.

Brooke received a generous stipend that would continue for as long as she lived, as long as she and Peter had been married, and not in the process of divorce, at the time of his death. The payments would be monthly, with no possibility of a onetime lump sum. The annuity could not be passed on in the event of her death. Additionally, she got their Boston condo and a second home in the location of her choosing. Though it seemed a little restrictive to me—and I got the distinct impression that she was being kicked out of the Anchorage— Brooke didn't look at all displeased by her share of the will. Of course, she didn't look like she'd grasped it all, either. She leaned toward Terry to ask a question, but he shook her hand off his arm and turned his head away. I noticed that Mrs. Bridges leaned in from the other side and explained it again in whispered tones.

There were a few more personal items listed, including a few art pieces and Peter's gun collection to Clive; some specific jewelry pieces to Emma and Amelia, which I assumed had been their mother's; Peter's library books and desk to Eric; and a few other art pieces to Terry.

The Anchorage was bequeathed to Amelia alone. A trust was available for the running of the estate, to pay the taxes in perpetuity. She could do what she wanted with the building, but was encouraged to discuss the future of the Anchorage with her siblings for input and advice. Amelia's tears, which had been close to the surface, now spilled over. Clive slid a box of tissues across the table. Emma handed one of them to her sister, and then put her arm around her. Amelia buried her head in Emma's shoulders and sobbed.

The company distribution was the last item outlined in the will. Gus had earlier explained to me that the company was privately owned, with 80 percent of it in Peter's name and five percent each in

Emma, Eric, Amelia, and Terry's names. Terry had been running the company, and Emma had a lot of say, but Peter had retained control. It didn't take an MBA to realize that this was the crux of the estate. Peter was calling the shots from the grave. And the shots were more like small grenades.

Terry was given 2.5 percent more of the company stock, and a monetary inheritance equal to 25 percent of net worth of the company at the time of Peter's death, provided he was still married to Emma and/or not in the process of divorce proceedings. Of Peter's remaining 77.5 percent of the stock, Emma was given 46 percent, Eric 25 percent, and Clive 6.5 percent. Quick calculations told me that Emma was now in charge, with 51 percent of the company. I looked at her carefully. This time she did seem surprised. But the bombshells didn't end there.

Terry was assured a position in the company for as long as he was married to Emma, or for as long as she wanted him to remain. If he left the company because of divorce, he would not get a payout. If he left the company by mutual consent, he would receive a payout determined by Emma and approved by the remaining partners. In other words, Terry worked for the company at the pleasure of his wife. He definitely did not look pleased.

The last part of the reading had to do with contesting the will itself. If anyone contested the will and lost, they would only receive $2,978. $2,978? I wonder what the significance of that number was.

Freddy finished reading the last part of the will and turned over the last page. He looked up at the clock and then around at the other people in the room.

"Per Mr. Whitehall's instructions, all company identification cards, pin numbers, and security codes were voided an hour ago. The Coexecutor of the will, Gus Knight, will oversee the distribution of the new codes and clearances pursuant to the terms outlined in this will. I've made copies of the will for each of you. Should you desire to challenge the contents of the will, you will have forty-eight hours in which to do so, otherwise the terms will go into effect as outlined. For these next forty-eight hours the company will be effectively closed."

"But, I have clients who—"

"You can't mean—"

"What am I supposed to tell—"

The cacophony of voices rang out clearly and quickly. Freddy's voice rang out just as clearly, and with more tenor.

"Ladies and gentleman, this is not open for debate. The company is closed for forty-eight hours. You do not have access to computers, to email, to phones, to anything having to do with company business. The founder of your company has died. Your clients will have to understand. Mr. Knight's office will send out an email to clients explaining the situation. Gus, maybe you can work with these folks on the wording, and on who should receive the email?"

Gus nodded his head and opened his mouth to say something.

"Why should he be telling us what to do? Why should you? What the hell is going on here ... are we supposed to believe that Peter Whitehall changed his will, cut us all out of ... why should we listen to you? Or to Gus?" Terry's face had gone from pale to pink. He looked as if he was going to blow.

"Mr. Holmes, I will provide whatever documentation you need to prove that these are the wishes of Mr. Whitehall."

Terry looked as if he was going to say something else, but the words didn't come. Finally Amelia stepped toward him and took his hand in hers.

"Let's go home, Terry," she said, pulling him toward the door. Brooke followed closely behind. "Emma, are you coming?"

"No, Amelia, you all go on. I'll work with Gus on this email…" Emma spoke in low tones to both Eric and Gus. They looked at me a couple of times, then back to the huddle. Terry took a step toward the group.

"Emma, maybe I should stay," Terry said.

"No, Terry, you go on back to the Anchorage," she said curtly. "I'll be back shortly."

Life had become much more complicated for Terry Holmes than it had been an hour earlier.

· Fourteen ·

Gus walked over to me as my cell phone rang. I'd silenced it for the reading and had only just turned it back on. I looked at the caller ID. The call was from Connie.

"Sully, where the hell are you?"

"In Boston, at a will reading."

"A will reading? Well, that's a hell of a thing during tech week. You okay?"

"I'm fine, thanks. Is Patrick behaving?"

"For the most part," Connie said. "It's turned into a bit of a pissing contest—Patrick keeps throwing Shakespearean quotes at Stewart, Stewart tosses them back. They're sharing war stories from road tours. Patrick's actually sober. Oh, yeah, and Stewart's stepping in as the Ghost of Christmas Future."

"What?"

"Everything's fine. It's only that … "

"It's too fine, isn't it?" Stewart Tracy was a fine actor and a great guy. But he was not without ego. Being willing to step in as the Ghost of Christmas Future, donning a cloak with a masked face, relegated to pointing for emoting—that was too much for an actor of Stewart's stature and ego. Something was up.

"It is a little calm for my taste, yes."

"I'll be back as soon as I can." I turned back toward Gus.

"Everything okay?" he asked.

"Too okay."

"Is there such a thing as too okay?"

"Oh yes." He looked confused, so I elaborated. "Friday we have our first preview, and next week we open the show. Too calm now might meant something's going to blow later this week."

"The calm before the storm," Gus said. "I need to stay in town for a bit to help Emma. I was hoping you'd be able to hang in there for a while. We could have a late lunch."

"I'd love to, I really would, but I need to get back. I can take a train from North Station, that's fine. There won't be heated seats, but I'll live."

"This isn't the time, I know, but we have some things to talk about. I want to tell you—"

"Gus, do we need Eric for this afternoon?" Emma said. "Oh, sorry, I'm so rude ... hello, Sully, how are you?" She leaned in toward my face and air kissed below my left ear. She looked tired but jazzed. Happy, almost. Happier than I'd seen her for a long time. "Gus, Eric would like to get back to Trevorton and see Harry," she went on. "Do you think we need him this afternoon?" Eric had come up and was standing next to her.

"No, probably not. If you have access to a computer, Eric, we can forward a draft to you in an hour or so. As a matter of fact, Sully needs to get back as well."

"I'll trade you time on the computer for a ride home," I said to Eric.

"Deal."

We said our goodbyes and Eric and I walked to the garage, the same one where Gus and I had parked earlier. I was right; it cost an arm and a leg to free Eric's car from the concrete underground. Happily, given that the walk back had been a brisk one, Eric's car had heated seats as well. A girl could get used to this kind of ride, but it was probably best not to.

We crossed the Tobin Bridge and headed up Route 1 toward home. As per usual, this old road was more of a bumper-car ride waiting to happen than a fast-moving highway. It beckoned to shoppers of varying tastes with a huge number and variety of stores directly off the road, enticing new shoppers while others waited for a half-car-length gap in the traffic flow to squeeze back onto the roadway. It was not a route to be taken lightly, or to be taken quickly. But Eric was a pro. He moved to the right lane to let those determined to bust the speed limit by, and paced himself, braking slightly to let drivers in. Being a Massachusetts driver born and bred, it went against my grain to let too many drivers in without a challenge. It could brand you a sissy in the unwritten rulebook of the roads.

"Sorry. It's from driving with Harry so much," he said.

"What is?"

Eric smiled and looked over at me. "Letting all the drivers in. Harry's from Maryland—his road etiquette has rubbed off."

"Probably not a bad thing, I guess. How did you know that was what I was thinking?"

"You've been a million miles away since we left Clive's office, and you don't look particularly happy. I figured it could be my driving. Or maybe it's something else?"

"A lot of things. And nothing. Nothing compared to what you're dealing with. How are you holding up?"

"This has been a bitch of a week, don't get me wrong. But it's also had its upsides."

"Such as?" I couldn't imagine how his father's murder and his encounters with the police could have any upsides. Eric was usually a fellow arbiter of gloom and doom, so this burst of optimism was confusing.

"For one, Harry's been a brick. I've come to appreciate him more and more. For two, you're on my side, and I don't think there could be anyone better to get me out of this mess."

"Thanks, Eric. I don't know that."

"I do. You're going to fix this situation. You and Gus. I have faith." He waited for a reply, but I didn't have one. I was hoping we'd be able to get him off the suspect list, but I wasn't sure how. Eric waited a minute longer, and then went on with his enumeration of blessings. "Such as, from the grave my father did the right thing by his family. He gave Amelia the house, which she loves. And he essentially kicked Brooke out of said house, but took care of her at the same time. He also gave Emma the credit she deserves for running the company, and he put Terry in his place. He did none of these things in life. It would have meant more then, but this is better than nothing."

"It is much better than nothing," I said, as Harry let another driver merge in from one of the strip malls. "Are you happy with the way things went this morning?"

"I am. I was so afraid he was going to leave me the business."

"'Cause that would have been terrible," I said.

"It would have been, because he would have done it for the wrong reasons. He was big into the male heir crap ... part of the reason I'd always been such a disappointment to him is that I didn't step up to the plate the way he wanted me to. I didn't have his killer business instinct. Emma inherited that. I'm too soft, too willing to negotiate ... they finally let me run a part of the company geared to nonprofits, let me work without the abstraction of a profit margin. Clive helped with that—showed Dad about the tax benefits of running part of the company at a loss. Thank God for Clive."

"Clive seems integral to your family," I said. "Were he and your father good friends?"

"He was my father's conscious."

"Did you really not want him to leave you the business?"

"Terry kind of pushed me out of the line of succession," Eric said. "When he became the anointed one, it took me off the hook but made Emma's life more difficult. She got passed over. I thought he'd leave it to Terry, or put him in control. Or leave us all equal parts. Any one of them would have kept Emma trapped. But he didn't do it, did he? He left Emma the business, and Clive and me with enough shares to have a say but not enough to override Emma. He trusted her with his legacy." As traffic was down to a crawl, Eric looked over at me and smiled. He looked so much lighter, I didn't want to remind him about the cloud that still hung over his head.

"But he left Terry a good chunk of change, didn't he?" I said. "What was it? An amount equal to 25 percent of the company? I have no idea what the company is worth, but that's not nothing … that's a lot of something."

"That's a lot of nothing, and won't be for a while. Sully, he left him 25 percent of the net worth of the company at the time of his death. The company is going through a huge transition right now. We were thinking of taking it public."

"Really? I hadn't heard that."

"No one has. Top secret stuff. That's the reason Dad brought Gus on board, to help get the groundwork laid."

"Meaning?"

"Meaning...I don't understand a lot of it, but what it meant for the short term was taking all of the company capital and reinvesting it in the company to strengthen the infrastructure."

"All of the capital? Isn't that a risky move?"

"Yes and no. Not having capital was risky, but it's not like we all weren't still drawing salaries. It did mean that the net worth of the company was next to nothing, though."

"How long was that going to be the case?"

"For the next few months at least. A year at the outside."

"So your father left Terry an amount that seemed very generous but was relatively worthless for the foreseeable future. But the gesture was there, so it would be tough to take to court. And he added that divorce or proceedings clause in Terry's part of the will."

"And the chances of an impending or actual divorce are pretty good."

"Really?" I said.

"Yeah. Something happened recently, I don't know what. Emma has seemed a lot better, especially lately. She told me that she was going to talk to Terry about a separation after the holidays."

"When did she tell you this?"

"About a month ago."

"Did your dad know?"

"I imagine so. She never would have kept something like that secret from him, especially since it was bound to impact the company. Maybe that's what prompted the change in his will."

Of course, my mind switched to a different gear. The new will actually gave Emma a motive to kill her father. And it gave one to Clive. And to Eric. I didn't want to burst his bubble, but the new will didn't take him off the suspect list. Instead, it put a star by his name.

For that matter, the new will added one more name, at least to my eyes. Gus Knight was now on the suspect list.

I needed to ask someone when, exactly, the new will had been drawn up. If it was within the last month, then the "no divorce" codicil had more sinister implications than a father's concern for his daughter and his family name. An idea that had been swirling around in my brain began to take some shape. But before I could nurture it further, I had to deal with some ghosts.

· Fifteen ·

Normally, *A Christmas Carol* opens the first Friday in December. Thankfully we'd decided to open a week later, adding extra rehearsals, more previews, and a grander opening. If only I knew then what I knew now. For this year's production, someone (okay, it was me) had come up with the brilliant idea to have the dress rehearsal for invited guests, which made it more like a performance. The size of the invited audience was fairly substantial—actors had generous ticket access, folks who couldn't afford to come were invited, and a couple of retirement homes made the trek in. In normal years, there were always opportunities to find room for a guest or two during the run, but this year the only comped tickets were for the dress rehearsal.

In my own defense, usually the show was so tight by Thursday that having an audience was actually helpful for the actors before the Friday night performance. This year, however, hours before an audience warmed the seats, Marley was being played by a last-minute replacement and Scrooge was ... troubled. The show needed a few more rehearsals, but, as good a general manager as I was, I couldn't stop time from ticking. Like it or not, Friday was our first preview.

The set looked much better than it had yesterday. Happily or not, depending on how you feel about one's potential being wasted, my well-honed observation skills got me up to speed about the status of the production within minutes; my skills in combination with Connie, who'd seen me come in and met me at the top of the aisle as I surveyed my kingdom.

"Hi Connie. How's it going? Still calm?"

She shrugged and smiled, but that told me little. Stage managers repurpose tension, so the smile could mean things were fine, or things were beyond horrible and she was in fixing mode. "Do you want the long or short version?"

"Short, for now. I assume your report will have the long version?" Connie's rehearsal reports were legend. They were frequently longer than the plays themselves, and occasionally more entertaining. "How's Stewart doing as the Ghost of Christmas Future?"

"That scene was the only one Patrick couldn't get a handle on. He kept pushing for Gabe Roberts—he was playing the part—to feed him the lines, but Gabe couldn't do it. The only way we got Gabe to play the Ghost in the first place was that he didn't have any lines. So Gabe decided he'd rather do crew ... and since Stewart is done with Marley early on, he agreed to play the part."

"Why?"

"Why what, Sully my darling?" Stewart's arms circled my waist from behind and he kissed the back of my neck.

I felt enough of a spark to know that I wasn't dead. Damn, life is complicated.

"I guess someone has recovered from their morning bike ride. Why are you willing to play a Ghost without a face?"

"The Christmas spirit has flowed forth ... you're not buying it, are you?" He lowered his voice and leaned in. "Okay, how about this. It's boring as hell to sit backstage for well over an hour to take my bow. And Patrick needs the help."

"And?"

Stewart leaned closer and whispered in my ear. "And there but for the grace of God go I."

I was about to make a smart retort, but the look on his face stopped me. "You're serious, aren't you?"

"It's a long story, Sully, but yes, I'm serious. You called and asked me to help, and I'm helping. And glad that you asked."

"Stewart, could you try this on again?" Gabe was on stage, holding up the Ghost of Christmas Future cloak. Regina's son was a head shorter than Stewart, so they'd obviously been reworking the costume. I was glad Gabe seemed happy. He was a good kid; I'd hate to lose him.

"Sure thing, Gabe. Be right there. Sully, will you be around a while?"

"For the rest of today."

"Great. Let's talk later, okay?"

∞

I found Dimitri and sat next to him. For the next two hours there were costume and tech checks and other flurries of activities that allowed Dimitri and me to have a mishmash of a conversation. I offered to cancel the audience for Thursday night, but he declined.

"It's the final dress, so we can start and stop if we need to. We always make that announcement before we start. This year we mean it. Who knows, maybe the audience will be thrilled by the chaos. Besides, I have a feeling that Patrick may be better with an audience. Even having Stewart as a new face to impress has given him more game."

"What's up with that? Stewart seems … "

"Yeah, I know. He's a big fan of Patrick's work, did you know that?"

"No, I didn't."

"I didn't either, until he confessed about an hour ago," Dimitri said. "I mean, a big fan. From childhood. Saw him on stage when he was a kid—it inspired him to be an actor. He hasn't worked with Patrick long enough to hate him, and Patrick is reveling in the idolatry. Go figure." I knew that Dimitri had been a similar fan before rehearsals started. I didn't doubt that he envied Stewart's naiveté, just a little.

Connie went to get food during the dinner break, and I went into my small office at the high school. Frank was using the computer.

"Oh hi, Sully." He blushed pink. I was afraid to see what he was looking at on the computer, but I walked over anyway. It looked blank.

"What's up?" I asked.

Frank looked really guilty about something. Not criminal guilty, but "I didn't want you to find this out" guilty. If I had kids of my own, I would have known how to break him, but I don't, so I didn't. My old techniques of intimidation might have been a little harsh.

"Um, you remember what I told you about Mr. Whitehall's house?" he said.

I nodded.

"Well, I, um, kinda went over there, to see if I could get the hard drive. I figured maybe whatever was on it might be useful, you know? I brought Gabe with me. I didn't tell him where we were going until we were almost there ... and then ... "

I waited for a few seconds, but I couldn't stand it anymore. I needed to put him out of his misery.

"And then he said he needed to tell his mother if we went in."

Good boy, Gabe, I thought. If Frank had gone to the house to look around, no matter how noble his intentions, it would have tainted the evidence. Regina needed to know.

"Did he tell her? Or did you?" I asked.

"I sent Gabe all the links, figuring he could pass them on. I don't like to get too involved. Some of this stuff skirts the law ... "

"Frank, do me a favor and send Regina the links yourself, okay? She might have some questions."

"Okay," he said.

There was a chill in the air that I needed to thaw. "What are you doing now?"

"I'm looking at the live feed to see if anything is going on at the house. So far, nothing. The hall isn't too focused. And Mr. Whitehall's study is dark." He flipped screens and showed me the two views. The study was in fact dark, too dark to make anything out. I recognized the hallway, but Frank was right. The sight lines were horrible, and the view seemed a little unfocused.

"I'm not sure what the problem is. It should be self-focusing. And I swear the camera was in a better position. I mean, this is pretty lame. You can barely see anything."

"Maybe you can see enough. I assume the police are watching this as well." I stared at the screen, willing some sort of answer to come into focus, but nothing. A thought occurred to me, and I looked at Frank. "Frank, *should* you be able to see this?"

At least he had the good grace to seem embarrassed. "Like I said, we weren't done with the setup yet. I don't even know where all the cameras were. The final step would've been to walk Mr. Whitehall through the password change and other administrative tasks. That would have shut me out of the system. And put him in control. We never got that far."

We both stared at the screen and saw the hallway by the library. "Do you have a view from the camera on the staircase in the main foyer?" I asked.

"He had one on a staircase?" Frank asked. "That must have been one of the new cameras he was playing with." He hit a couple of buttons. Nothing. He looked at another website. Still nothing.

"Was there one in the library?" I asked.

"Not that I could see, but it was tough to really look around. Why do you ask?"

Again, Frank looked embarrassed. He was studying the keyboard with great intensity. I walked over and shut the door to the office.

"Frank..."

"You used to be a cop, didn't you?"

"I was a police officer, yes."

"Don't you take some sort of oath? That you'll always pursue criminals, no matter what?"

"There isn't that kind of oath." Frank looked relieved. I hoped he wasn't about to confess to some horrible crime. There wasn't an oath, but there was a code. A code I still followed.

"Mr. Whitehall, see, he wanted to put a camera in the library..." Frank began.

"In Terry's office."

"I guess. Anyway, someone, probably this Terry, put a lock on the door. Mr. Whitehall needed to get into the room but he didn't want to ask for a key... so he asked me for some ideas. I know this guy, who knows this guy... who can get his hands on state-of-the-art lock picks. I put in an order."

"Did you use lock picks?"

"I gave them to Mr. Whitehall for him to use. Showed him how. Not that I know how," he said quickly. "It was pretty simple."

"When did you give them to him?"

"A couple of weeks ago... yeah, three weeks ago today. I remember because that was the day the DMDEAD virus came out."

We all mark time in our own way. So Peter Whitehall had obtained some lock picks about a week and a half before he was murdered.

"Did he contact you afterward?"

"DMDEAD kept me pretty busy for a few days. We'd made an appointment for December 4 to finish up the install."

"That was the day of his funeral." I wondered what Peter had found in that week while he played with new technology. "Do you think he figured it out on his own?"

As if he were answering my question, I saw Terry walk into his office. Before he pulled the library door closed behind him, he looked down the hall toward Peter's study—and the camera—and made a rude gesture with his left hand and middle finger.

Could it be that simple?

· Sixteen ·

$\mathcal{I}$t was almost six thirty. In a little more than twenty-four hours an audience would be sitting in these seats, watching a public performance. I shuddered at the thought. An invited dress, and there hadn't been a complete run-through yet.

As I waited for things to begin, I mulled over what I knew now that I hadn't two days ago. On the one hand, there was the new will, Peter's surveillance predilection, Brooke's strange behavior, Terry's fall from grace. On the other hand, though, it added up to nothing. My gut told me to look in Terry's direction. So far, evidence implicating him didn't exist. I wanted to go back and look through Peter's study. Without Mrs. Bridges standing guard.

The lights went down and I watched the run-through of the first act. At first I tried to pay attention to both the play and my thoughts, but after a couple of minutes I realized I was too tired to pull it off. So I decided to pay attention to the play and give the rest of it a rest. For now.

Run-throughs this late in the game are often a little painful to sit through, and this was no exception. The realization that your show isn't going to be everything everyone dreamed of starts to sink in, and the product of weeks of rehearsal seems much worse than it actually is. There were costume malfunctions, missed cues, lighting problems, and a horrific Fezziwig dance scene that resulted in two cast members sprawled on the floor and more than a couple of bruises. Now, if it had been my first year running the theater, I would have been convinced that my professional life was going to come to a grinding halt after the reviews came out. But I'd been around for a while and sat through a lot of rehearsals, and I knew Dimitri's process. The show wasn't half bad. It wasn't as solid as it had been at this point in years past, but the bones were solid. It even had flashes of brilliance.

I told Dimitri as much during the break before the second act. He started to list all of the problems, but I could tell he was pleased by my praise. I let him go on for a couple of minutes, then interrupted him. "True, true. It's all true. But that scene with Belle made me verklempt. Dimitri, have you ever seen me verklempt? And the Fezziwig scene needs more rehearsal, true, but it's lovely. Stewart was wonderful as Marley. Not surprising, since he's a great actor, but he's only been here a day. And I love the scene with the ghosts outside Scrooge's window. That is such an important scene, I'm glad we put it back in ... "

By now Dimitri was almost beaming, but I didn't stop. He deserved the praise. I'd been warned by both him and Connie that the first act was perfection compared to the second. They warned me in particular about the Ghost of Christmas Future scene. Hopefully, though, Stewart Tracy and a hidden earbud would give us our own Christmas miracle. I knew Dimitri would dismiss my praise as pity if I held back, and I was about to go on, when my phone vibrated in my pocket. "We'll talk more after the show, Dimitri. I need to grab a soda before we start up again." I squeezed his arm and walked out of the theater before answering the phone. Dimitri would have had a fit if I'd left him to answer a phone call.

The phone stopped vibrating by the time I cleared the door. I was checking the number when it vibrated again. I didn't recognize the phone number as I hit the button.

"Sullivan here." Rude way to answer the phone, I know, but it was a habit from the old days, and I hadn't bothered to retrain myself. Better if people know they got the person they want right away.

"Sully, thank God. I didn't know what I'd do if I couldn't get hold of you—"

"Emma, is that you? What's wrong?"

"Can you come over here now? I'm at the Anchorage."

"Emma, I'm in the middle of—"

"Please, Sully, please. Someone … Terry … just get here, okay?" The phone went dead in my hand. I hesitated a minute before going to the back office to get my coat. And for the fourth time in the past week, I headed to the Anchorage.

· Seventeen ·

Emma met me at the door. She still had her suit bottom and blouse on, but she was wearing an oversized cardigan over the top of it. The front of the blouse looked damp, as if she'd dribbled something down her front and tried to clean it up. She wordlessly led me toward the library, pushing the door open and stepping back for me to enter. I was about to go in when the pungent stench of old pennies hit me. I recognized the smell from my prior career. Looking up, I saw Terry, or what had been Terry, slumped over his desk. Most of the back of his head appeared to be on the headrest of the chair. The rest of it was sprayed across the curtains. I took the rest of the room in quickly. The only other thing that was different from the last time I'd been there was the gun on the floor by Terry's hand. I did some quick mental calculations and swept the scene again.

Emma moved as if to pass me, but I stopped her on the threshold. "Have you called the police?"

"No, I called you first. I thought you should—"

"Call them, now." She looked at me blankly. I turned and saw Mrs. Bridges coming down the hall from Peter's study, wiping her hands on her pants. "Mrs. Bridges, call the police. Ask for Regina Roberts. Tell her what happened." Mrs. Bridges nodded her head and walked down the hall toward the kitchen.

"Have you gone in there?" I asked, sounding sharper than I intended. Years of training kicked in as if I'd only been off the job for a few weeks rather than a few years. Terry ceased being a man I'd known; he was now the victim. His office was no longer the library; it was now the crime scene. Emma wasn't the widow, she was … another victim, or a suspect. It was hard to tell. She seemed awfully steady for someone who'd just found her husband with half of his brain spattered across the room.

"Yes, to check and make sure … I thought he'd gone, but then I saw his number light up … we were on a conference call, so I had to go down the hall and check … " Emma's shoulders hunched over and she began shaking. I put my arm around her shoulders and steered her away from the room. I noticed a slight stench and looked down at her shirt again, at the damp patch down the front. I looked back at the hall and noticed that a large area of the floor had recently been washed, the part closest to Peter's study.

"Emma, let's go sit in the living room and talk this through."

"Don't you want to look around and see if there's anything—"

"No, I don't. It's called contaminating a crime scene. I can't do it. But I can be here while you talk to the police. I'm here for you, Emma, but I don't want to get in the way of a murder investigation."

"But he killed himself. Didn't you see the gun?"

"Maybe. But the police have to see the scene—"

"He left a note. On his computer. He said he was sorry, that he killed Daddy … " Emma started shaking again, and I led her over to the couch.

171

"Is the note still there?" I asked as gently as I could, which, I'll admit, was far from the dictionary definition of the word.

"Of course it is."

"Did you touch the keyboard?"

"No, at least I don't think so. Why?"

"Because if he wrote the note, his fingerprints might be on the keys he used."

"If?"

"Emma, let's wait for the police to get here, okay?" But sitting and waiting wasn't doing much for my nerves, or Emma's. "Who else was home tonight?" I asked.

Emma looked startled, then found her composure again. "Shouldn't we wait for the police?"

Mocking. That's what I needed at this moment. Mocking from someone I wanted to help. "Fine, that's fine. I was curious, making small talk."

"Sorry, Sully, its ... so ... unbelievable. I never thought, never wanted Terry to be pushed to kill himself ... I just wanted me back. You know? I wanted to try and be happy for the first time in a while. I didn't want him to ... I only wanted him gone."

"What do you mean, Emma?"

"I asked him to leave the house."

I had to lean in to hear her, she spoke so softly. "When?"

"This afternoon. After I got home from the reading of the will. He was waiting ... Gus was with me, I'd asked him to stay. I was afraid I'd back down, but I didn't. It was really easy. Terry made noise about the will, and then he started to use his charm. I could see it coming. Thing is, it usually works. Really well. Too well. But this time the charm offensive didn't work. Daddy had believed me. He took my side. What a vote of confidence. I told Terry I wanted him out."

"And?"

"And he agreed to go. And I agreed we could talk about it some more tomorrow. At ten. We were going to meet at our office. Gus was going to be there as well."

She still hadn't told me who was home, but we ran out of time. I heard a short, shrill beep come through the intercom on the wall, and then a pair of headlights wiped themselves across the room. The beep must have come from the guard's booth, a heads-up that the police had arrived. I was tempted to get up and meet them at the front door, but I didn't want to leave Emma. I also had the feeling that if I left, I wouldn't be offered the chance to rejoin her. I know I would have kept me away.

Regina Roberts strode into the room and glared at me. "How the hell did you get here so fast? And for that matter, what the hell are you doing here?"

I couldn't blame her, not at all. The pressure on her department must have been formidable. Still, I didn't like the look she was giving me and I felt my hackles rise.

"Emma called me on my cell, at the theater. She didn't tell me why, but she asked me to come over…"

"I didn't realize you were at the Whitehalls' beck and call," Regina said.

I stared at her until she looked away. "When I got here and realized that Terry Holmes was dead, I asked Mrs. Bridges to call the department and ask for you." I held up my hand to stop what I presumed were her follow-up questions. At least they would have been mine. "I did not go into the room. I did not touch anything, including the door. I was in the room yesterday, so there may be my prints in there, but I didn't touch the keyboard. Emma did go into the room to check…"

"Maybe she can tell me herself. Mrs. Holmes?"

"I was in the kitchen on a conference call. I saw the light from Terry's extension on, and didn't think he was home. I went down to check. I saw a light under the library door, and so I went over to see ... " She stopped talking and looked down at her hands, which were clasped in her lap. I knew that she'd be telling the story a few dozen more times before the sun rose in the morning, so I wasn't surprised that Regina moved on.

"Did you see anyone else?"

"No."

"Who else was home this evening?"

"I think we all were home."

"Who is we all?"

"Clive Willis was working with me. My sister Amelia and Mrs. Bridges were working on the Christmas decorations. Brooke was here, but she went to Boston around five, I think. You could check with the guard."

"And your brother?"

"Eric? He was helping Amelia for a while, then he went over to the theater to have dinner with his boyfriend. Did you see him, Sully? He came back around 7:30—right before I found ... Terry. Amelia was pretty upset. He took her upstairs. He's with her now."

I hoped that Regina didn't ask me to confirm Eric's theater alibi. I couldn't. I never saw him, but then I hadn't gone backstage at all.

Regina looked at us both for a minute, and then nodded her head as if she'd made up her mind about something.

"Okay, I might as well take a look for myself. Ms. Holmes, stay put, okay? And Sully, why don't you come with me?" I squeezed Emma's hand and followed Regina out of the living room.

"I assume this separation is so we don't coordinate stories?" I said. "I doubt that you want my professional opinion, since you apparently don't hold me in very high regard. I can wait here, stay out of your way. Believe it or not, I want you to find the killer. I'm on your side."

Regina stopped outside the library door and looked in. She looked back at me and took a deep breath. "You keep catching me on the rebound. When I saw you here the other day, I'd just been chewed out about how we handled the Peter Whitehall scene. Apparently we'd trampled, we'd contaminated, we'd proven ourselves to be bumpkins that a good defense attorney could use to squash the case in court. It wasn't fair, and it wasn't accurate, and I was pissed. You happened to be in the line of fire. And now it's going to hit the fan again, and here you are. I've got to make sure we handle this really carefully, because it's going to crash a few houses of cards that people have been constructing."

"And you're going to get the brunt of the blame. I've been there more than once."

Regina paused. She almost looked embarrassed when she asked, "Is that why you left the force?"

"One of the reasons. It's complicated. I'll tell you over that beer sometime. Meanwhile, tell me if I can do anything to help." I smiled and was glad that she smiled back, signaling a truce.

"I've called a team in to go over the scene. From the state. No need to confirm that he's dead?"

"I'd say not, no." We both looked at the scene with critical eyes.

"Damn, I'd love to look this room over, but I need forensics to go over it first," she said. "You sure you didn't go in?"

I took this less as an accusation and more as a jab at securing information. "I'm sure. Emma did, though."

"She the one who happened to wash the floor?"

"No, I think that was Mrs. Bridges. I'm not sure, but it's possible Emma was trying to make it to the bathroom off Peter's study but failed in her attempt."

"Did she tell you she was sick?"

"No, but her blouse was damp in the front, and when I got here Mrs. Bridges was coming from the study. The floor was still wet. I think she'd been cleaning up, but I haven't seen her since."

"God knows what else got cleaned up," Regina said. I nodded. I'd been thinking the same thing. Who knew what footprints there'd been, or what other trace evidence in the hall had been lost.

"She tell you anything?" Regina asked.

"Emma? Only that she thinks it's a suicide. Apparently there's a note on the computer. She doesn't think she touched the keys. I asked."

Regina peered into the room as far as she could without stepping on the carpet. She and I both took it in again: the body, the computer, the gun on the floor beside the desk not too far from Terry's dangling hand.

"Does she really think it's suicide, or ... "

"I don't think she's that good of an actress," I said. "She really thinks it's suicide."

"She seems to be holding up, considering."

I shook my head and smiled. "She's not holding up that well. Not if I'm right about her getting sick. Plus, I think the shock is starting to wear off and set in at the same time."

"Well, if she thinks it's suicide, she's in for another shock."

· Eighteen ·

It was almost eleven o'clock, and I was sipping a cup of very cold, very strong, and very old tea. The crime scene investigators were still at work, and a plethora of police had descended on the house. In any other circumstance, I'd imagine people would be dragged to the station. But not the Whitehalls. The Whitehalls were questioned at home.

This thought wasn't particularly fair of me. After all, two people had been murdered within a hundred yards of each other, both shot. The family had been through a lot. But still. I hated that justice wasn't blind. I'd hated it the first time I realized it, and I'd hated it ever since. But I'd given up trying the change the system. So did Gus, I guess. So who was left to fight the good fight?

Another thing that didn't seem fair was the way Regina had been relegated to the background as soon as the state suits arrived. I'd recognized a couple of them. They'd looked right past me once they realized I wasn't on the suspect list. I'm sure there were those among them who would have loved to be able to nail me for the murder, but I'd been in a theater across town when it occurred. Of course, the exact timing of Terry's death was difficult to determine. The last time anyone had seen him was around six o'clock, when the guard spotted him entering his office on the live feed. Or at least they assumed it was him, like I did—I realized I'd been looking at the same video, at almost the same time, in the theater office with Frank. I hadn't shared this with Regina or anyone else. Why get Frank, or myself for that matter, into unnecessary trouble?

So Emma had been home, as were Eric, Mrs. Bridges, and Amelia. Hell, even Clive was in the house. He and Emma alibied each other—they'd been on a conference call in the kitchen. Since they still weren't using Peter's study, and apparently Terry's office seemed inappropriate for company business now, comfortable space was at a minimum. Personally, I think working in the kitchen makes a lot of sense, but that's me. Always best to have food within easy reach.

Regina had been sent to babysit me. I told her about *A Christmas Carol* trials and tribulations. She'd heard a lot of it from Gabe, but some of it was news, including the fact that Stewart Tracy was back in town.

"Well, that must be making life interesting for you," she said.

"What do you mean?"

"You've been seeing your ex-husband, haven't you? And now Stewart is in town ... an embarrassment of riches of exes."

"Seeing my ex-husband? Who ..."

"Sully, Sully, Sully. It's a small town. He was seen coming out of your house yesterday morning, early, and then again this morning."

"Is this Officer Regina talking, or the town gossip Regina?"

"Sometimes I wonder if there's much difference," she said. "But it's the town gossip talking. You're big news, ever since people connected you to Eric's handsome lawyer. I'm sure it's perfectly reasonable, but it has caused some tongues to wag." She paused, waiting for me to explain what was going on.

I had no intention of doing so, of course. For one, it was no one's business. For two, I had no idea what was going on; how was I going to explain it? Instead I figured I'd throw out a morsel of information and see if I could get her off the track.

"Gus drove me down to Boston for the will reading this morning. Peter left me a small inheritance."

"Really?" It worked. I could tell she was dying to know more.

"Yes, a coin collection and tea set that had been owned by my grandfather and namesake, Edwin Temple."

"Did you expect to be remembered?"

"No, not at all. I'm surprised he remembered my name, frankly."

"I heard that it was quite the morning."

"It was that. Jeez, I can't believe it was only this morning." I looked at my watch. "Almost yesterday morning." Again with the stare. This time I didn't ignore it. "Regina, if you have a question, ask it. I'll answer it if I can. I'm too freaking tired to play games."

"Okay. What—"

"Only," I interrupted. I know it's rude to interrupt, but I thought it would be ruder to ask for quid pro quo afterward. "Only, I also get to ask a question or two. If you can't answer, cool. But if you can…"

"Deal," Regina said. "My first question: Frank." Whoops, I was hoping she'd skip that question. "Why didn't you let me know about the cameras?"

"Frank told me that they weren't recording, as far as he knew. If he'd found something, I would have turned it over, I promise. Did the website help at all?"

"What website?"

"The live feed from the cameras?" The look on her face made it clear she had no idea what I was talking about. Boy, I was out of practice. I'd said to Frank that he should send the links to Regina. I assumed he did it. He'd never told me I was right.

Regina looked like she was about to explode, but her voice was surprisingly calm. "Tell me," she said quietly.

So I did, at least what little I knew. The most important thing I contributed was the confirmation of a Terry sighting at six o'clock. Frank would need to supply the rest.

"You're sure about the time?"

"Give or take five minutes at the most. We had a half hour for dinner, from five-fifty to six-twenty."

"Was the feed recorded?"

"I'm not sure. Frank would know. I'm sorry, Regina. I thought he'd told you about it."

She shot me a look and went out to the hallway to talk to one of the other officers. She was back in a couple of minutes.

"You promise me you didn't check out the crime scene tonight?"

"Did they find my footprints in there?" The lab had taken my shoes for print identification.

"Not yet."

"They won't. Regina, I'm not an idiot. I wouldn't fool around with a crime scene."

"Okay. I guess I know that. This morning—"

"Wait a sec. My turn for a question. Was there anything on the hard drive from the old surveillance system?"

"Yes."

Damn, she was playing rough. But I was tough, I'd hang in. Besides, I had no shoes.

"Tell me about this morning." Regina said.

"You've probably heard most of it already. Peter changed his will. Seems to have cut Terry out."

"Well, he left him a good amount of money."

"No, not really." I explained the business angles to her.

"Was this public knowledge? About the company?" she asked.

I thought about it for a second and then shook my head. "I don't know. Maybe not. Eric told me, and he didn't swear me to secrecy, but he probably expected discretion. Which he would have gotten, had Terry not have been killed."

"He still will. I'll use it as background, ask some questions." And use it to make everyone think you're a freaking genius, I thought. Ah well, good for her. You had to use what you could, when you could. "The question is, did Terry know what Peter was planning? Even if he didn't know exactly what was up, he must have sensed something. I'm sure that Peter was doing other things to make Terry wonder if the tide had turned." I thought back to Terry's one-finger salute toward the camera. Did he know where the camera was, or was he showing his father-in-law the respect he'd been given that day?

"All of which nicely provides motive," Regina said. "Even before the will I would have said, strictly on gut, that Terry was the guy. I couldn't figure out the proof." She looked at me for a while, trying to make up her mind about something. "Apparently he did it, if you can believe the note on the computer."

"Which said?"

"Can't, sorry Sully."

Damn. I tried a different tack. "Fingerprints?"

"Don't know yet," she said.

"Gun?"

"It's the same caliber as the one that killed Peter Whitehall. The one we found Eric Whitehall dumping was also that caliber."

"Didn't ballistics show that the gun you found Eric with was the gun that had killed his father?" I asked.

Regina looked around and lowered her voice. "Not conclusively, no."

Not conclusively? They were going to hang Eric out on the rails on inconclusive proof? What was that all about? Unless they weren't going to hang Eric at all. Unless they were taunting their suspects with a false sense of security. And then the noose started to tighten, and Terry started to panic.

"Hell, Regina, this doesn't make sense. Maybe it *was* suicide?"

"C'mon, Sully, you saw what I saw. The blood spatter, the way the body fell. The angle was wrong. If he'd shot himself like that, no way he would have ended up face down on the desk."

She was right, of course. That's what had bothered me too. That, and the gun by the dangling hand. If he'd shot himself, slumped back and then fallen forward, there was no way his hand would have ended up at his side like that.

"No one else in or out?" I asked.

"Not according to the guard."

"And you've checked him out?"

"He's clean. He was on the phone to Ireland this evening, talking to his family. His wife was in the booth with him."

"Maybe Terry didn't kill Peter?" It was hard for me to believe. But if both men had been killed by the same gun, and Terry also had been murdered, it just didn't make sense.

"The guard caught Terry spraying the lens of the camera that faced his study, the day before the murder. It was probably hair spray. Just made it all fuzzy."

"He sprayed the lens?" I thought back to the feed Frank had been watching. It explained the focus problems with the camera. "How do you know?"

"There was another camera facing Peter's study door that Terry didn't know about. And that camera caught Terry in the act of spraying the other lens. It also caught him coming in and out of the study that evening, possibly around the time of death."

"Evening? I thought Peter died around daybreak?"

Regina hesitated, probably wondering how much to divulge. I could understand the battle. She considered me a source of potential information. Priming the pump with information could bring forth a well. That said, she'd begun to cross a line. Some of this information was police knowledge only. But since she'd crossed it, she must have decided to keep going. Maybe she trusted me more than I thought. Maybe she was sick of being relegated to babysitting. Maybe she was as tired as I was.

"No, closer to midnight, near as we can figure," she finally said. "Someone had started a large fire that warmed up the room considerably, so it makes pinpointing a time of death pretty tough."

"The warm room kept the body warm—"

"Which throws things off," Regina said. "We know Peter was alive at midnight. Cameras, household members, and a long-distance call all confirm that. The time of death could be anywhere from shortly after midnight to 6:00 a.m."

We both sighed. The fact of the scientific matter was, and is, that time of death, absent an eyewitness to pinpoint the time, can only be narrowed down to a four-hour span. A warm fire would prevent the body from cooling off at a normal pace, which would further complicate the time. Whoever murdered Peter was either lucky or very smart. Regina's next comment made me bet on the side of luck.

"The camera did pick Terry up around two a.m. It looked like he was carrying something."

"Any idea what it was?"

"The lab is working on it."

I repeated those last few words with her. Television has made the lives of forensic scientists difficult—everyone expects it to take less than the time of a thirty-minute episode to run tests and get photo enhancements, DNA, and ballistic results. In real life, crime labs are understaffed and underfunded, and science takes a while. Especially if you want the evidence to stand up in court. And if the Trevorton Police were going to arrest Terry Holmes for murder, it damned well better stand up in court. Because with guys like him, you didn't get a second chance.

I wondered if that was why he was killed. To make sure he didn't get a chance to get away with the murder?

Once again, then, the list of suspects would include anyone in the house. And considering that Eric had been set up for Peter's murder—presumably by Terry—this put my old friend near the top of the list. Damn.

· Nineteen ·

As if on cue, the door to the living room opened and Eric walked in. He was about to say something when he noticed Regina sitting on the second couch. I smiled and shrugged my shoulders.

"Hi, Sully. I didn't know you were still here, and then Mrs. Bridges asked me to come in and get your keys. They need to move your car to make room."

"Should I move it to the street?"

"That may be easier said than done. There are a lot of cars out there. I think I may have seen a news van, but I'm not sure."

"Damn."

"My thoughts exactly. Being trapped in this house again ... I don't know if I can take it."

"Conscience getting to you, Mr. Whitehall?" That was from one of the suits who'd come in earlier. I had no idea who he was, but I knew what I thought of him. "Pompous jackass" came to mind. I looked around the room and noticed that the opinion seemed shared. From the look on Eric's face, I guessed that the two weren't strangers.

"As I told you earlier, Lieutenant, my sister Amelia and I were together all afternoon until I went to the theater. Then she went to the greenhouse. Our gardener was with her, they were doing a—"

"Hardly the most rock-solid alibi."

"Perhaps your sister would not be a good alibi, Officer. My sister, however, is an impeccable alibi. Obviously your colleagues agree."

"For now."

"Can Ms. Sullivan leave, Lieutenant?" Regina asked.

"I suppose so, but I want her to stay around town."

"She's not going anywhere."

"Fine. We're getting ready to move the body. You want to come back?"

"Sure." Regina took a final sip of her cold tea, then turned to me. "See you later, Sully. Will you be at the theater tomorrow?"

"Yeah, but I have to go by my office first. Call me on my cell if you need me. It's the best way to get in touch."

I watched Regina follow Lieutenant Nameless back toward Terry's office. Man, I'd been there, more often than I cared to remember. Ignored for hours, then thrown a bone that I accepted gratefully. Technically, this was Regina's case, since she was the first on the scene. But again, Whitehall justice worked a little differently, and the case seemed to have landed much higher in the food chain. At least they were keeping her in the loop. I wondered if that extended to Eric.

He flopped onto the couch Regina had vacated. He lowered his head into his hands and stared at the floor. I sat on the couch's arm and put my arm around his shoulder, squeezing it gently.

"Can you leave?" I asked.

Eric shook his head. "I don't know. Probably not. Besides, I want to stick around for Emma and Amelia."

"Emma seems to be coping pretty well."

"Emma always seems to be coping pretty well. And she usually is. But this isn't usual. Hell, there was no love lost between Terry and me, but even I'm sorry that he felt he had to ... "

I debated the ethics of holding back but decided against it, since it was so contrary to my nature. I've always found that holding information back should be done sparingly. If you have a reputation for forthrightness, which I do, then occasions when this principle is not true are rarely, if ever, apparent.

I stood and started to fiddle with the tchotchkes on the mantle. Nice tchotchkes, but tchotchkes nonetheless. I wondered who had put them there—Brooke, a decorator, or maybe even Peter's first wife? Did they mean anything, or were they here for show? The room seemed rarely used, probably a company-only room like most living rooms, so I guessed that the objects were probably here for show. Offices, sitting rooms, and bedrooms were more reflective of individual taste. I pulled my mind back to the present and turned and looked at Eric, who was still studying the carpet.

"Eric, he didn't kill himself. Someone else did."

"What? But why didn't someone say something? Ah, so that's why all the questions? Not a formality? I assumed Terry had confessed to killing Dad and they were trying to tie up loose ends."

Eric seemed so dumbfounded that I felt bad about telling him the rest. But better me than someone else, someone who didn't care as much about him or his sisters.

"Eric, I hate to be the one ... the thing is, I don't think you're off the hook. Knowing the way the police think, you may be one of the prime suspects in Terry's death. After all, you're the man he framed."

"Now it makes sense, why they were asking me all those questions ... why they seemed so pissed I had an alibi. I didn't do it, and they couldn't pin it on me."

"What alibi?"

"I was with Amelia."

"Eric, Lieutenant Sunshine had a point. That's hardly airtight."

"We were giving the North Shore Birding Society a tour of the gardens. Amelia does it every year around the holidays. It's less of a tour, actually, and more of a party for the birders. She didn't feel up to it this year, but she didn't want to cancel either. So I was with fifteen or so devoted amateur ornithologists in the greenhouse, toasting the holidays and discussing Amelia's plans for the Anchorage. She's thinking about putting an aviary on the grounds and opening it up to the public."

"I'm sorry—"

"No, I'm sorry. You let me know what they're thinking, which is really helpful. Once I knew Amelia was okay, I left her with her birder friends making plans. Then I headed over to the theater."

"I was there," I said. "I didn't see you."

Eric paused and looked hurt. "Et tu, Sully?" he asked. "I snuck backstage to see Harry. We shared a sandwich in the dressing room. Stewart was there."

"Good. I just want to make sure you can account for your time."

"I appreciate it, I really do." He paused. "Are you sure Terry was murdered?"

"Shhh, I don't know if that's for broadcast. I don't know anything for sure, but it looked like murder to me, and if it looks like that to an ex-cop who isn't even in the room, it's murder." I sat back on the arm and stared at the tea service. "Eric, do you know where everyone else was from six p.m. on?"

"Six?"

"He was seen at six, found at seven thirty."

"Checking up on us?"

"Just curious, you know how that is. Was Mrs. Bridges in the greenhouse with you?"

"Off and on. Mostly on. Wait, let me think. She was in the house during that time."

"Where was Brooke?"

"She left around five, five thirty. She was going into the city."

"Really? Why didn't she just stay there after the reading?"

"She came back home with everyone else. Then she decided she wanted to leave. Really, it was the first decision she'd made all week. No one tried too hard to talk her out of it—she's been more difficult than normal, which is considerable. Besides, she had the right idea—it was a little tense around here this afternoon, to put it mildly. From what Amelia told me, Emma and Terry had really gone at it when she got back. She asked him to leave."

Not quite the same scenario Emma had painted. "Did he go?"

"Emma said they'd taken a break and were going to talk again later. I told her I'd go with her. He was going, one way or the other."

The timing was tight, but maybe Emma had done more than talk.

· Twenty ·

$\mathcal{I}$ had to wait in my car for a couple of minutes while the police cleared a path for me to leave. I called Connie on my cell and got her voicemail, which made me think that the run-through was still going on. The disconnect between the two activities was difficult to comprehend—Terry's murder and the ensuing police deluge had seemed to take forever, but meanwhile, a tech run-through was still plodding along at the high school. I didn't want to be alone anyway, so I decided to stop by the theater and see how it was going. I hoped I wouldn't find the Ghost of Christmas Present stuck mid-flight, or the Cratchit children running amok backstage, but even those diversions would be welcome.

I kept flashing back to Terry's body and knew the images would keep me awake tonight, at least. I'd never gotten hardened to unnatural death, even when I was on the job. Being horrified kept me on my toes. Violent death should never be routine. Even when the victim is far from an ideal human being, he, or she, deserves better. I shivered and turned up the heat in the car.

As I drove, media vans were approaching from the other direction. Eric was right. The Anchorage was going to be a media zoo. Lucky Brooke. She'd made it out just in time.

Dimitri was in the process of giving technical notes to the production staff when I walked into the theater. Connie sat by his side, prompt script splayed across her lap, writing furiously. Dimitri stopped talking when he saw me coming down the aisle. I was waiting for the "where the hell have you been?" barrage, but it didn't come. Connie must have warned him off giving me a hard time. She was pretty good at assessing when I could be pushed and when I couldn't. Another one of those stage manager traits.

"I hope to hell you can run sound," he said, hands on hips. "We think that our sound engineer has been arrested."

"Dimitri, we don't know that," Connie said. "They said they had questions for him. No one said anything about being arrested."

I was caught between worlds for a minute. Should I fill them all in, or let it go and catch hell tomorrow for not keeping them ahead of the gossip wave? I decided that hell tomorrow was a better deal, because I couldn't take much more tonight. I did have to talk to Harry. I'd promised Eric that I'd let him know what had happened.

"How is rehearsal going?" I asked.

"Aside from our sound engineer being gone?"

I didn't bite. I knew Frank would still be tweaking things, but that Connie and her assistant stage manager would be running the sound for the show. Worse came to worst, we'd make it through.

"Aside from our sound engineer being gone," Dimitri intoned a little less dramatically, "it was not nearly as horrific as I had feared."

"Not nearly as horrific" are not words a general manager wants to hear. Granted, the show was sold out for the most part, but I didn't like the idea of delivering a bomb to our community for the holidays. I looked to Connie for clarification.

"The second act needs work. A lot of work. Stewart has asked for a rehearsal tomorrow afternoon to go over the Future scene, and Patrick agreed." I winced. Overtime for union actors. I didn't even have to say it aloud; Connie knew. "I know, Sully, but it could help it go from passable to pretty good."

"Just pretty good?"

"After a couple of performances, it may even be great. The earbud Frank suggested is working out very well. Patrick only needs it during the third act. We do have some fine-tuning to do … I hope we get Frank back before tomorrow afternoon."

Connie caught me up on some more of the production issues. She also told me that Stewart, Harry, and most of the rest of the cast had just gone out for a drink. She was heading over to join them; did I want to go? I didn't have to ask where they were. Despite it being decidedly off-season, there were several local watering holes available, yet the theater folk, such as it were, all went to the same place: the Beef and Ale.

The Beef and Ale was a decidedly not-hipster-chic bar that had a dozen kinds of local draft beer and really cheap, comforting, dense, fat-filled food. Tired as I was, I knew that I was too wired to sleep. Good greasy food and a couple of beers might cure what ailed me. Probably not, but it was worth a shot.

The Beef and Ale was close enough that driving seemed like a wasted effort, so I left my car at the high school. Connie decided to drive, since it was on her way home. I was grateful for the peace and quiet. I was dancing the limbo between incredible physical exhaustion and mental insomnia. The beautiful winter night at least helped me feel more in balance with these two warring factions. The cold night air woke my physical self, while the sharp beauty of the isolated harbor helped my mind find a modicum of peace. The high school was on the midpoint of the harbor, set back a few blocks from the water. When I walked toward the shore, to the left I could see the summer home of the Cliffside Theater Company butting up to the edge of the water. I even saw the potential site of our new production center, and made a wish upon a star that we could make that happen this summer. On the other side of the harbor was the Beef and Ale, and the rest of what passed as the waterfront of Trevorton. I'd been spoiled since moving back. Daily water views were my new elixir.

Walking at night provided an opportunity to look into some of the more picturesque houses on the harbor. Few, if any, people drew their curtains to the street traffic, light as it was. This time of year, with the holiday decorations both inside and out, the voyeuristic walk was particularly lovely.

Trevorton in the winter was much different from Trevorton in the summer. As beautiful as the summer was, the winter suited me more. That's when the true community of Trevorton was defined, relied on, and celebrated. The few establishments open were refuges, and the winter folk sought them out. It was easy to be friends in the summer. It was the winter that defined a person's true character. This is not to say that January, February, and most of March were a cakewalk. Far from it. But places like the Beef and Ale helped make it bearable.

In the summertime, with its abundance of bars and restaurants to choose from, I still visited the Beef and Ale, but mostly off-hours. It was a winter retreat, with dark-paneled walls and a musty smell that overpowered you in the summer but was masked by the wood fire in the winter. Dartboards on walls, checkerboards and backgammon boards painted on tables, no music, no pinball, no loud lights. A foosball table was as rambunctious as the entertainment got. Well, at least the coordinated entertainment. Great conversation, drunken brawls, and clandestine rendezvous were the real entertainment of the Beef and Ale. Authentic rather than manufactured charm, in addition to good company and comforting food, were the winter sports it provided. Tonight I looked forward to seeing a friendly face or two.

Or three. The first person I saw there was Stewart, sitting with Patrick at the bar. It seemed the moratorium on drinks was lifted, as they both held nearly finished pints with new ones waiting next to them. At least there was food in front of them. Stewart smiled when he saw me, rising from the bar to give me a friendly kiss. Usually I didn't like public displays of affection, particularly with someone technically working for me, but tonight the human contact felt good.

"Sully, it wasn't that bad, was it? The run-through? You look done in."

"It's not that. It's been a hell of a day. I was meeting up with Connie; have you seen her?"

"She's over talking to Cassandra."

Cassandra was a very, very good costume designer, but she never let you forget it, or the favor that she was doing you by working for your small company with its shockingly low budget. Our costume budgets weren't wonderful, but she could keep what she didn't spend, as long as the show didn't suffer. Given her incredible stock from years of costuming, I felt fairly certain that the Cliffside did fairly well by Cassandra. Still, the ego stroking was part of the deal. On the best of days I wasn't up to it, and this had not been the best of days.

Stewart, who knew the effect that Cassandra had on me, kissed me on the forehead and nodded toward the bar. "Join us, Sully. We can ask people to move down a little."

Patrick looked pained but recovered quickly. "Yes, do join us," he said with forced charm.

"No thanks. I see Harry over there ... I need to talk to him for a minute, and then I'm going home. I'll see you both tomorrow."

I gave Stewart a kiss on the cheek and walked toward Harry's table through the maze of people. Actually sitting at the bar was optional, and not necessarily optimal. Most people stood three-deep in the general vicinity of it. Gene, the bartender, was more than able to serve everyone, keep their tabs, and cut them off when necessary despite the density of the crowd. He winked at me as I moved by and handed me a cold pint. I reached for my purse, but he waved me off. I'd try to settle with him later, but chances were I wouldn't be allowed to pay if I kept it to one. Gene always bought me my first pint and offered it up to the memory of my father. They'd been best friends, and Gene and I had adopted each other as family since my father's death. I'd missed seeing him these past few days and looked forward to catching up.

I lifted my glass toward the ceiling and smiled. He picked up his own glass and mimicked my toast. Like many of the bartenders I knew, his drink was ginger rather than Bass ale.

I caught another glimpse of Harry and worked to part the crowd. As his table came into view, he offered me a watery smile and inclined his head toward his table companion. My ex-husband looked as frosty as the moorings in the harbor, but I didn't worry too much about it. He'd had as long a day as I had, and I was about to make it longer.

I'd barely sat down when Harry asked me the same question Stewart had asked: if the run-through had been that bad. Actors are remarkably myopic. It wouldn't occur to a one of them that something else might have impacted me today. Before I could reply, Gus answered for me.

"I don't think she saw the run-through, did you, Sully? I mean, I didn't see you in the theater. And I was there for quite a while."

"When did you get there?"

"About six or so. I was at the Anchorage and then thought I'd come by."

"And you stayed for the rehearsal?" I probably sounded as incredulous as I felt. Why would anyone with a choice sit through a four-hour rehearsal for an hour-long act?

"He wanted to see you, Sully." Harry shared the same scolding tone my mother once had, and I almost reacted as well to him as I had to her back in the day. The underlying "he was being nice, be nice back" reproach was a favorite while I was growing up. Even then I didn't suffer fools easily. I almost flared, but I decided to let it go, though I didn't relish my friend telling me by tone to be nice to my ex-husband. The intersections of my life with Gus's had been a little disconcerting. Irrationally, I wanted Harry on my side.

"Have you talked to Eric or Emma, either of you?" I asked.

"Not since this afternoon," Harry said.

Gus shook his head. "Has something happened?"

I nodded and tried to get the words out, but found that I couldn't. My mouth had a cotton texture, but I didn't take a sip of beer to quell it. I was afraid that I wouldn't be able to keep it down. I'd never puked on the job, but I wasn't a professional police officer anymore, and the veneer that had protected me back at the house was beginning to crack.

"Sully, what is it? Is it Eric? Is he okay?" Harry grabbed my hand and leaned his pale face close to mine.

"No, no. Nothing's happened to Eric. It's Terry. He's been ... he's dead." Both of them pulled out their phones and furiously sent texts while they listened to me.

So much for subtlety. "Careful, boys. You might want the cops to inform you."

"How was he killed?" Gus asked.

"Shot. Emma called me from the house. I went over before the second act. I just got back."

The cotton was still there, but my stomach felt more stable. I decided to risk the beer, and drank most of it in one long pull. Harry and Gus waited for me to tell them more, but the words weren't coming. The beer helped equalize my physical and mental selves, but exhaustion was winning. I leaned back in my chair and started to pick from the leftover fries on Gus's plate. He pushed it toward me and motioned to the waitress.

"Another round, and a bacon cheeseburger, medium rare." He looked at me with his eyebrows raised. I nodded, and he thanked the waitress as she hustled off. I suddenly flashed back to our marriage. Not a particular day, but rather a particular routine. Gus and I always talked about our work, usually without too much detail. We both were well aware of the traps of professional breaches in personal relationships, particularly when both professions are in the law. But the broad strokes were enough—we could fill in the details easily enough.

There was one period when I was working a heinous murder. Gus was prosecuting a rapist who would probably walk. We knew the toll our work was taking on our souls. I would come home very late some nights, and Gus would either be waiting for me or would have left me a note with dinner instructions and permission to wake him up. I'd have takeout sent over to his office. We took good care of each other in a lot of ways, but lousy care of our marriage. Suddenly I couldn't bear to look at him anymore, so I turned to Harry.

"I have no idea what's going on, what happened. But it looks like Eric is in the clear. He was helping Amelia with some tour."

"The birdwatchers."

"Yes."

"Ironic, isn't it?" Harry said. "Eric was bitching and moaning this afternoon because Amelia wanted him to help her with the tour. He hadn't wanted her to cancel, and she thought it was important for him to act as if nothing's wrong, so they agreed to work the event together. It's one of the few social engagements Amelia looks forward to."

"They were in the right place at the right time," I said.

"Do you think the police will take Eric off the suspect list for Peter's death?"

"I have no idea, Harry. No idea." Not likely, I thought.

"Depending on the timing, the list may be morphing a bit," Gus said. "If the murders are related."

"Is Eric still at the house?" Harry asked.

"Yes, I think he wants to stick around for Emma and Amelia. Did he text back?"

"No. I better call him and check in. Will you be here for a bit? Can I leave my stuff?"

"Yes, I've got to eat my burger. And get a little drunk. And then I need to get some sleep."

Harry walked toward the front door, dialing his phone as he went. I watched him go, and then turned to find Gus staring at me. I used to prize myself on being able to read his face, but tonight I'd lost the power. I had no idea what he was thinking. And at that moment, I didn't really care. The comforting familiarity of him disconcerted me on one level, an intellectual level that remembered it all, including the hurt. But the other part of me wanted him closer. I tentatively reached my hand halfway across the table. He broached the other half and took it in his.

"Are you going to go over?" I asked Gus.

"I'd rather not, unless they need me. I feel like a second murder counts me out."

"I feel the same way, even though I care a lot about what happened. Time to step out and let the professionals take over. Which is hard," I said.

"Sully, I need to—"

"Sully, love, see you tomorrow?" Stewart was calling my name from the doorway. He and Patrick and a couple of other actors were heading out the door, undoubtedly to another bar.

"Good night, Stewart," I called back. "Behave yourselves."

"Always, darling, always." A huge wink and a slight bow. So dramatic, yet so charming.

I was still smiling when I turned back to Gus. He let go of my hand, and his face had the frosty expression again.

"You could go with them, if you'd like," he said. He sounded petulant.

"I didn't want to and I wasn't invited." I refrained from explaining who Stewart was in my life. If Gus had a question, he could ask. Or he could be as grown up as I was and not ask. The way I'd not asked who Kate was. And that was different, since Gus had nothing to fear from Stewart. Stewart was my past. I had a feeling Kate was Gus's present. But she wasn't here, and I was. I reached back and took his hand again.

Then I took a deep breath and leaned across the table. He leaned toward me, and I felt his warm breath caress my face. "Gus, this is what I do want. I want to forget today for a little while. I want to finish my beer. I want to eat my burger. And I want you to take me home. And stay. How does that sound?"

His response was a grin that curled my toes.

· Twenty-One ·

I woke up on Thursday with my hangover only outdone by my mood. A few more hours of sleep would have done a world of good, but the image of Terry prevented a blissful slumber. The alcohol had offered a brief respite, but when I woke up at six, I was up. There was nothing else to do but to get out of bed and make coffee.

I supposed I could be grateful that the inevitably awkward morning-after was avoided, but that wasn't my style. I'd known when I propositioned Gus that there would be music to face in the a.m., and I'd been willing to risk it for a night of... of what? Passion? Gus and I were capable of passion, but if passion was all I'd wanted, I could have called Stewart. I wanted more than passion. I wanted a familiar connection. I wondered now if we would have found the connection again. But thanks to Harry, I didn't find out.

Gus had been up at the bar paying our tab. He hadn't even waited for the waitress to come back to the table with our check. I was finishing my burger in record time when I saw Harry coming back in, heading over to Gus at the bar, and handing him his cell phone. Professional responsibilities—Gus's—came crashing back. He turned to me as he was talking on the phone. He shook his head and shrugged his shoulders, and had the good grace to look upset. I slowed down eating my burger.

Harry came over to the table and sat back down. He looked at me, and then at Gus, and then back at me.

"Did I interrupt something?"

"Who's on the phone?"

"Eric, with Emma in the background. They want Gus to help deal with the police and the press."

"How did they know he was here?"

"I told them."

"Helpful Harry, that's you. Always Mr. Helpful."

"Sully, did I step in something?"

At that moment, Gus arrived at the table and handed him the cell phone.

"Sully, I . . ."

"Have to go. I know, Harry told me."

Gus glanced at Harry and then squatted beside me. He lowered his voice and leaned in toward me. "Sully, I'm so, so sorry about this."

"So am I. But you've got to do what you've got to do. It's fine. Really." It wasn't, but what could I say? I kissed him on the forehead.

Gus winced and then turned to our mood-wrecker. "Harry, Eric said that if you want to come with me, that would be fine with him."

"No, that's fine. I'll stay with Sully."

We watched him leave. I sighed dramatically and finished my beer, as did Harry.

"You got what you wished for. Eric invited you over. Why didn't you go?"

"Eric's got it together, and it sounds like a zoo. I figure I'll wait for him to come over to my place when he can."

"Did he say what was going on?"

"I don't think he knows much. He's holed up with Emma and Clive from the sound of it. He said more and more people keep arriving, and no one seems to be leaving."

"Good thing it's a big house." I said.

Harry twirled the bottom of his pint around in his glass. I signaled to the waitress for two more and then turned back to my silent tablemate. "What's wrong, Harry?"

"Just something Eric mentioned. I asked him how everyone was holding up, and he said Mrs. Bridges was taking care of Amelia, and that he and Emma and Clive were stuck in the kitchen. I asked about the merry widow, and Eric said she went back to Boston, late afternoon. He said that he talked to her before she left. She was planning on going to see the show at the Colonial..."

I hesitated to interrupt, but I wasn't sure if this Brooke fixation was a conversation consideration or something of import. He had a look that I recognized from the mirror. Come to think of it, I probably wore a similar look by now. This whole business with Terry wasn't holding together. If the same gun that killed Terry had killed Peter, my theory that Terry was the murderer went down the toilet. The waitress came over and put two beers down. I'd forgotten that I'd ordered them, which meant they weren't a good idea. Nonetheless, I took a long pull and noticed that Harry did the same.

"Sully, this is probably nothing, but I'd swear I saw Brooke at the theater around five or so."

"Maybe she didn't go right back to the city."

"I mentioned it to Eric, and he told me I must be mistaken. He'd called her around then, and she was at the Beacon Hill apartment. He said, in that imperious tone of his, that she couldn't be two places at once. But really, she could, if she was lying on the phone and talking on her cell. So I figure I was right. She was at the theater."

I let the "imperious tone" remark pass. I knew what Harry was talking about, but bitching about boyfriends could be a long detour and I wanted to stay focused on Brooke, or at least try.

"I wonder what she was doing at the theater," I said.

"No idea. I saw her backstage, near the prop table. Maybe she was looking for you."

"I was there. She could have found me. Come to think of it, wasn't Eric there too?"

"He came a little later," Harry said.

"So, she wasn't there to see me." Why would Brooke possibly be looking for me? I remembered her angry face from this morning when I walked into the will reading. Wow, was it only this morning? Damn, it had been a full, full day.

"I was going to ask her, but then Connie called me onstage for a fight call. When I turned away, she left."

My conversation with Harry ended when Gene took my keys and asked one of the tea-totaling patrons, yet another friend of my late father's, to drive both of us home. I argued for a second, then realized it was a good idea. Is it any wonder that I stayed in Trevorton even after my father died? His memory was protecting me from myself at every turn. These guardian angels were local. In Boston, I'd have been on my own.

I was sober enough to thank our chauffeur for the ride and offer him a pair of tickets to the show. I was also sober enough to call the box office and leave a message with his name, in case he actually called. My final act was to feed Max the cat and take off my shoes before falling into bed. I wanted to do more, to think more, but the day had finally caught up with me.

∞

While the coffee was brewing, I took off my clothes and splashed cold water in my face. A shower would have made me feel better, but I couldn't muster the energy. Instead, I wrapped myself in my robe and went upstairs to the living room, cup in hand. I turned on my laptop and leaned back on the pillows, waiting for it to boot up. The next thing I heard was the loud warning call of the coffee pot turning itself off after two hours. My neck was so stiff from my head leaning back that I thought it would snap in half if I moved my chin to my chest too quickly. Once I'd finally wrenched my aching body off the couch and did a couple of yoga stretches, I realized that I felt a lot better. Not good, but better. Well enough to start thinking about what I knew, what it meant.

I opened a new document on the computer and wrote notes on the events that transpired after Peter had died. Back in the day, I would have kept copious notes all along. I'd gotten sloppy in retirement and had to recreate a lot of it from memory. Fortunately, despite the webs from the beers, my memory was still pretty good. I stuck with the facts the first time through. I went back through to add my impressions and thoughts, coloring that font blue. I used to use different color highlighters, but the computer was more fun. The third time through, I added the outstanding questions in lime green. Then I added my best guesses at the answers to those questions in red. There was more green than red on the pages, but at least I knew where to start. I picked up the phone and dialed.

· Twenty-Two ·

"Whitehall residence."

"Mrs. Bridges, it's Sully. Hope I didn't wake you."

"Good morning, Edwina. No, we've been up for a while."

Edwina? I'd hoped we were progressing to Sully. Ah well, maybe last night had put me back at arm's reach.

"When did everyone leave?"

"I'll let you know."

Ah, so they were still there. Good. "Mrs. Bridges, I'd like to come over this morning to, um …"

"To see the things Mr. Whitehall left you? Certainly. What time can we expect you?"

∞

The Anchorage zoo was in full splendor, both in front of the gates and behind them. In front, there was an amazing maze of media vehicles parked. Fortunately for me, they couldn't completely block the gate since they had to keep the street clear. I explained who I was to the

205

officer outside the house and he waved me into the grounds. Another officer directed me to park alongside of the house, out of the driveway. Official vehicles only. Gus's car was there. He must have spent the night.

I wished I'd put on lipstick, and immediately shook myself. What was I doing, feeling like a lovesick teenager? Worse, a middle-aged woman acting like a lovesick teenager. Shake it off, Sully. Get your head in the game.

Ah, the game. The rules had changed in the past twenty-four hours, but the end game was the same. First, get Eric in the clear. Legally, I suspected there was enough reasonable doubt to ensure that he would never be convicted of his father's murder, even if it got that far. But there would always be that question hanging over Eric's head. Was he innocent, or was he another example of what a high-priced lawyer like Gus could do to the course of justice? For that matter, the sword of thwarted justice was hanging over a lot of heads now. Were I another type of person, I would have embraced the reasonable doubt, left the whole thing in Gus's more-than-capable hands, and been done with it. Of course, if I were that type of person I would never have ruffled so many feathers that I ruined my own career.

I had to admit, curiosity was driving me forward today as much as the elusive search for justice. I had as many questions as I had answers. The more answers I got, the more questions I found. By now I'd expected that a picture would be beginning to form, but not this time. This time Terry's death had blurred the picture just as it had started to come into focus. Who killed Peter Whitehall? Who killed Terry Holmes? Were they the same person?

Mrs. Bridges had suggested I come to the back door instead of the front. I still had to run a minor gauntlet of police and other people in suits who were busy talking on cell phones. I was stopped briefly by an officer standing sentry, but he must have been expecting me because he barely looked at my ID, though he did use his walkie-talkie right after he waved me past.

The back entrance was actually a side entrance, since the house backed up on the cliffs. Whatever its location, it was hardly a second-rate entry to the Anchorage. The cobblestone walk led to a large oak door with leaded glass panels. I knocked, and the door swung open at my touch. I stepped into a flagstone mudroom, paneled in oak with a built-in bench, shelves, and cubbies around the room. There were two other doors in the space. One glass door provided entry to the greenhouse. The window panels were so foggy I couldn't see inside. The other door, glass also, led to a small hallway. I wasn't sure what to do next but was saved from my indecision by the arrival of Mrs. Bridges at the second door. She opened it and stepped back for me to enter.

"Edwina, I'm sorry. I thought I'd hear the knocker."

"Sorry if I startled you. I didn't knock too hard since the door was already open."

"Probably from all of the police 'testing' that's been going on. They keep opening and closing the doors, running around timing entrances and exits, fingerprinting everything that doesn't move, taking everything out of the cupboards." She sighed.

I stopped mid-step and turned back to her.

"Taking everything out? What do you mean?"

"All those benches in the mudroom? All storage. That and the coat hooks."

"What was in the bench storage?"

"Anything we wanted to keep available but out of the way. Smocks and clogs for the greenhouse, boots, raincoats, gloves, towels. Leftover summer detritus like suntan lotion and gardening hats. That sort of thing. They boxed it all up and took it with them."

"All of it?"

"All of it. Plus from the things they found in the cubbies. Tomatoes I'd canned, some jellies. I stored it there during the winter, cold and dark storage. Oh, and of course, some of Brooke's medicine."

"Medicine?"

"That's what she called it. Her father's secret recipe. It was hooch, pure and simple. Well, hardly pure, but fairly simple. Homemade alcohol."

"Homemade? Was that what she had in the flask?" I'd seen her topping off her tea on Tuesday. "I would have assumed it was rare and expensive brandy."

"An old family recipe. Her father sends her a case for her birthday, and for Christmas. Horrible stuff. Tastes like cough medicine."

"So she was willing to share?"

"Yes and no. She offers, but only if you're with her one on one, watching television or chatting. She never brings it out for social gatherings. Usually. Lately it has been her constant companion. Giving her comfort, poor thing."

By now we were in the kitchen. I settled at the table, draping my coat over one of the chairs. Mrs. Bridges handed me a cup of coffee and then went back to what she'd been doing, making sandwiches. I hoped one of them was for me. I must have drooled, because she took a small plate and put a couple of the finger sandwiches on it.

"Don't stand on ceremony, Edwina. I'm too tired. Help yourself. There's plenty."

"I'm trying to picture Brooke drinking homemade hooch." I picked up a sandwich.

"Well, it can't be too far of a stretch to imagine her drinking, surely."

Meow. She *was* tired.

"The depth of her grief over Mr. Whitehall's passing has been heartening, I will say that," Mrs. Bridges went on, reclaiming her manners. "Any doubts I may have had have been released. She's been the picture of despair."

"How is she holding up since Terry's death?"

Mrs. Bridges shook her head. "I wouldn't know. No one has been able to reach her to tell her. I'd hate for her to hear it on the news. Or to be met by reporters."

That seemed odd. It hadn't yet been twenty-four hours since Terry died, but surely there had been enough time to contact Brooke. "Isn't she in Boston?"

"She was supposed to be, but she's not at the condo. I called a neighbor and asked him to check."

"Did you tell the police?"

"They know she is missing," she said.

"Mrs. Bridges, is the coffee ready?" Gus came into the kitchen and acknowledged my presence with a brief smile. He looked done in. If he'd slept, it was probably sitting up. He moved slowly, keeping his hips in check. I was betting on some back pain. I reached into my bag and pulled out some ibuprofen, handing him the bottle. He shook out a few, swallowed a couple, and put some others in his pocket.

"Thanks, Sully. You must have been a helluva Girl Scout. Always prepared."

"I try."

"What brings you over here this morning?" he asked me.

"I decided to come over and talk to Mrs. Bridges about my inheritance." Gus raised one of his eyebrows and then went to get a cup of coffee. I didn't try to defend myself, especially from Gus. He knew me too well. "Odd timing, I know. Mrs. Bridges was telling me that Brooke is AWOL. Odd, that."

"Odd indeed. I'm a little worried, actually," Gus said. He leaned back against the counter, a few feet away from Mrs. Bridges, facing me.

Mrs. Bridges stopped making sandwiches and looked over at Gus. "You're worried?"

Concern was etched across the housekeeper's face, and Gus responded by backpedaling. "Only a little. I've never known Brooke not to answer her cell, or at the worst respond to a text within the hour. She's not responding to either texts or calls."

"Maybe she left her phone somewhere," Mrs. Bridges said.

Gus smiled at Mrs. Bridges and lightened his voice purposefully. "Or it ran out of juice. You're probably right. I'd prefer it if she didn't hear about Terry's death on the news. We'll find her. Don't worry."

He glanced over at me. I recognized the look, and knew he was having trouble following his own advice.

$$\infty$$

I offered to help Gus carry the coffee and sandwiches to the living room. We didn't see anyone on our way, but there was a low hum indicating a hive of activity somewhere nearby. We were alone in the living room, but I thought it was a good idea to keep my voice low. Walls have ears.

"Hi." I felt myself blushing.

"Hi." Gus was smiling, but he looked like hell. Handsome hell, but hell nonetheless. "I feel like I haven't seen you for days."

"I know, but it's only been a few hours. How's it going here? Eric in the clear yet?" I wondered if Gus was worried about whether he might be on a suspect list as well. Or would he just let me worry about that?

Gus shook his head. "Looks like Eric is out, but Emma might be in."

"Emma? I thought she was on a conference call."

"Which she had to leave a few times to retrieve some documents from Peter's study. Enough of a window, I guess."

"Do you know she's a suspect for a fact, or are you guessing?"

"Mostly guessing, but educated guessing."

Gus had been in the DA's office for a few years. He probably knew what investigators were thinking before they did. "Have they tested her hands for gunpowder?"

"They've taken some samples from everyone who was in the house at the time. Including me."

A smart move. If they waited too long, the evidence would be more tainted than it already was. And given the number of vans in the driveway, I guessed there was a traveling lab that was more than capable of gathering evidence. And processing it before they made any move toward bringing someone in for questioning.

I put myself in Emma's place, a habit from the old days. Empathy was part of what made me good at my job. It's also what had almost killed me. I'd routinely put myself in the place of victims, trying to figure out their final moments to see if I could find a clue I'd missed otherwise.

I would also put myself in the place of the perpetrator, walking through the crime as it was recreated. Then I'd look at my list of suspects and try to imagine their motivations and methods. I'd also look at other people I met to see if they fit the scenario. The exercise was effective, but it took its toll. No matter what I did, I couldn't help the victim. And occasionally I'd find my suspect but not enough evidence to bring him to trial. Those were the cases that still woke me up at night. I had a couple of cases that I kept in my personal active file. I'd do searches on the names of the suspects every few weeks, trying to keep track of what they were up to. When the folks on my personal list slipped, and they would, I'd be there. Even if I was in the middle of rehearsals at the time, I'd be there.

My investigative muscles weren't as sharp as they used to be, but they were warming up. Empathetic pondering came back easily. And the exercise did not bode well for Emma regarding Terry's death, no matter which angle I used. Spouses were almost always the prime suspect, and for good reason. Emma had spousal motivation to kill Terry. I knew firsthand that she'd suspected him of having an affair. Additionally, they were in business together. For all I knew, Peter hadn't tied it all up in his will and Terry still had a card to play. And finally, there was Peter. If I thought that Terry killed Peter, and the police thought that Terry killed Peter, then Emma must have at least suspected this too. And whatever else he was, Peter was her father.

A part of my subconscious must have been working on this puzzle already, because the exercise took just a few seconds. I looked at Gus, and knew that he'd reached the same conclusion.

"Do you think … " I began.

"I don't think she did it. She has too much to lose."

"What do you mean?" The activity in the hallway sounded closer.

"It's complicated. We have a few issues that need to be addressed if the company is going to move forward. Losing Peter, then Terry, hasn't made it any easier. The people we're working with aren't going to give us any more latitude. And Emma is the only one who can finish these negotiations."

"What about Eric?"

"Terry took him off the project when he was brought in for questioning. Emma signed off on the change. He can't be reinstated at this point, since it would be a conflict of interest on Emma's part. And I don't have the power to do it on my own."

"So if Emma is arrested..."

"Have you heard of the Cunningham Corporation and their Century Projects?"

I nodded. "They have a foundation I'm trying to approach for theater funding."

"The Cunninghams have been talking to Peter and Emma about working together on a project up here near Trevorton. Negotiations have been challenging. That's putting it nicely. If the Cunninghams have an opportunity to buy the company in a takeover, they'll take it."

"Even though it's a private company? How?"

"By getting folks to call in loans. It would be risky, and it would tarnish their image as a community-minded corporation. Especially under the circumstances. Mimi and Jerry are nothing if not self-aware, but if Emma is arrested, it'll provide an opening they won't ignore."

I didn't know Emma well, but Gus was probably right. She was a business woman. Which convinced me even more that she didn't do it. She wouldn't jeopardize her business, her standing in the community, her world by killing Terry. She'd find another way to get rid of her husband.

"Sully, you've got to figure this out," Gus said. "They aren't going to arrest her without being very careful, but they aren't going to wait too long. Especially now that Terry's dead."

Regina walked into the room and looked at me. She was wearing the same clothes she had on last night. I poured her a cup of coffee and added some cream. She took a long swig. "What the hell are you doing here?" she barked, as usual.

"Good morning to you, too, Regina. Came by to check in with Mrs. Bridges."

"About?"

"I wanted to show her the items Mr. Whitehall left her in his will." Mrs. Bridges had arrived with another plate of sandwiches. She put two on a plate and handed them to Regina. Regina put her cup down on a coaster, then took a bite. She sighed and smiled slightly. Mrs. Bridges' sandwiches were an elixir.

"Is this the best time for Sully to take a look at her bounty?" Regina asked between bites.

"It isn't a bounty. It's a lovely remembrance. It was my idea that she come over," she lied. "I wanted something besides all this to focus on. Perhaps it was callous of me."

I put my arm around Mrs. Bridges shoulders. She'd made up the excuse, but not the emotion behind it. For the first time, I would have described her as old. She'd spent most of her life holding the Whitehall family together and, despite her Herculean efforts, it was falling apart.

"Show me my teapot, Mrs. Bridges," I said. "If that's all right with you, Regina."

"That's fine. You'll need to keep it here, but sure, take a look." Regina grabbed another sandwich and sat back on a chair.

Mrs. Bridges and I walked into the dining room. I'd seen the room before but never ate a meal there; the kitchen had a table, and there was also a breakfast room. Interestingly, even back in the day when my mother was alive and visits were allowed, we'd been relegated to those two rooms or the back patio in the summer. I'm not sure if it was a slight, or a sign of the level of intimacy my mother shared with her cousin. My father would have guessed the former. I might have agreed with him at one point, but today I settled on the later.

The Whitehall dining room had once been a showplace. My childhood memories were of antique mahogany pieces—a long table, high-backed chairs, a china cabinet, a sideboard, and a buffet. The walls had been painted a dark green, with a dark chair rail and wainscoting and candlelight, creating a dark, somber effect that fit the era of the room itself. I paused in the doorway, taken aback by the redo of the room. My gut told me it was by Brooke's hand. A huge table took up most of the center real estate. Rather than wood, the top was glass and held up by three large black cylinders. The chairs, twenty on quick count, were upholstered in white brocade. The walls were now dark red, as was the wainscoting. There was a sideboard with a granite top. Only the built-ins were the same, but even these had been painted the same shade as the walls. I ran my hand over one of the doors, hoping they'd been primed carefully so someday they could be taken back down to the wood.

"Did Brooke redecorate this room?"

Mrs. Bridges sighed. "She wanted to modernize it. Her words."

"What did everyone else think?"

"This room, and the living room, weren't used too often by the family, so she was allowed to do what she wanted. Mr. Whitehall didn't much like it, and neither did the children, but they lived with it."

"And you? Do you like it?"

"No, but I understood why she did it. The first Mrs. Whitehall was a wonderful woman who cast a long shadow, even after her death. It was a formidable task for Brooke to make her own mark."

"I wouldn't have thought she'd care that much." I looked at the window treatments. They were very expensive, fit the décor of the room perfectly, and were devoid of any personality.

"Oh, she cares. She's got a fairly vulnerable side to her. She wasn't to the manor born, and it makes her insecure. So she puts on airs and tries to play a part. Now, let's take a look at your tea set."

"Do you need help?" I asked.

"I know where it is," she said. "Give me a moment."

She turned back to the sideboard and started opening doors and drawers. There was a lot of stuff, mostly in different closed containers. I sat down on one of the horrifically uncomfortable chairs and watched Mrs. Bridges search the cabinet. The short period of silence allowed me to think. Ideas were taking shape, but I was hard-pressed to articulate them without more information.

"Mrs. Bridges, can I ask you a couple of questions?" I asked.

"You may ask. I'll answer if I can." She'd pulled out a couple of pieces and put them on the table. She went back to the cabinet to keep looking.

"Fair enough. Apparently Brooke came by the theater last night. Do you have any idea why she would do that?"

Mrs. Bridges paused in her search and looked toward the dining room door. It was still closed. "I hate to speculate. Perhaps you could ask her yourself when she gets back home … "

"I promise I'll ask Brooke when she gets back, but there are a couple of advantages to asking you now. First of all, you won't lie to me. Brooke may. And secondly, time is of the essence. Gus thinks, and I agree, that the police are taking a hard look at Emma for Terry's murder. They may not wait to act until Brooke gets home." Mrs. Bridges stood up from the cabinet and collapsed on a nearby chair. I felt bad for pushing, but I needed answers. Now.

"She was at your theater?"

"Yes, last night. Around five thirty."

"This is just speculation, you realize, but there's a young man who works at the theater—"

"Frank?"

"Yes, Frank. He's been meeting with Mr. Whitehall, doing some sort of computer work. He was given free reign of the house while he was working. Brooke and Frank became friendly while he was here."

"Friendly."

She looked at her hands while she answered. "I walked in one day and seemed to have caught them in a moment. I don't know anything for certain, mind you."

Frank and Brooke? That seemed a little odd. "I thought that Frank was working when no one was home." As I said it, I realize that probably wasn't possible, since someone was likely always home. "What did you know about the work?"

"Mr. Whitehall asked me to help facilitate letting Frank into different areas of the house." She stopped again. The short sentences were wearing on my patience, but I wasn't sure of the tack to take.

"Mrs. Bridges, I know that you were, and are, very faithful to Peter Whitehall and his wishes. I think that's commendable. Now, I didn't know him that well, but I'd imagine that he'd be okay with your breaking a confidence, especially if it would help Emma. Wouldn't you imagine he'd want to help Emma?"

"Of course he would. It's just that all of this is supposition on my part. I'd hate for you to go in the wrong direction."

"I wouldn't use what you say as proof without verifying it. I'm missing some pieces, and I think you may be able to fill in the gaps. Okay?" Mrs. Bridges nodded and turned back to the cabinet. She pulled out a large wooden box and laid it on the table, and then put the rest of the containers back in the cabinet while we talked.

"Did Brooke know about the work?"

"No one else knew. But Mr. Whitehall was less concerned about her being home while the work was underway than he was about others."

"Terry?"

"Yes. It seemed to me that he didn't want the children there either."

"He was installing new digital surveillance equipment. You know that, right?"

"I surmised as much, but I have no idea why."

"If he didn't mind if Brooke was home when the work was being done, I'd assume that he wasn't spying on her."

"The work was being done in the East Wing of the house, where the offices are, and the library. And the kitchen. Brooke didn't go to that side of the house too often, so I assume Mr. Whitehall didn't think she'd encounter the installation work."

"But she did, obviously, if she met Frank. And you caught them in a 'moment,' which could have been a one-time situation or an affair. I know Frank, and I've got to tell you, I'm a little surprised at the idea of him having an affair with Brooke. And I can't imagine her being that stupid."

"Agreed. It was probably nothing, or it was simply a momentary diversion for her."

But it added yet another morsel to ponder, and my plate was already full. She ran her hand over the top of the wooden box and turned it toward me.

"Here it is, Sully," she said. "This tea set is over two hundred years old—a Revere set purchased by your grandfather for his wife on their twenty-fifth anniversary. I think that the history of the set is in the box as well." She opened the lid and turned the box toward me. It was beautiful. I wasn't sure I would ever use it, but I'd display it. It seemed a shame to keep it boxed up.

The set had two pots, one for coffee, one for tea. I pulled the teapot out to look at it and heard something clink against the inside of the pot. I lifted the lid and saw a flash drive clipped to an envelope. I considered giving these to Regina, but there was nothing to indicate they were evidence in the case. And the envelope had my name on it. Finders keepers?

"I doubt Edwin used a flash drive," I said to Mrs. Bridges. "Do you recognize the handwriting?"

"Looks like Mr. Whitehall's, but I can't be sure."

Before I had a chance to question her further, the dining room door swung open and Regina entered. I put the envelope in my pocket.

"You done yet, Sully?" she asked.

Mrs. Bridges shot her a look that would have scared me, but it didn't appear to have much effect on Regina. She was tough, I had to give her that.

"No, still looking at my treasures." I lifted the coffee pot to show her. Damned if I didn't hear a clink there too. I lifted the lid and looked inside. There was a small bottle with an eyedropper top, along with an envelope that resembled the one in my pocket. This envelope wasn't addressed to me, however. Instead, it said, *IN THE EVENT OF MY DEATH*. I didn't pick either item up, just tipped it toward Regina.

"Put it down on the table, Sully." Regina put gloves on and carefully removed the bottle and envelope from the pot. "Don't touch anything else in the box," she warned us.

"What is it?" Mrs. Bridges asked.

"Do you recognize the handwriting, ma'am?" Regina asked Mrs. Bridges.

When she didn't answer, I did it for her. "Maybe it's Peter's?"

We heard a phone ring, and Mrs. Bridges reached into her pocket. After her initial greeting, she listened for several moments and then reached behind her for the chair. She sat heavily and rested her head in her hands.

"What is it?" I crouched down beside her and took her hand.

"There's been a car accident. Brooke—"

· Twenty-Three ·

Regina left the dining room quickly, pulling her cell phone out as she walked. She stood in the grand hallway barking questions, clearly pissed that she hadn't gotten the news first. After a couple of minutes, she walked back in. I walked over to her and spoke in quiet tones.

"They found her an hour or so ago, identified her, and made the call here. Damn."

"Do they know what happened?" I asked.

"She went off the road and crashed into a tree sometime last night. I don't have a good window of time. There weren't any skid marks. She may have had a heart attack or stroke. They won't know for sure until they open her up and run some tests."

"Was it an accident?" Mrs. Bridges asked.

"That's what they are assuming," Regina said more loudly, with a layer of compassion in her voice. "But I should tell you, ma'am, I spoke with the supervisor and gave him an update on what's going on here. They're going to move slowly, make sure they cover all of the possibilities. Just in case."

"In case?"

"In case there was foul play," I said gently.

There was nothing more to do. Mrs. Bridges answered a few questions, but Regina didn't balk when I suggested she be allowed to go up to her room.

"Do you want me to walk up with you?" I wanted Mrs. Bridges to finish telling me about Frank.

She shook her head. "I'll be fine, thank you. I'd rather be alone for a few minutes, if that's all right."

"Should I see if someone can get you something to help you sleep?"

"Thank you, Edwina, but no. I don't want to cloud my mind at this point. I'm sorry I wasn't able to show you the rest of the set and finish our conversation."

"Another time. Here's my card. Call me anytime, day or night, if you need anything. Anything at all."

"Thank you, my dear," she said. I watched as she made her way up the rounded staircase, holding on to the railing with one hand as she hoisted herself up each step. The last few days definitely seemed to have aged her.

I turned back to find Regina staring at me. I stared back.

"Sully, do you think it's a coincidence that Brooke died last night?"

"Regina, I don't believe in coincidence."

"Neither do I. Still, I wish to hell I knew what was going on."

"Going on where? Where's Mrs. Bridges?" Gus was carrying the now-empty plates from the living room back toward the kitchen.

I explained what had happened, and he handed me the plates and went back toward the front of the house.

I brought the plates into the kitchen. I washed them, tidied up the sandwich debris, and pondered my next step. I felt my pocket. I knew

I should hand it over to Regina, but I wanted to look at it first. It was wrong, and went against all of my training, but at this point I didn't care. This whole thing was wrong. First Peter, then Terry, now Brooke? Maybe I should tell Gus about the flash drive? No, not a good idea. As a lawyer, he might feel obligated to turn it over to the police. I might soon end up in the same place, but I wanted to look at the contents of the flash drive first.

Gus came back into the kitchen. He smiled and stood as close as he could without touching me. I matched the gesture. He looked over his shoulder and took my hands in his, then leaned his forehead against mine. Any complicating thoughts about withholding evidence from him disappeared when I felt his touch.

"I checked in with the local cop—"

"Officer. Regina."

"Regina. She said you could head out if you want, but that you should come by the station later to sign a statement about the evidence you found."

I explained about the eyedropper and the note. Since neither of us knew what it meant, I asked if I should stay around.

He shook his head and kissed me quickly. Then he stood up straight, still holding my hands. "I'd rather go with you, frankly. But you should get out of here before they change their minds."

"Thanks. I should probably go to the theater. Tonight is the invited dress. Call me later?"

"Absolutely."

I stood up and kissed him lightly on the lips. The kisses may have been quick, but they were potent. I didn't dare look back as I left.

· Twenty-Four ·

The temporary office the high school had made available to us during our stay was tiny, but at least it was all mine. I'd moved a few things in so I could work on payroll and do some social media. I went there now on the pretense of catching up on paperwork. Actually, it wasn't a pretense. I was behind in sending an email update to the board of directors, and I also owed the actors' union a call to explain the cast changes. I decided not to pursue anything against our former Marley. The Christmas spirit had invaded me. Plus, his side of the story would probably get us company hazard pay assessments for his having to work with Patrick. I wondered if I could get someone to tell me anything, off the record, about Patrick's history. So yes, I had a lot to do. But first there was a note to read.

∞

I grabbed some latex gloves from the shop, put them on, and pulled the flash drive out of the teapot. The note addressed to me was typed and unsigned:

Sully,

If you are reading this note, it is because the situation I outlined in my first note must have come to fruition. The files referenced are all included on this flash drive. Again, I thank you for your help.

~PW

On quick perusal, the documents looked to be the same as the ones Gus had brought to my place. But Peter had added comments to explain his thoughts, so they began to make a little more sense. These weren't the PDFs—they were the full spreadsheets. I looked at one of the cells and followed the references in it, backward. There were many pages and workbooks Peter hadn't included in the files he'd sent to Gus. It would take days to go through these, and I felt an expert should probably do it so the evidence wouldn't get lost somehow.

The spreadsheets tracked the movement of large amounts of cash from one account to another, then back to the first account after a delay of anywhere from a day or two to a few weeks. Thanks to Peter's careful notes, it was clear he hadn't approved of these moves and considered them theft. The problem for Peter was that he didn't have proof of who was doing the moving, and he must have wanted to keep his theories within the family before he made accusations. Given the recent turns of events, I put my money on Terry. The final spreadsheet hypothesized about the amount of money that had been taken by holding these investments—close to $2 million. It must have taken a long time for that amount of money to build up. Had Emma's hiring Jack Megan triggered all of this? Or was Peter thinking this earlier? I wondered if he'd told anyone else, like Terry, about what he'd discovered.

I suppose it made sense for Peter to pass the information to me once he'd decided he could trust me. He probably wouldn't have thought that Gus and I would be working together. Although if someone had asked me a week ago, I wouldn't have thought that Gus and I would be working together either.

The other envelope, unfortunately now in Regina's possession, had been addressed *To be opened in the event of my death.* I wished I'd opened the coffee pot first and pocketed the contents. Curiosity was killing me. Assuming that note was from Peter also, what did it say? What was in the bottle? Had someone been trying to poison Peter? If so, why did he, or she, decide to shoot him instead? Did he or she know about these notes?

My money was still on Terry, but now that someone had murdered him, that envelope might provide clues. I needed to figure out how to get Regina to tell me what it said. Chances were good, damned good, that she wouldn't. I wouldn't have. Maybe I'd try to get it out of her later if she came to the theater to pick up Gabe.

I'd also give her a copy of the spreadsheets. I still needed to decide whether she'd get the note to me as well. I could give her the spreadsheets and tell her they were from Gus—which they were, at first. But the note would be trickier to explain. My conscience started to bother me. She needed the whole package.

The spreadsheets were beginning to swim before my eyes. I refocused on preparations for opening night next week. Programs needed to be proofread again, since Stewart had to be added and David had to be deleted. Ushers needed to be confirmed, press lists checked, social media updated, and photographers contacted. A million details, all ending up in my purview at some point during the day. I made lists and sent out a flurry of emails.

Just at the point when I realized I was starving, there was a knock on the door. Harry arrived at the door with a white to-go container. A blue cheddar burger and fries from the Beef and Ale. He handed me a diet soda and sat on the other side of the desk, opening his own container of nirvana.

"How did you know where I was?" I asked him.

"Your car was in the parking lot, and I took a chance. Gene always gives me a second burger for you, so it's great that I can actually give it to you this time. Normally it feeds Dimitri."

"Food soothes the savage beast," I said. I took out a fry and munched on it.

"Is it true about Brooke?" he asked, dipping his fries into the container of ketchup he'd placed in the middle of the desk. I pushed it back to him. Compromising the perfect, fried greatness of Beef and Ale fries was sacrilege.

"Car accident, from what I know. How did you hear?"

"Are you kidding? It's all over the news. Peter, then Terry, then Brooke? The national press has picked it up."

"Have you spoken to Eric?"

"No. He isn't replying to texts. They seem to be under lockdown."

"They're using the house as an interrogation center for the family, rather than making them run the gauntlet past the press into the station. Emma has given them permission to do what they need to do."

"Is that smart? Letting them into the house?" he asked.

"It's probably still a crime scene, so they don't have a choice. Besides, it's much better for them to cooperate." Harry looked skeptical, so I continued. "The presumption is that whoever killed Peter was in the house that night, right? Well, for my money, the prime suspect was Terry. Then he's killed. No accident. Killed. Probably with the same caliber gun as Peter—"

"How do you know that?"

"Peter was killed by a 25mm. I didn't see Terry up close, but he still had a good amount of his skull, so it was probably a small caliber."

"Thanks for the image." Harry tossed his fries into his container and closed the lid. I grabbed it and dumped his fries into mine. Yes, it was upsetting, but I'd seen a lot worse than Terry, a lot closer up. Besides, the puzzle had me. If Terry killed Peter, then who killed Terry? And what about Brooke? Did someone help her move to the great beyond? The timing was too coincidental, but it made no sense.

"Hello, earth to Sully ... where were you just then?"

"Trying to make sense of something that doesn't. Sorry, Harry. Let's change the subject. You ready for tonight's dress?"

"Jeez, Sully, I don't know. Thank God Stewart's here, that's for sure. He and Patrick have been working together all day. And Frank's got the place pretty well wired so Connie can feed Patrick lines or direction."

"Let's hope Connie can rewire if needed."

"It's under control. Besides, Frank came back a little while ago."

Frank was back? And there were two hours before the show? That bit of information got me to leave my fries.

· Twenty-Five ·

I finally found him downstairs, in the trap room—the room beneath the stage that can be used for storage, for trap doors, for access to the orchestra pit, for actors to move from one place to another, and for errant sound designers to hide out. I could never find the trap room easily and had spent five minutes wandering the downstairs halls. I was tired and confused, and couldn't quite remember what I knew versus what I was supposed to know, and what I was at liberty to say. Brooke's death was common knowledge at this point, as was Terry's. I felt as though there were tumblers in my brain that should have been sorting the details into the truth, but something was stuck. Hopefully Frank would help loosen it up.

He was hunched over his laptop tapping away, oblivious to my presence. I watched for a few seconds.

Finally he noticed me standing in the doorway. "Sully," he said, semi-lowering the lid of his laptop and turning it away from me.

"Hey Frank. Heard you had a conversation with the police last night? Sorry, that was probably my fault. I told them about the website."

"It's okay. They wanted to confirm that we saw Mr. Holmes going into his office, and to find out more about the new setup."

Frank looked miserable, which, under the circumstances, was understandable. But he couldn't look me in the eye. Again, could be understandable since I'd gotten him dragged into a police station, but he didn't seem pissed. Just miserable.

"Did you hear about Brooke?" I asked gently.

"Yeah, saw it on the web."

"You knew her, didn't you?" I pulled up a rehearsal cube and sat down across from him.

"Yeah." His voice caught.

"I'd heard that you knew her pretty well." For the first time, Frank looked at me. I shrugged and smiled.

It was his turn to smile, or at least try to. "I didn't know her that well. She, uh, tried to, uh … "

"She made a pass at you?"

"Yeah, a couple of times." He gave me a "can you believe it?" look. "But I didn't, you know."

"Why not?" I asked.

He shrugged his shoulders and looked down at the laptop. "It seemed wrong. She was pretty wasted half the time. And besides, I knew Mr. Whitehall and thought that sleeping with his wife wouldn't be cool."

That was one way to put it. "Did Peter know she'd made advances?"

"Not from me. I kinda felt sorry for her, you know? We got caught a couple of times. Mrs. Bridges walked in once, and Mr. Holmes walked in another time. After that, she stopped making passes. She even apologized."

"She did?"

"Yeah, she said something like 'Terry said it was unkind of me to put you in that position.' Then, it was weird, you know, but she asked if we could be friends. So when I came over to do work, I'd make sure to check in with her, and we'd talk."

"About what you were doing?"

"No, I'd promised Mr. Whitehall I wouldn't tell anyone about that. Mostly about family, stuff like that. We both had family in Western Mass. She didn't visit a lot, but I did. We'd talk about the kielbasa festival, polkas, stuff like that."

It seemed Frank knew a Brooke that few if any other people knew. It was interesting that she seemed to be trying to reconnect to a part of herself that she'd tried, successfully, to ignore. I wondered if drinking her father's hooch had been part of embracing her roots.

"You said she'd been drinking? Was it the stuff her father made?"

"The samogon? Yeah, mostly."

"She spilled some of it on me once. Smelled like cough medicine."

"It's grain alcohol and raspberries. Takes a while to make, but it cures what ails you."

Connie's voice came over the loudspeaker that was piped into the trap room. "It's four o'clock. Just reminding everyone we're going to do a tech run with the Ghost of Christmas Future in fifteen minutes."

"That's me, Sully. I have to run a couple more tests." Frank started to lift the top of his computer back to a viewable level.

"A few more questions first. I heard that Brooke came by the theater last night. Is that true?"

The lid was being lowered again, physically and emotionally.

"Frank, if I found that out, someone else will. With her accident—"

"So it was an accident?" Frank's relief was palatable.

"So far as I know, it was an accident. Why?"

"I was afraid she'd done it on purpose."

"Because of something she said?"

"No. I was worried, is all. Sorry, Sully, I really need to get back to work." He turned back to his computer and away from me. I left the room to go up to the office. But we both knew I'd be back.

∞

While producing a show, a creative set designer can, very early in the process, talk a director and general manager into a stylistic set enhanced by projections. Early in the process, this seems like a good idea. But so did hiring Patrick King. The projections weren't going well, and there hadn't been a run-through with them working yet. Instead, there had been slides with helpful descriptions like "cloud" or "sunny day." Connie assured me this was the least of our problems, and that Frank was working with the images the set designer had created, trying to make them work with our projection system. I had no idea what that meant and wondered when Frank was finding the time. Or the mind space.

I grabbed a cup of coffee, a pad, and a pen from my desk and went into the theater. Dimitri and Connie were conferring with Frank, who now had his laptop sitting next to another laptop at the tech table. Connie called for quiet and they did a quick run-through of the first projection, which, to my untrained eye, looked pretty good. I walked toward them as they discussed the logistics.

"It does look much better, Frank, but are you sure it'll run on the computer in the booth? Or does it have to run on yours?" Connie asked.

"I'm copying all my files to the booth computer, so it should be okay. I need to take my laptop with me to run the sound cue for..." Frank was saying.

"Frank, Patrick can't hear…" Gabe called from backstage.

"Be right there," Frank called back. "Connie, can you finish copying these files over? Just the ones in this folder." Connie and I looked at where he was pointing, and she nodded. Frank picked up a box and headed backstage, Dimitri in tow, presumably giving more notes.

Connie was clicking the files over when her headset buzzed. She put it on and grunted a few times. "Sully, I need to go backstage. Don't ask. Can you copy these? It takes a while, not sure why. And you need to do them one at a time."

"Sure. Glad to be able to do something useful." And I was. Almost as glad as I was to get a chance to look at Frank's computer.

I selected the first file and started to copy it over. It was called CC_actI_scene4_ghosts. All of the files had similar naming patterns—Christmas Carol, Act I, Scene 4, Ghosts. Pretty easy to follow, which was good, depending on who was running the cues from the booth.

Connie was right; the copying was really slow. Thankfully it seemed that the booth computer was the slow one, not Frank's, so I was able to look around while the files copied. I did a search; Frank's naming convention seemed to hold true for everything—he clearly and concisely named files in an easily recognizable format. Given the number of projects he was balancing, it made sense that he kept things clear. And it was a break for me. I looked for files that were last accessed within the last twenty-four hours—ever since Frank and I had seen the feed showing Terry going into his office. Then I sorted the files by type and ran down the list, quickly. A couple were called TH_office. Terry Holmes? I copied those and a few others from yesterday to the booth computer, in a folder on the C drive.

I wasn't sure how much more time I had, but I opened Frank's web browser anyway. The wireless network he'd installed in the theater was up and running. I logged into my Gmail account and sent myself the TH_office files. I would have sent more if I'd had time. I copied another file for the show to the booth computer, and then went back to the browser. It was 25 percent done. My email was taking forever to go through, so I kept my pointer on the X on the upper right corner. Now 55 percent. I'd figure out how to get them off the booth computer later if I had to. Up to 70 percent.

Frank was coming through the curtain. Heading toward me. Did he walk more quickly when he realized I was copying the files, or was that my imagination? Up to 89 percent. Connie came out, called to Frank. He stopped, but he never stopped looking at me. Email sent. Sign out. Clear cache. Just like you taught me, Frank, I thought. I closed the search window and starting copying the last projection file as Frank and Connie walked up to the table.

"The last file is being copied now," I said, getting up from the chair.

"Thanks, Sully. Gabe," Connie said into her headset, "could you come out once Patrick is set? We need to run through a few things before we start." She turned to me. "I called half hour," she started to explain. "We needed to do a run through of the Ghost of Christmas Future graveyard scene, but we didn't get to it."

Half hour, the half hour before a performance, was sacrosanct. It was time for the actors to get ready to run the show.

"Not a problem." I was careful to look Frank straight in the eye, and smile. "I'll go check my email."

∞

I closed and latched the office door. It was probably paranoid, but I wanted to see what these TH_office files were in peace. Watching the projections on screen had got me to thinking. I clicked on the link on my email and was thrilled when the file picked a program to open automatically, rather than making me pick one. I hated it when my computer wanted me to think for it, since it was usually for something I really couldn't figure out on my own. Sometimes new media made me feel old.

Frank and I had seen Terry going into his office over the web. Or had we? Frank had told me that we were looking at a live picture, and I took his word for it. Why wouldn't I? But maybe … I watched as a small snippet of Terry Holmes walking down the hall to his office filled the web window. I tried to remember if it was the same thing I'd seen yesterday, but the lovely hand gesture at the end was absent. I clicked open the second file, and this one was what I remembered, complete with Terry flipping the bird at the end of the video clip. Was this a recording of the actual moment I'd seen? Or had I been watching a recording?

If so, that meant Terry could have been dead when I "saw" him flip the bird. The idea made my head hurt. If the timeline I was keeping was screwed up, the suspect list had shifted again.

At this rate, I was never going to see the last act of *A Christmas Carol*. I couldn't decide what to do. Should I call Gus and give him a heads-up, or call Regina? A knock at the door prolonged my decision-making.

"Sully, you in there?" It was Regina. She won. But who, besides me, was going to lose?

∞

I opened the door. "Do you want to come in?" I asked Regina.

"I came by to watch rehearsal for a while and get Gabe, but I had trouble focusing. Connie said you'd be in here."

"Want some coffee? I have one of those cup-at-a-time coffee makers in here. Hot chocolate too."

"Do you have decaf? I want to be able to grab some sleep tonight."

"Grabbing some shut-eye between shifts?"

"More like dismissed, with thanks." Regina sounded like she felt a mixture of incredibly pissed-off and hurt, in equal measure. I'd been there more than once, but I didn't think camaraderie was the reason for her visit.

"Let me guess. The chief got a phone call—"

"Text."

"From the mayor?"

"A state rep."

"Who was worried about … ?"

"Oh, who knows? Whatever it was, my boss decided to take over the case, which is fine. But I guess he didn't like hearing my opinions."

"Which isn't fine."

"Which sucks."

"Sure does." I handed her a cup of coffee and watched her take a sip.

I figured I'd start with the files and go from there. I would take a risk and go for full disclosure. Regina would be upset, could even drag me over to the station, but the only way I would win her trust was by being honest.

So I told her about the flash drive and the note from Peter. As I told her the story, I handed both items over.

"I don't suppose you have printouts?"

"I do, but not here. They were all PDFs. I could copy some out if you want."

"Do you have the spreadsheets on your computer?" she asked, nodding toward the laptop on my desk.

"No," I answered, patting my laptop. And I didn't. This was my work computer. Technically, the Cliffside's computer. The files were on my personal computer, which was in the knapsack under my desk. I'd learned long ago to keep work and my personal life separate. Even though the lines were blurry, I dedicated the office computer to accounting files and office correspondence. That way, if I ever left the theater for good, the work would stay. And if anyone wanted to check up on me, they could. Full disclosure, just not of my personal stuff.

"Tell me what they say."

"Here's what I was able to understand from the one I was looking at. They track money being shuttled from account A to account B for a short period. The principle would be shipped back to account A, but the interest stayed in account B. The money wouldn't stay for long, but it was a lot of cash, so the interest seemed to add up."

"To?"

"A couple million dollars."

Regina whistled. "Any notes on who was doing the moving?"

"No, none. The more I think about it, the more I think it may not have been provable, at least not yet. I think the spreadsheets are the incredibly well-educated guesses of Peter Whitehall."

"Which he sent to you because?"

"I think he'd asked around and knew he could trust me." The story of Emma wanting to hire me was Emma's story to tell, with Gus in the room with her. "I noticed the other note said 'In the event of my death' or something like that? Was that from Peter?"

"Yeah, it was. There also was a report and a bottle."

"I saw the bottle. Was the report on what was in the bottle?"

Regina shook her head. "Sorry, I can't go there." She started to shift toward the front of her seat, ready to hoist herself up.

"Hold on. I have something else to show you." She settled back in the chair and watched as I clicked on the two files I'd emailed to myself. She watched them each twice more before she turned to me.

"Tell me," she said.

So I did. I told her about the projections for the show and how Frank had named the files. I told her about thinking back to the picture of Terry giving us the finger and how something seemed wrong. "So, if you're using my statement that Terry was in the hallway at six o'clock, it doesn't stand up anymore.

"I didn't mean for you to be involved, Sully. Really I didn't." Frank had pushed the door open a little and was standing at the doorway. Who knew how long he'd been standing there. I looked at Regina, and she looked at me, shaking her head gently.

"Why don't you sit down and tell me about it, Frank?" I asked, working hard to keep my voice gentle and forgiving.

Regina hauled herself off the chair and motioned for Frank to sit there. She stood next to me. The office was cramped, really cramped, but Frank closed the door anyway. I looked at her, and this time she nodded. If I asked Frank questions, it was one civilian to another. Technically she could ask him questions, but it would be less messy if I did it.

"Brooke came by the theater yesterday around five thirty. She was freaked. She asked for my help. She needed me to tell people she'd been at the theater earlier too, to give her an alibi. But I told her that I'd been with other people all afternoon and couldn't give her an alibi."

"An alibi?" I asked.

"She'd found Mr. Holmes ... you know."

"Dead?" I asked. Frank nodded and looked down at his hands, which he then wiped on his jeans.

"Did she kill him?" I asked. I was being obtuse, but I wanted to make sure to get the whole picture.

"No, man, no, she couldn't."

"What time did she find him, did she say?"

"Around four."

"But you couldn't provide an alibi for that time. So you couldn't help her."

"I couldn't tell anyone she'd been at the theater. But I could figure out a way to make people think Terry had been alive later."

"Other people being me?"

"Yeah. Gabe was supposed to come in before you. I figured he'd tell his mom, like he did with the other stuff. I had some footage I'd taped while we did a test run on camera locations a few weeks ago. I was getting ready to play it for Gabe when you came in."

A faint buzzing sound interrupted the stunned silence that followed Frank's admission. Connie's tinny voice called out, "Frank? Frank, are you there?"

Frank pulled the walkie-talkie from his belt and considered it for a second before he pushed the talk button.

"Yeah, I'm here."

"Could you come back in here? The computer is frozen again and we're stuck in the future Cratchit house."

"Be right there," Frank said. "That's how I knew you found the files, Sully. I had to go back onto my computer to reload the files, and went in to see if I could find an earlier file. Noticed that other things had been looked at, figured it was you."

"It was her all right," Regina said, sounding slightly disgusted. I wasn't sure if it was at Frank or at me. "Frank," she continued, "you need to come down to the station with me. And we should grab your computer."

"Yes ma'am. Can I go and reboot the computer for Connie first? My laptop is in there. I won't be a sec."

"You have two minutes. And do not, I repeat, do not make me come after you, do you understand me? Do not leave the building. Do not take the wrong computer by mistake, because if you do, by God, I'll take every computer in this building into custody. Am I clear?"

"Yes ma'am." Frank ran out of the room. I had little doubt that he'd be back. Regina took her coat off the back of the chair and put it on.

"Regina, do you want me to come and make a statement?"

"No, let's see what we have first. I know where you are. Besides, you may want to call that handsome ex of yours. Frank may need some help."

"Frank definitely needs some help, but Gus can't help him. Conflict of interest," I said.

"Off the record, Sully, do you think Frank is mixed up in this?" Regina asked.

"Mixed up as in helping Brooke with an alibi? Yes. As in murder? I don't think so. But I've got to admit, he makes a pretty good suspect, doesn't he?"

"An excellent suspect," Regina agreed. "He made an excellent suspect before, and this isn't going to help his case. Yup, Frank will need some help." Frank had taken Gabe under his wing, helping Regina navigate some pretty rough waters stirred up by her teenage boy. I knew she considered him a friend, as did I.

"I'll call Freddy Sands and get someone down there. If you think it will help, I'll come down to the station."

Regina shook her head. "Sully, I appreciate that you're not pushing me for more details. And for coming clean with information as you get it. I know that you understand, hell, you understand better than anyone what a bitch this job can be."

I nodded.

"And you could have called in favors from me, gotten more details, played PI. But you didn't," she said. "At least not that I can tell. Not that knowing that the bottle Peter Whitehall had tested was full of ethylene glycol would have told you anything. Or that he was worried that a certain recently deceased son-in-law might be poisoning him. Nope, you didn't push for any of that. I appreciate it. Call Freddy. Then call handsome Gus and let him know what's going on. Keep in touch, okay, Sully?"

$$\infty$$

Ethylene glycol. Ethylene glycol. Ethylene glycol. I kept repeating it as I typed it into Google, or did the best I could. Fortunately, Google thought for me and let me know how it was supposed to be spelled. A toxin. Syrupy-sweet tasting. Death resulted from renal failure. According to the medical WikiDoc on the subject, "Symptoms of ethylene glycol poisoning usually follow a three-step progression, although poisoned individuals will not always develop each stage or follow a specific time frame." I kept reading. "Stage 1 consists of neurological symptoms including victims appearing to be intoxicated, exhibiting symptoms such as dizziness, headaches, slurred speech, and confusion. Over time, the body metabolizes ethylene glycol into other toxins; it is first metabolized to glycoaldehyde, which is then oxidized to glycolic acid, glyoxylic acid, and finally oxalic acid. Stage 2 is a result of accumulation of these metabolites and consists of tachycardia, hypertension, hyperventilation, and metabolic acidosis. Stage 3 of ethylene glycol poisoning is the result of kidney injury, leading to acute kidney failure. Oxalic acid reacts with calcium and forms calcium oxalate crystals in the kidney."

Neurological symptoms included seeming intoxicated, experiencing dizziness, slurred speech, confusion ... I hadn't seen Peter Whitehall in a while, so I didn't know whether he'd showed those symptoms. But I had met someone who'd exhibited them—and she'd died last night in a car crash.

I drove to the Anchorage, my mind still in a muddle, but clarity was starting to prevail, at least a bit. And I had a good idea of someone who could illuminate things more. To what degree, was the real question. And the very real concern.

$$\infty$$

There was still a considerable army at the house, and I had to run a gauntlet again in order to gain entrance. I must have been on some sort of list, because they directed me to Gus without an escort. I found him in the dining room, hunched over an open laptop at one end of the long table. The cabinets still hadn't been repacked from earlier in the day. There was caution tape all around the area, but the room hadn't been cordoned off.

"Did you crash the crime scene?" I asked as I slid into the chair to his left.

"I couldn't use Peter's study or Terry's office, and the living room and kitchen are taken over by various officials. This was the quietest place for me to work."

"For a mansion there really isn't a lot of practical space, is there?" I asked, looking around.

"Don't you have a show tonight? What are you doing here?" he asked, ignoring my pithy observation.

"I came by to check something with Mrs. Bridges. Thought I'd check up on, um, everyone. How is it going? Is Emma okay?"

"For now. They're being very careful and solicitous. Too solicitous, if you ask me. I'd feel better if they did something instead of stomping around, resentfully doing nothing."

"I think that I'm getting a sense of what happened, but proof is going to be a problem. And without proof, this family is going to live under one hell of a cloud." Someone walked by the door, slowing her pace when he realized that Gus wasn't alone. I turned. Emma was hovering in the doorway.

"Sully, you came back?"

"I did, to talk to Gus, but I'm leaving again soon."

"Not on my account, please. I came in to tell him that I'm done in. I don't know the protocol. Can we make them leave soon? Do you think they're going to make any of us go with them? Eric passed out an hour ago, and Amelia has locked herself in her room. Mrs. Bridges has run away to the greenhouse. Clive is still here, holding down the fort, but he's pretty exhausted as well."

"Let me go and speak with Lieutenant Black," Gus said. "He's the one in charge now, right?"

"I think so, I've lost track."

Gus got up and crossed over to Emma, squeezing her arm before going into the hall. I led her back to the table, giving her my seat and taking Gus's. I closed his laptop without reading the screen, a rare moment of decorum. But I didn't want the distraction for Emma or myself. I had questions for Emma, and probably not much time to ask them.

"Sully, Gus is a wonder. He's been a—"

"Emma, do you still want me to help you?"

"Of course. Anything you can do."

"Emma, I wish there was an easy way to ask this, but I don't have time and I don't see how the effort could help. Who killed Terry?"

She had the good grace to look taken aback, and the better grace not to comment on it. "I honestly don't know, Sully. We argued, I told Terry he needed to leave. He tried to talk to me about it, but I went into my office with Clive. He stormed into his office, and it was the last any of us saw him."

"And your office is—"

"On the other side of Terry's office. We made the old library into two offices. Had a wall built between them eventually."

"Eventually?"

"Last summer. It seemed like a good idea. Daddy agreed. We put the telecommunications room between them. You know, servers, wiring."

"Could Terry access the server from his office?"

"No, the only door is from my office. But Daddy had the only key."

"So the only way into Terry's office was … ?"

"The hallway. I didn't hear anything, but then I couldn't. The tech room is climate controlled, with thick walls. Terry and I couldn't hear anything in each other's offices."

"Why did you go to his office?"

"Like I said, I was on the phone in the kitchen, on a call. I noticed that Terry's line was lit up. I was angry that he was still there, and I went down to confront him."

"What did you do?"

"I didn't really see him at first, you know. I went in and only … only then I saw how he was … the blood, and his eyes. His eyes were wide open. It was awful. I screamed. And then turned and puked in the hallway."

She looked over her shoulder and turned back to me, leaning over the table even closer to me. "I also found something in the office. It may have been there for days. Or maybe someone dropped it—"

"What was it?"

"Mrs. Bridge's key chain. Only Mrs. Bridges and my father had keys to the entire kingdom. She never let the keys out of her sight. But there they were on the floor, next to Terry."

Mrs. Bridges?

"What did you do with them?" I asked.

"I gave them back to her, of course." And then Emma looked straight at me, daring me to say aloud what we both were thinking but couldn't possibly be true.

∞

I found Mrs. Bridges in the greenhouse, tying an apron around her waist and surrounded by a seemingly organized cacophony of pots, plants, soil, and gardening implements. "What a nice surprise," she said. She didn't bother to take her hands out of the dirt she was mixing.

I felt like a cad.

"Hello, Mrs. Bridges. I hope you don't mind my coming over like this. Unannounced."

"Surely we're past formalities, aren't we, Edwina? Do you think you could call me Clara?"

"I could try, but it's going to be tough. Clara. Do you mind if I talk to you a bit?"

"No, not at all. If you'll help me with these orchids. They haven't been touched since Mr. Whitehall passed, and they're in a sorry state." She handed me an apron and a pair of gloves, both of which I took reluctantly.

"I'll help, but I warn you, I'm not very handy with plants."

"It isn't that difficult. Just some separating and repotting that needs to be done. I'll show you." For the next few minutes she explained the procedure of taking the old plant out, dividing it, trimming the excess, and repotting. It didn't seem difficult, but it did seem complicated, at least at first. After a while we developed a rhythm. Mrs. Bridges, her division-of-labor experiment quickly abandoned, took the riskier job of separating, and I took the repotting task.

After a few minutes of quiet work, she finally broke the silence. "You wanted to talk?"

"I do," I said, taking my gloved hand out of the pot I was working on and placing it on her arm. "Please know that you don't have to answer my questions, though. It's all really none of my business."

"Answering your questions will be good practice for others, who will likely be asking similar ones later."

"Not all of them, I shouldn't think. Like what your keys were doing next to Terry's body?" I asked.

She paused and looked right at me. "So you've seen Emma? Good. That couldn't have been easy for her, carrying that around all day. My keys. Edwina, I don't know what they were doing there. I lay down after we got back from the reading, and when I got up, I couldn't find them. I went looking for them, thinking I must have mislaid them, but had no luck."

"Mrs. Bridges, did you know what we would find in the tea set?" I asked.

"Your tea set?" she asked innocently.

"Don't," I said, gently.

She smiled and shrugged her shoulders, as if to say, "It was worth a try."

"I went into Brooke's room to look for my keys. She'd been in such a state, I didn't know if she'd left for a drive or gone for an overnight. Her room was a mess. I found some notes from Mr. Whitehall to myself, and to Emma. I barely had time to register their existence when I heard the scream ... Emma had found Mr. Holmes. I went down to help with that and put the notes in my pocket. I didn't even remember I had them until later that night."

"What did the notes say?" I prodded gently. "Are you sure they were from Peter?"

"Oh, they were from him all right. His note to me was to let me know about certain arrangements he'd made in the event of his death."

"That's awfully dramatic, isn't it? When was the note written, do you know?"

"Last summer, I'd imagine. A little dramatic, certainly. But he'd been under some strain. He had a heart attack around the 4th of July. Nothing he couldn't get past, but it had made him feel vulnerable in a way that he wasn't accustomed to. He started taking stock. That, coupled with Emma's meeting with you about Terry. I think he wanted to get his house in order."

"Did he know Emma thought Terry was having an affair?"

"Yes. And that she'd hired someone to follow Terry."

"Who found nothing."

"Found enough to get Mr. Whitehall thinking. And doing some investigating on his own. Prompted him to make some changes."

"The will," I said.

"And other things." She went back to futzing with the plants but kept talking. "Sometimes I think his heart attack was one of the best things to have happened to him. It helped him realize what was important."

More likely he got scared of the chains of hell that awaited him, I thought uncharitably.

"We had a long talk, Mr. Whitehall and I, around Veteran's Day. He wanted to let me know about some changes that were coming up in the household. We hadn't had a talk like that in a long, long time. He'd thought of himself for so long, he'd forgotten he had a family he could count on. Anyway, he told me that Mr. Holmes wouldn't be living at the Anchorage much past the new year, if that long. He asked me to keep an eye out for Emma. And he asked me to clear out the guest quarters over the garage for after the new year."

"For whom, did he say?"

"I asked, but he told me that it would all be dealt with after the new year." Mrs. Bridges took off a glove and wiped at the tears running down her face. "Poor man. If only he'd let me know."

"You know who it was for, don't you, Mrs. Bridges?"

"I can guess now. For Brooke, I'd imagine."

"Brooke?"

"I found out right after Mr. Whitehall's death. You and Mr. Knight had visited. Brooke was distraught, even more than normal. Terry was trying to calm her down, but she kept screaming and crying. I finally went in to see what I could do, and she clung to me as if she were a child. I told Terry I'd take her upstairs and put her in bed. That perhaps we should call someone, but he told me no, she'd be all right. She started crying even more. I finally got her up the stairs. Told her I'd sit with her until she fell asleep. Just as I thought she'd drifted off, she said to me, 'He killed Peter, you know, Clara.'"

I'd stopped repotting in the middle of her story, and she looked surprised when she handed me the next plant.

"He being?" I asked, going back to the task.

"Terry Holmes, of course."

"How did she know?"

"He told her."

"He *told* her? But why?"

"To keep her complicit, I'd imagine. Mind you, she was in quite a state, so it took a while for the story to come out." She moved on to the next plant, and handed me a new pot.

I was losing my mind, controlling my urge to shake her until the truth rattled out of her. Breathe in. Breathe out. Soil in pots. Keep her talking.

"Mrs. Bridges, please tell me the story. It's the only way we can figure out what to do. Time is of the essence." I hoped I was keeping my impatience out of my voice.

"She and Mr. Holmes had become very close."

"Very close?"

"Do you think I would have, for one moment in my house, allowed ... " As if to emphasize the point, she struck one of the pots too hard and it broke on the table. The ruckus seemed to calm her. "No, I can't believe that. Terry had gotten Brooke on his side, against Mr. Whitehall. Brooke told me she'd tried to separate from Terry's plans several times, but Terry was having none of it."

As I'd seen, Peter had tracked his money carefully enough to follow it back to Terry. Most likely he assumed that Terry had a mistress and was getting the money for her. Or was the embezzlement the true crime in Peter's eyes? The reason for Terry's fall? Did I think so little of Peter that I believed his daughter's marital misery weighed on him less than money? I'm afraid, being my father's daughter, that I did.

"When you and Peter spoke, how much had he told you about the money?"

"The money? Nothing. When he told me that Terry would be leaving, I thought it was because of the affair."

"But he wanted to wait until after the holidays to kick him out? I can't imagine that was because of Christmas charity?"

"Why didn't he kick Terry out earlier? Surely you would have," I said.

"I did ask him that," Mrs. Bridges confessed. "Apparently there was some business that needed to be finished up before Mr. Whitehall felt Terry could be let go."

"Do you think Terry knew he was on his way out?"

"The night Mr. Whitehall died, he and Terry argued. Loudly. I couldn't hear the words—they were in his study—but the door was slightly ajar and I heard the voices. Terry stormed out. I went into the study afterward, to check on Mr. Whitehall. He asked me to leave a note for Mr. Willis and Emma to meet with him first thing. I asked if he didn't want me to call them in right then, and he said no, let them rest. It would be the last good night for a few. And so I said good night and left him. Poor man."

We finished repotting the orchids in companionable silence, both lost in our own thoughts. I left her, at her insistence, to clean up the green house and went in search of Gus.

∞

The process of clearing the cops out of the house had started, at the instigation of Clive Willis and Gus. The wing with the offices was closed off, with a police officer on duty. There were a couple other official-looking people hovering around. I decided that they were likely working for the Whitehalls when they pointedly ignored the police. Gus confirmed they would be setting up camp in the living room. Having spent a little time in the for-show-only room, I decided that the policeman sitting on the settee in the hallway was likely to have a more comfortable night.

Clive was going to stay at the house again, and he insisted that Gus leave and get some rest.

"It's a long ride back to Boston. Be careful on Route 1. It's a bear this time of night," he admonished.

So really, it was only in the cause of public safety that I suggested Gus come back to my house.

· Twenty-Six ·

I called Connie. She reminded me about the bad dress/good show adage and said that we were going to have a brilliant hit on our hands if that was true. I asked if I should come by, but they'd called a rehearsal for tomorrow afternoon, so everyone was heading home.

I made a second call, to the Beef and Ale, and we picked up dinner on the way home. Another fine meal of burgers and fries. At some point I needed to grow up and eat like a middle-aged woman concerned with trans fats and cholesterol. Who was I kidding? My life would have room for the Beef and Ale's blue cheese burgers. Besides, I did eat the tomatoes and lettuce. That's got to count for something.

I poured Gus another glass of my fine three-dollar Cabernet. During the drive and over dinner, I filled him in on Frank and the phony live feed incident, as well as my conversations with Emma and Mrs. Bridges.

"You've had a busy few hours. In comparison, I've done nothing today."

"Busy, yes, gathering lots of information. Working on lots of ideas. But nothing hangs together. And there's no proof."

"No proof?"

"It's like when I thought that Terry did it. I had a gut feeling. He did do it, according to Mrs. Bridges, and that's according to what Brooke told her. Hearsay. No proof. Brooke asked Frank for an alibi, or so he says. He said it was because she knew she'd be accused of the murder. But, again, hearsay."

"So you think Brooke killed Terry?" Gus sounded dubious.

"According to the threads I've been gathering, that's the story that comes together. Then she came by the theater and asked Frank to help her with her alibi." Gus had taken another bite of his burger, so his mouth was full. He shook his head while he chewed.

"No," he finally squeaked out, taking a long swig of wine to wash down the burger. He cleared his throat and started again. "From what you said, Peter believed he was being poisoned, right? With eth ... "

"It's in antifreeze. Causes kidney failure. Makes you look like you're drunk, along with other side effects."

"Drunk and confused? Like Brooke?"

"Like Brooke," I agreed.

"Brooke who could barely stand up the past few days? That's the same Brooke who could overpower Terry, stage a suicide, clean herself up, and go to the theater to ask Frank for help? Doesn't track, Sully. Besides, didn't you say that she and Terry were having an affair? Why would she kill her lover?"

"Why would he kill *his* lover? Terry must have been the one who was poisoning Brooke, right? Unless ... why did Peter think that it was Terry who was trying to kill him?"

"Don't know. Maybe Mrs. Bridges could tell us."

"Maybe," I said. I made a note to myself. "We can ask her tomorrow. But suppose Peter was wrong. Maybe it wasn't Terry who was trying to kill him. Suppose someone was trying to frame Terry for poisoning Brooke? Or someone else poisoning Brooke?"

Gus wiped the vestiges of his last bite of burger from his mouth. He took a healthy swig of wine and, shaking his head, leaned toward me across the table. And then he smiled. That smile. The train of thought that had been gathering steam in my mind derailed, leaving nothing. Nothing but wondering how the sleeping arrangements were going to work out.

"Sully, what do you think we should do?"

"About?" I asked, wanting to make sure we were thinking about the same thing. But the chirping of his cell phone brought us both back to earth. I handed him his phone, glancing down at the display. *Kate*, it read. Gus's voice dropped and he turned away, walking across the room to speak.

Who was Kate to Gus? How serious was it? How could I ask? Should I ask? Why did I feel like I was in high school again?

While recalling how much I hated high school, I was pulled back from falling into the abyss of self-doubt by the chorus of "Silver Bells" coming from my own phone. *Stewart*, said the display. Time for my own lowered voice and back-turning.

"Sully here," I said.

"Sully where?" Stewart asked, his voice both teasing and tired.

"At home. How did it go tonight?"

"Let me come over and tell you."

I blushed. My tryst with Stewart was long over, but I had no doubt that the two of us, consenting adults both, might be willing to pursue a "friends with benefits" arrangement. I'd been considering it when I called Stewart with our Scrooge SOS. But that was before the Gus effect had rolled back into my life. And turned me upside down.

"I have company, Stewart."

"Ah, so it is true. The ex is back in the picture."

"No. Yes. I don't know. Where are you?"

"Calm down, sweetheart. Didn't mean to fluster you." I heard a door open, and Stewart spoke a little louder. "Is that better? Good. I actually am calling for another reason. I've been a good Watson for you. Connie and Harry have both caught me up, separately, on this business with Eric Whitehall's family. Tragic, isn't it? Shakespearean, actually. Is Frank involved? He went back to the police station before the tech run."

Many people expect actors to be outgoing and boisterous at all times. And while they can be, some, the good ones, are also reflective students of human nature. It becomes second nature after a while. A similar second nature to what the police develop. Always questioning, wondering, gathering seemingly unimportant facts into a semblance of truth about a character. The murder of Peter Whitehall had been the talk of the town all week. But with his outsider's view, Stewart was likely to be working on gathering his own characterizations, and conclusions, about the people involved. For him, it was a character study. For me, it might be insight.

"So I thought I'd call you and see if you knew what they brought him in for," he finished.

"I'm not sure. I think they had some questions for him. He did some work for the family." I hoped that was vague enough. I didn't want to upset Regina by disclosing news.

"Work, is that what they're calling it these days?" Stewart laughed. "I wouldn't think that romancing the gorgeous blonde would be considered work."

"Romancing?"

"A Victorian term I used for you, my dear Sully. It means—"

"I know what it means. But what do you mean? Who told you they were sleeping together?"

"Frank."

"Frank, when? Why? How?"

"So many questions. More than happy to discuss it if you'll have a drink with me."

"Stewart..."

"Sully, you'd be surprised what I've heard. In all seriousness, I thought I should call and let you know as soon as..."

And then the phone fell. Stewart was gone.

∞

I called the Beef and Ale on my landline and asked Gene to look for Stewart. Though he hadn't said where he was, there were few choices in Trevorton and the bar seemed the most likely. While I waited, I gave Gus the briefest of outlines about our conversation.

"He's not here. I haven't seen him tonight," Gene said.

I hung up the phone and listened to my cell. The line was still connected. I grabbed my coat.

"Where are you going, Sully?" Gus asked.

"Gene couldn't find Stewart, so I think I'll go look for him. Something must have happened. See, the line is still connected." I handed him my phone.

Gus listened for a moment, and then clicked it shut. I grabbed it back but the connection was gone.

"What did you do that for?"

"He probably forgot to turn it off when his next drink arrived."

"He was in the middle of a sentence. You're such a jerk," I said, searching for my keys.

Gus handed them to me and put his own coat on.

"What are you doing?" I asked.

"Going with you, at least as far as the Beef and Ale goes. I'll grab a ride out to the Anchorage and get my car. I've decided to go back to Boston tonight."

And so we stood there, all the good tidings of the past few days forgotten and our rapprochement giving way to old, tired habits of anger and sniping.

$$\infty$$

It felt like the brief ride was going to be spent in complete silence, but Gus tried one more time. "Just who is Stewart?" he asked.

I knew he wasn't asking for Stewart's acting resume. "A friend."

"Just a friend?"

"Not 'just a friend,' no. I don't have many friends, Gus. The ones I have don't deserve a 'just a' qualifier. Stewart Tracy is my friend. And I'm pretty sure the definition of our friendship isn't any of your business."

Gus looked out the window for a few moments before turning toward me. "You're right, of course. It's none of my business. Sorry I asked."

I was tired and frustrated on more levels than I cared to admit. Damn you, Gus Knight. I thought I'd worked him out of my system, but I was wrong. Damn.

"Listen, Stewart is a friend and he didn't hang up. I need to be sure he's okay. I'm sorry that you have a problem with that. Really sorry."

The rest of the ride was in silence.

$$\infty$$

Gus and I parted ways in the Beef and Ale. He ordered a draft and took it to a back table where he started to work his phone, flipping between emails, studiously ignoring me.

Patrick King was sitting at the bar, finishing his ale while a new one awaited him.

"Hi Patrick. How are you this evening?"

I swear he tried to hide his beer from me. Please.

"Well, thank you, Sully, I am well. Though it hasn't been easy, has it? No, indeed, it has been a tough run ... "

"I thought I'd find Stewart with you."

"He was here for a bit, but went out a bit ago." With that he turned back to his beer.

Though part of me wanted to smash his beer off the bar, for effect, finding Stewart gave me a more urgent gut ache. It was the same gut ache I'd ignored when we hired Patrick, and my early New Year's resolution was never to ignore my gut again.

Connie and Dimitri were huddled over a table near Gus. "Hi guys," I said as I walked over. "I'm looking for Stewart."

Dimitri, never subtle under the best of circumstances, looked pointedly toward Gus, who just as pointedly ignored both of us. "Really?" he asked.

"He called and we got cut off. He sounded a little odd. I want to check in on him."

"He stayed at the theater to help Gabe finish the wiring on Patrick's costume," Connie said. "It kept cutting out, and Gabe needed someone to run the system through its paces to make sure it holds up."

"And Patrick?" I asked.

"Couldn't be bothered." Connie shrugged and swatted the air in the general vicinity of Patrick's back. "Got to say, getting Stewart up here was genius, Sully. He's been like a tonic for all of us, right, Dimitri?"

"He has indeed. Speaking of which, we should discuss—"

"Sorry, Dimitri. Let me go and check on Stewart."

"Is everything okay?" Connie looked concerned.

"I'm sure it is. Just being a worrywart is all. I'll try and get back here soon. If not, I'll see you both at the theater tomorrow. And I'll be on email later."

∞

There were no cars in the high school parking lot, but I decided to check inside anyway. I let myself in and called out. No one answered, but the place wasn't buttoned up either. There are always a few lights left on in a theater, since walking in the pitch black can be very dangerous, depending on the state the theater was left in. A trap door might be left open, or a piece of scenery down. The recognized practice is to have some bare light bulbs on top of poles, called ghost lights, burning in the middle of the stage.

Tonight the normal ghost lights were on, but so were the house lights. Full force. I walked down toward the edge of the stage, where an empty bottle of bourbon was tilted on its side.

Maybe they'd left to get something. I punched Stewart's number into my cell again. I heard the faint ring of a phone. I hung up and repeated the experiment. With the same results. Stewart's cell phone was somewhere in the theater. But where was Stewart?

As general manager, my purview is the front of house. The inner workings of a theater belong to actors, stage managers, and technicians. From childhood summers following my mother around, I felt at home at the Cliffside, going up to the fly rails, down to the trap room, and off to the wings. But this theater wasn't mine.

I called Stewart's cell again. And again, trying to figure out the source of the ringing. It seemed to be coming from the trap room. Maybe Stewart was taking a nap down there? And he didn't hear his cell? Lots of maybes. I'd find out for sure once I figured out how to get down there from the stage. I certainly wasn't going to drop down through one of the trap doors. At least that wasn't my first choice.

I called once more, but this time I heard a crash, a blow, and the phone stopped mid-ring. And then I heard the moan.

∞

It was the moan that propelled me back into cop mode. I called Regina's cell but got her voicemail. I explained where I was and asked her to come by. I used the term "backup." She'd know I wouldn't use that word lightly.

I hesitated for a moment before calling Gus. I got his voicemail as well, but my message was a little different—just to let him know that I was at the high school, afraid Stewart was hurt, and to let Connie know. He could choose to read between the lines or not. I called Connie and left a similar message on her voicemail.

I'd left my bag in the car, so I put my cell and keys in my pocket. There was a wimpy Swiss knife on my key chain, and I looked at it in disgust. God, had I gotten soft. I used to have a serious Swiss knife, but I'd lost it at an airport. At the security checkpoint. I hadn't replaced it in kind—frankly, these days I mostly used the corkscrew. Hopefully I wouldn't need anything more serious, but my gut still ached. Something was wrong.

I walked around the stage and scenery as quietly as I could, looking for the entrance down to the trap room. It took some maneuvering, since most of the scenery was down, not flown or raised about the stage. Probably a short cut for a touch-up work call before the actors came in tomorrow, but still a major pain in the neck. Huge flats with exterior scenes of Victorian England, the inside of the counting house, the Cratchit house. Smaller flats with doorways and fire and brimstone and a mountain of fake food made my path more circuitous. Finally I got far enough upstage that I could see the path to the dressing rooms and then the small staircase down to the trap room. I was careful not to move too quickly lest I hit a piece of scenery and make a noise.

Finally, I stood by the staircase. I was careful when I looked down the stairs, alert for shadows or noises or the unknown. At first I didn't see anything other than a pile of laundry at the bottom of the steps. It was when the pile of laundry moved and moaned that I almost forgot my police training and rushed down. Almost. Instead I moved as quietly as I could, walking down the stairs on tiptoe, tearing my eyes away from the pile at the bottom of the stairs and forcing them to survey the area as soon as my head cleared the stage. I didn't see anything, but I couldn't. What little light there was, was focused on the staircase. The rest of the room was in a blue light. I knew my eyes would adjust, but I didn't want to wait.

As I got closer to the pile of laundry and recognized Stewart, I was shocked I could have thought of him as a heap of clothes. I reached for his neck, ignoring the blood while I searched for a pulse. I said a silent prayer when I found one. I'd found more than one corpse in my career, but never one that I cared about.

My phone wouldn't get a signal, so I whispered to Stewart to hold on and made my way up the stairs, cell phone in front of me waiting for a sign my phone service was active. I only made it up three steps before I heard him.

"Put the cell phone down, Sully. Please."

"Frank? Is that you? I can't see you."

"Please, Sully. I have a gun."

I hit redial and mute, putting the phone on the highest step before I turned around. Damn. I hated it when I liked the suspect.

"Walk toward me," he said.

"Can I check on Stewart first, Frank? That gash is pretty rough … did he fall down the stairs? He was always a little clumsy after a couple of drinks."

"He didn't fall."

"Really? What happened?"

"Don't play dumb, Sully." Frank stepped out into a pool of light so I could finally see him. He did, indeed, have a gun. It was pointed right at me.

"Frank, let me go over and help him. I don't know what happened here but I know you, Frank, and I know you wouldn't hurt Stewart on purpose. It must have been some sort of mistake. So let me go and help him."

Gaining his trust was critical if I was going to get Stewart and myself out of this. After what seemed like an eternity, Frank nodded.

"Don't do anything stupid," he said.

"Just checking on my friend is all." I put my arms out from my side in a good faith gesture and moved toward Stewart, keeping my eyes on Frank. He and I did a dance, keeping an equidistant arc.

I reached Stewart, my friend. Had Frank shot him? I took off my scarf, giving Frank a running commentary as I was using it to stem the flow of blood from Stewart's brow. From what I could tell it was a surface wound, but head wounds bleed like a bastard. And he'd already lost a lot of blood.

"Stewart, please don't die," I whispered.

I almost screamed when his eyes fluttered slightly and he whispered, "If you insist, love." He tried to smile, but a look of pain stopped the effort.

"What's happening over there?" Frank asked.

"I'm trying to stop the bleeding."

"I didn't mean to shoot him," Frank said. "The gun just went off."

"That can happen."

"I don't like you there, Sully. Move him over here."

"That may not be a good idea, Frank." I really wanted to keep Stewart visible at the bottom of the stairs.

"Move him." I looked over at Frank, and realized that he and I weren't dealing with the same reality anymore.

I dragged Stewart over to the mattress under the center trap in the stage. Frank gestured for me to get down, so I sat on my knees beside my prostrate friend. I rewrapped the scarf around his head, using my hat as an extra bandage. I hoped the bleeding would let up soon. Stewart had either passed out again or was pretending. I took his hand in mine. Nurse ministrations over, I turned back to Frank. "What happened? Let me see if I can help you figure this out."

"Stop it. You can't help. It's all so bad," he said. He didn't bother to stop the tears as they streamed down his face. "How could I really believe she loved me? She used me. But she didn't deserve to die." Frank started to gesture with his gun, which should have made him vulnerable and given me an opportunity. But his finger was on the trigger, and I doubted he'd put the safety back on after shooting Stewart.

"Okay, so you loved Brooke. And you thought she loved you. But now you don't think so? What changed your mind?" I kept my voice reasonable, although louder than absolutely necessary. The only thing I could hope was that Regina had gotten my message and would hear my voice. Or maybe Gus ... no, Regina was my best bet.

"We were from the same neighborhood in Chicopee. I didn't know her growing up, she was a little older, but still, what were the chances? I think she liked talking about home. We got, um, close, you know? I lied before. You believed me then. Who would ever want to sleep with Frank, right? Brooke liked me. A lot. She said no one understood her like I did. I felt bad at first, because I liked Mr. Whitehall. But she was so pretty. And she needed me. She said she was in way over her head."

Once he started, he barely took a breath, waxing on about his relationship with Brooke. It was tough to try and imagine what Brooke had been thinking. I hoped it had meant something to her, but given what I knew about her, I doubted it. It seemed to have meant the world to Frank.

"She wanted to leave Mr. Whitehall, and she was going to, but she needed money first. She told me she'd signed a pre-nup and wouldn't get anything if she left. She told me she had a plan, but she needed to get into Mr. Whitehall's study without anyone knowing. So she asked me how to trick the new security system. I told her and offered to help. But she said she'd take care of it, that she didn't want me to get involved.

"I thought she was going to take some money or something. I never, ever thought she'd ... I swear. She promised that Mr. Whitehall was the only thing between us. I wanted to be with her so badly. When Mr. Whitehall was killed. I freaked a little, I'll admit it. Brooke sent me an email and asked me to give her time. And not to call. Or text.

"So I waited, but finally I decided I had to call. And so I did. A few times. And I emailed. Brooke came by the theater yesterday and asked me to stop calling. She was going to leave. And then she told me that Terry was going with her. She said she hadn't been well and Terry promised to take care of her. She was going to go to Boston, and

Terry was coming later. She said she had one last present for me, and then she gave me this package, saying it was from her and Terry. It had a gun in it. This gun," he said, gesturing again.

Frank's agitation was palpable and contagious. My legs were falling asleep from sitting on the floor. But jumping up seemed like a bad idea under the circumstances, so I rolled my legs from side to side to keep them awake. I needed to be able to move if I got the opportunity. But until then, I needed to keep Frank talking.

"Do you think they were trying to set you up?" I asked.

"I think Terry gave it to Brooke for her to get rid of," Frank said. "Such a coward—why did she like him better than me?"

"So what did you do?" I asked. I thought I heard a sound coming from upstairs.

"I drove to the Anchorage this afternoon. Mr. Whitehall hadn't changed the passwords. I know where all the cameras are. I got past the gates. No one stopped me. So I kept going and let myself into the house. I found Terry in his office. I asked what the hell he was doing. And he laughed at me. *Laughed at me.* And then he thanked me for my fingerprints, and for my help."

"What help?" I asked.

"Terry told me he'd been pretty pissed when he found out about Brooke and me. Said she was his and he didn't like to share. But he said Brooke would come back to him. He must have thought that with enough money he could woo Brooke away from Mr. Whitehall and the Anchorage. I guess he was right."

"What a bastard," I said, partly to continue to build rapport with Frank, but mostly because it was true. Terry and Brooke? That explained why Jack Megan hadn't been able to track anything about Terry's affair for Emma. Terry was having an affair with his father-in-law's wife. And they all lived in the same house. Jeez. I wondered if

Peter had known. This would definitely have bothered him. For a whole lot of reasons.

"Then he laughed again," Frank said. "He told me to get out. Didn't even wait to see if I would. He sat down at his desk and turned toward his computer. He wasn't scared, even though I had the gun. So I walked up behind him and shot him. I tried to do it so it would look like he'd shot himself, but I must have missed something. I missed something, didn't I, Sully? Tell me what I did wrong."

"The angle was off," I said quietly.

"Damn, I really thought. I went up behind him and put the gun here." To my horror, Frank knelt on the other side of Stewart, rolled him over slightly, and put the gun right next to his ear. Frank had gone around a bend, and I wasn't sure if I could keep him on the road. Or from shooting Stewart.

"Frank, Terry poisoned Brooke. Did you know that? I think the poisoning was what caused her to crash. You actually did the world a favor. If anyone deserved killing, it was Terry Holmes. Honestly. Frank, you know I was a cop back in the day. I can't see how they could get enough evidence to convict you."

Suddenly I heard something stumble down the staircase. My cell phone was now at the bottom in a half-dozen pieces. Damn, I still had a year to go on my contract.

"Who is that?" Frank said.

"She's right, son. There isn't nearly enough evidence to convict you." Gus walked down the stairs, hands outstretched in front of him.

"Who the hell—"

"Gus Knight. A friend of Sully's."

"How did you find us?" Frank asked. The hand holding the gun was still against Stewart's ear. I moved my legs a little to wake them up and tried to figure out how to get into a squat without Frank noticing. My New Year's resolution included finally signing up for that yoga class. And applying for a license to carry a concealed weapon. Of course, who would have figured at the beginning of the day that I'd need a gun? Certainly not me.

"Sully was going to give me a ride back to Boston. When she didn't come back, I decided to come and get her."

"How much did you hear?"

"Nothing really. Just Sully toward the end. But I know her well enough to know that if she says that there isn't evidence, there isn't evidence. So, let's fix this."

"You can't. No one can."

I hoped Gus wasn't alone. But if he was, it was up to the two of us to end this. Now. Before Frank decided he had no way out but to hurt Stewart. Or himself.

"Gus is a fixer." I slowly moved my weight back on my heels, making an awkward squat. My legs still had pins and needles, and it took every ounce of my self-control not to stand up and stretch them. Resisting the temptation, I shuffled closer to Frank and Stewart. "A real fixer. He's a defense lawyer, and he's gotten some real slime off. He'd really enjoy getting someone like you off, someone with a good excuse for what he did. Wouldn't you, Gus?"

"Well, I'd need to know what he did first. Frank, do you want to tell me about it?" Gus moved around so that Frank turned a bit toward him. In doing so, the gun shifted away from Stewart's temple. Sensing this, Frank pointed it toward me. He was too close to miss.

"Move over here," he told Gus, who complied. Frank looked at both of us, and then at Stewart, still sprawled on the ground. Either he'd passed out again or he was an even better actor than I thought.

"Get over here, lawyer. Lean up against this column and put your hands behind you." Gus did what he was told, and Frank took some gaff tape out of the front pocket of his hoodie, using it in a one-handed tie-up technique to lash Gus to the column. It also tore easily, particularly with the tooth-tearing method Frank now employed. Years of taping down electric cables made him deft with the tape; Gus wasn't going anywhere. After he was finished, he turned around and looked at me. "I don't know what to do...I didn't think...I didn't want..."

"Of course you didn't, Frank," I said, straightening my legs out slowly until I was vertical. Well, not completely vertical. Still a little bent in the legs. Definitely yoga class this winter. "You got in the middle of something bigger than you. It sucked you in. Could have happened to anyone. Let us help you, Frank. Hurting more people isn't the answer."

"It's too late. I probably killed him already," Frank said, motioning with the gun toward Stewart. As if on cue, Stewart moaned slowly. I stepped in between them. In front of Gus too, sort of.

"Frank, here's what we're going to do. You're going to give me the gun. And I'm going to go with you—"

"No, I don't think that's a good plan. I'm sorry, Sully." He trained the gun on me again.

"Okay, here's another plan Frank."

I had never been so glad to hear Regina's voice, or any voice for that matter. Frank and I turned toward the staircase, where Regina was slowly creeping down, her gun aimed at Frank. "You hand the gun to Sully, take a step toward me, and lie down on the ground, hands outstretched."

Frank stood there, turned slightly toward Regina with the gun still focused on me. In three steps I could reach him, but those three steps would put me in point blank range.

"Or, I could shoot you right here." Still no reaction from Frank. Except, I noticed, to grip the gun a little more tightly and focus all of his attention back on me.

"Sully, I'm so sorry," Frank whispered. "I never meant for any of this to happen. It's just that I loved her, you know? It was crazy, but I did." Frank slowly raised the gun to his own temple.

"Not on my watch, Frank." I leapt across the short space between us. Frank hesitated, as surprised by my action as I was. Out of the corner of my eye, I saw Gus straining against his tape restraints and Regina running down the steep staircase, both hands on her gun, leaning against the banister to keep her bulky frame in balance. Stewart rolled over, toward us. I pushed the gun upward with one hand while elbowing Frank as hard as I could with the other. The gun fired upward, but Frank didn't let go. He tripped backward over Stewart's prone body and I fell on top of him, still holding onto the hand with the gun. The full impact of my not-inconsiderable frame knocked the wind out of him, and I kept slamming his hand against the ground until he lost control of the gun. It skidded away toward Gus. I put one hand on each of Frank's wrists, sitting on his chest and trying to calm him. Stewart threw his legs over Frank's, but still he struggled. Regina had been yelling in the background, but it wasn't until I felt someone's hands around my waist, pulling me off of Frank, that I realized she'd been calling in the troops.

Someone had cut Gus loose during the melee, and he took over the job of subduing me. He was a little bit effective, pulling me toward him and whispering that I was okay, it was all okay. For a second, I believed him. But then I saw Stewart, bleeding and barely conscious, and I knew it was a lie. I pulled out of Gus's arms and knelt by my friend. And started my own string of lies, telling Stewart that it was okay, everything was okay.

· Twenty-Seven ·

I rode with Stewart to the hospital. Gus met us there. Stewart got a few stitches and was admitted for observation. Gus and I were in the waiting area, about to go to his room, when Regina arrived.

"Staties took over," she said.

"Are you freaking kidding me? And they didn't even let you sit in?"

Regina seemed pleased that I was so pissed on her behalf. I'd been there too many times, of course, doing the work and losing the credit.

"No, they sent me down here to get statements. From all three of you."

"Can you talk to all of us at the same time? We were going down to talk to Stewart."

"He's awake?"

"Yes, he is now. They want to keep him up for a while to check for a possible concussion."

"Talking about what happened is probably a good way to do that. Let's go."

∞

Stewart looked as pale as the hospital sheets, but he was flirting shamelessly with the nurse. Then again, he'd likely be flirting shamelessly with someone five minutes before he died, so that was hardly proof positive that he was okay. So I asked.

"Stewart, you okay?" I rested my hand against his cheek, which felt warm to my touch.

He turned his face and kissed my palm. "I'm told by this lovely woman that I'm going to be fine."

The nurse blushed. "He needs some rest," she admonished the three of us.

Regina flashed her badge and identified herself. "We won't keep him long, only need to confirm a few details."

The nurse nodded and left, glaring at Gus and me.

"Well?" Regina asked Stewart.

"Well? Is that how you say hello, you sexy thing you?" Stewart teased. Regina smiled and Gus rolled his eyes.

"He's very charming," I said in a stage whisper.

"Obviously," Gus said.

Regina said, "I'm on duty, sweetie. As soon as we're done, I'll say hello properly." She raised her eyebrows a few times and took out a small digital recorder. "I'm going to record this, if it's okay with all of you." Each of us nodded, so she turned on the recorder and identified herself, Gus, Stewart, and me. Then she asked Stewart to explain the events of the evening.

"Frank had left Gabe to work with me on the mic'ing system for Patrick's costumes. We were experimenting with different earpieces, trying to find ones that couldn't be seen and could work without interrupting other frequencies. We weren't having a lot of luck. Gabe was doing well, but he kept having to call Frank for help. I asked why

Frank wasn't there, and Gabe said he was doing 'stuff.' He didn't expound on that—"

"He's a teenager, so he doesn't expound on much these days," Regina apologized.

"I remember it well," Stewart said. "But he was worried enough to tell me Frank was a little freaked. Gabe's description, not mine. But when Frank returned later, he seemed serene. Offered to step in for Gabe.

"We worked for a little while, and he took notes about what wasn't working. He finally said he needed to buy a new transmitter or something, and that we couldn't do anything more tonight. Then he offered me a drink. I suggested we go to the Beef and Ale, but Frank said he wasn't up to seeing anyone and he had a bottle in the trap room. He sounded so pitiful that I couldn't ... I went down with him and had a drink. And I told him I was sorry for his troubles. He broke down, said something about Brooke bringing him a gun yesterday. He didn't make much sense after that, so I told him I'd be going. I went up the stairs and called you, Sully. The next thing I knew, I fell down the stairs. My head was bleeding. Then Sully came riding in to the rescue."

"Hardly riding in," I said.

"If you hadn't, he would have killed me. I'm fairly sure of that. He was mustering up the courage when you came down. Poor bastard."

"What do you mean, 'poor'? He tried to kill you," Gus said.

"He wasn't himself. I'll testify to that, if he needs it. He really got screwed up by this Brooke woman. What was she doing having an affair with a guy like Frank? She was way out of his league."

"Not so far out of his league," I said. "They had similar backgrounds. She may have even started to care. I wonder if Terry didn't put her up to it? Maybe he realized that Emma had started to suspect he was having an affair." I paused, assessing the pieces that had all started to come together. "But Terry must have realized Brooke was a liability, and so he started to poison her. Still hard for me to believe."

"Not so hard, Sully," Regina said. "From what I've gathered, Terry had a bit of a sociopathic streak. It worked well for him for a long time. He charmed his wife and her family. Positioned himself to take over the whole thing. But then he fell for Brooke and they started their affair. The affair started to unravel his plan. So he had to stop it."

"But poison? Jeez, that's a tough way to kill someone. Especially someone you see every day," Stewart said.

"Love is pretty close to hate on the passion scale."

"I guess. But this is more dramatic than anything in *A Christmas Carol*. Speaking of which, when can I get out of here? We have a paying audience tomorrow night."

"You got shot, Stewart." Silently I blessed him for worrying more about the show than he did his own health. Bless actors—"the show must go on" wasn't just a quaint motto.

"Grazed. The bike spill caused me more pain."

"You got shot. You may have hit your head. Don't underestimate the power of the pain meds, my friend. You need to stick around for a while longer. Once they give you the okay, we'll get you out of here. But I think we need to postpone Friday's show. The Saturday matinee can be our first paid audience."

"We need all the previews we can get," Stewart said. He tried to sit up but fell back against the pillows. The color was coming back into his cheeks. Could he perform on pain meds? I hated myself for wondering—and hated myself more for hoping so.

"How about if we add a show on Sunday?" I said. "That way you can rest, but we can get the previews in. What do you think?"

"Sounds like a plan," Stewart said. "Of course, I'll need a nurse to take care of me once I get out of here." He reached his hand out, and I took it and squeezed.

"Connie has already said you can stay with her family for the next few days," I reminded him.

"Damn. There goes the party. Gus, will you be staying in town to see the show?"

"Actually, I'd love to. I can't wait to see how it turns out after all of this. Think I could get a ticket for opening night?"

"You're in luck," Regina said. "I know the box office staff. Will that be one ticket or two?"

Acknowledgments

I am so grateful to Terri Bischoff and the Midnight Ink team for bringing this book to life. It was a long-held dream that this series would get published, and I couldn't be more thrilled.

There are so many groups of folks who worked with me on this manuscript throughout the years. Thank you to the Natick Writing Group, Guppy swaps, Sisters in Crime, Dana Cameron, Sherry Harris, Ruth Polleys, Jason Allen-Forrest, and the dozens of other folks who read this manuscript in varying stages of development.

Thank you to my agent, John Talbot, for being on this ride with me.

Thank you to the wonderful Wicked Cozy Authors. Barbara Ross, Liz Mugavero, Edith Maxwell, Jessie Crocket Estevao, and Sherry Harris are my cheerleaders, and my friends. WickedCozyAuthors.com is one of the great joys in my writing life. A special thanks to our readers who are so supportive.

Thank you to the New England theater community, and to the board and staff of StageSource. I love my theater life and will be forever grateful for the support from the arts community. #ArtsMatter

Thank you to my wonderful parents, Paul and Cindy Hennrikus.

Thank you to my sisters Kristen and Caroline; my brothers-in-law Bryan and Glenn; my nieces Tori, Becca, and Mallory; my nephews Chase and Harrison; my godchildren Emma and Evan. I have the greatest family in the world. Your love means the world to me.

© Meg Manion

About the Author

J. A. Hennrikus writes the Theater Cop series for Midnight Ink. As Julianne Holmes, she writes the Agatha-nominated Clock Shop Mystery series for Berkley Prime Crime. Julie blogs with the Wicked Cozy Authors, is on the board of Sisters in Crime, and is a member of Mystery Writers of America. She is an arts administrator who lives in Massachusetts.

Twitter: @JHAuthors
www.JHAuthors.com